THE LOST GIRLS OF PENZANCE

SALLY RIGBY

To request permissions, contact the publisher at rights@stormpublishing.co

Ebook ISBN: 978-1-80508-255-2
Paperback ISBN: 9978-1-80508-257-6

Cover design: Lisa Horton
Cover images: Shutterstock

Published by Storm Publishing.
For further information, visit:
www.stormpublishing.co

ALSO BY SALLY RIGBY

A Cornwall Murder Mystery

The Lost Girls of Penzance

The Hidden Graves of St Ives

Cavendish & Walker Series

Deadly Games

Fatal Justice

Death Track

Lethal Secret

Last Breath

Final Verdict

Ritual Demise

Mortal Remains

Silent Graves

Kill Shot

Dark Secrets

Broken Screams

Detective Sebastian Clifford Series

Web of Lies

Speak No Evil

Never Too Late

Hidden From Sight

Fear the Truth

PROLOGUE

- Memorise staff shifts......✓
- Locate security cameras......✓
- Draw up exit plan......✓
- Air-tight alibi in place......✓
- Purchase means for sedation......✓
- Choose which girls to take......✓

With a self-satisfied sigh, I survey my checklist. Every step complete.

Now the time has come for the first one.

I've always been meticulous in my planning. Focusing on every detail. Scrutinising every element. Rehearsing every step until it's second nature. These skills can't be learnt overnight. They take years of practice.

I've also perfected the art of being unseen. Unnoticed. Until people only see what they want to see. Or should that be what *I* want them to see.

I reach for the open bottle of red wine standing next to the fridge. I can't have too much – only half a glass, in case it dulls my senses.

I need to be at the top of my game to pull this off.

But how could it go wrong?

I've examined every corner, every potential hideout, every possible escape route. No one can stop me.

I wander into the dimly lit lounge, and head over to my laptop. My eyes fixate on the screen which displays her image. Soon she'll be mine.

I'm going to take what I want. And no one's going to stop me.

I know what people will say. That I'm a monster. The lowest of the low. But what do they know?

It's all about balance. The cruel fairness of life. For every child who experiences the joy of play, there's another who knows only loneliness and fear.

That was me.

And now I want to redress the balance.

It's my turn now.

ONE

MONDAY, 24 OCTOBER

Detective Inspector Lauren Pengelly sighed as several drops of rain bounced off her fingers, which were tightly wrapped around the handlebars of her mountain bike. Sinister grey clouds gathered overhead. There had been a storm forecasted for later, but it could be arriving sooner. She'd been forced by her boss, Detective Chief Inspector Mistry, to take some of her accrued annual leave, despite her insisting that it wasn't necessary. He'd informed her that it was policy and so she'd acquiesced. She liked to choose her battles carefully, and this wasn't important enough to engage in for any length of time.

To fill the time she had off, she'd booked herself onto a two-week cycling holiday to undertake the iconic Land's End to John O'Groats route. This 874-mile ride was something she'd wanted to do for a long time because it would take her across the whole of the United Kingdom, from the southwest tip of Cornwall to the most northern point of Scotland. And she loved a challenge. Even so, it wasn't for the faint-hearted.

Her two beloved dogs, Tia and Ben – both border collies that she'd rescued when they were only a few months old – were safely ensconced in excellent boarding kennels a few miles away and her rucksack was filled with everything she needed for the trip, and comfortably resting across her back.

The rain held off with just a few spits while Lauren rode the forty minutes from the detached late-Victorian town house that she rented in St Just, past the old stone farmhouses nestled amid the landscape with their moss-covered roofs. Turning down the stony gravel path leading to the meeting point, she spotted the tour company organiser and guide, Dale Gray, in the distance. He'd come dressed for the weather in head-to-toe waterproof gear. Three keen cyclists stood nearby, admiring each other's bikes.

She'd met him once in the past, when she was investigating a series of burglaries at the Land's End shops, but whether he'd remember her or not, she had no idea. She jumped off her bike and wheeled it over, introducing herself.

'Morning, Dale. I'm here to sign in – I'm Lauren Pengelly.'

'Well, I'm certainly surprised to see you,' Dale replied, frowning. 'I was expecting a call saying that you'd have to cancel.'

Why on earth would he think she'd cancel? 'I don't understand. What makes you say that?' Did he think she wasn't up to it?

'Well, er... because of the human remains they've found on the Trenowden Estate. Didn't you know about it? Some kids on holiday were playing and found human bones. Including a skull – or so I've been told.'

This was big – so why was this the first she'd heard of it? Even if she was on leave, it wasn't like she'd already left town. There had better be a very good reason for her team not contacting her.

But, more to the point, how was Dale Gray aware of it – and she wasn't?

'How do you know about this?'

'I stopped off at the newsagents on the way here and they

were all talking about it. One of the women working in the shop knows the family whose kids found the bones.'

Nothing could be kept a secret around here. At least it had only just happened; she'd let her team off the hook.

The estate was only a twenty-minute cycle away – she might be able to squeeze in a visit to check it out before the tour set off...

'Thank you, Dale. I'm going to go take a look but I still intend to come on the trip. What exact time are you planning to leave?'

They'd been told to arrive sometime between eight and nine. It was typical of the laidback attitude in the area. Nothing set in stone. She could probably persuade him to hang on until she'd visited the scene.

Dale glanced at his watch. 'There are still three more cyclists to arrive, so within the next half an hour, maybe longer, depending on the weather...'

'The forecast is mixed for the whole trip – we're going to get wet at some stage.'

She'd been checking regularly and had brought plenty of wet weather gear with her.

'If it stays like this, we'll leave on time, but if the forecasted storm comes in sooner than expected, we may well delay a couple of hours. The first leg to St Austell can be quite tough for even the hardiest cyclist.'

Great. That could go in her favour. Then again, depending on what she found, she may well have to insist that she was needed on the ground and defer her leave. It wasn't like they had a large team. There was no one she'd be happy leaving in charge of a potential murder case. Her new sergeant was due to be starting next week, but as she'd never even met him, she certainly wasn't going to put him in charge of the investigation.

'Look, I'll head to the estate to see what's happening. You've got my number. If you need to leave before I get back, give me a call and I'll catch you up.'

She swung her leg over the bike and rode away before he had time to reply. The vicious wind whipped off the ocean and lashed at her cheeks. It was like having a free facial. If she got onto the National Cycle Route 3, she could easily be there in twenty minutes. The road was winding but it wasn't too hilly, which meant she could go at quite a speed.

News of the body would be a huge shock for the town. And it would certainly give her team some much-needed experience. She'd made the decision to return to Cornwall from Luton as a detective inspector because the only other option for promotion would have been to head further north and she hadn't wanted to do that. She much preferred the south for the weather and the way of life. She had no intention of staying long term, though. She viewed working for Devon and Cornwall Police, based permanently at Penzance station, as a stopgap until she was promoted to detective chief inspector at a larger force. Ideally, the London Met, or somewhere else coastal, like Brighton and Hove.

After university she'd joined the force through the fast-track scheme and had every intention of becoming a DCI before she turned forty. The trouble with working at Penzance was it was quiet and there weren't many juicy cases to get her teeth into, and bolster her reputation. It also meant that the team she led wasn't exactly dynamic and sometimes needed a rocket up their arses. But she'd inherited them and they were slowly coming around to her way of working.

The police did have their fair share of dead bodies, but they were mainly from drownings, in particular the tourists who were reckless when it came to swimming in the ocean. Other than that, the work was routine. Penzance was a quiet, parochial town. Not that she'd made an attempt to integrate much in the eighteen months she'd been back in Cornwall. Why would she when it was only a temporary post?

Arriving at the estate, the discovery site was unmistakable. The area had been cordoned off and there was a crowd of people staring. Thunder rumbled in the distance, hinting at the storm's arrival. She shivered, not just from the cold. Whose remains had been discovered and how did they get there?

She cycled over, stopping in front of a man who appeared to be in charge and was standing about twenty metres behind the cordon. He was in his mid-thirties and walked with a slight limp. She didn't recognise him. Was he from a different station?

She wheeled her bike over to the cordon, and held her hand up to the side of her mouth. 'Hey,' she shouted. He turned his head in her direction. 'I'm with the police.'

'ID?'

Damn. She'd left it at home. It hadn't entered her head to bring it with her. Why would she when she was on holiday?

'I don't have it with me,' she yelled back, shrugging. 'But I'm not lying. I'm with the force.'

'No ID, no entry. Sorry.'

She knew why he was doing this. If he was one of her team, it was what she'd expect. But that didn't help her situation. If he'd come over and spoken to her instead of shouting, she'd have been able to convince him who she was. But she got it. Maybe he didn't want to move too much because of his bad leg.

'Oi, what's going on?' the short, overweight man who had moved in beside her shouted. He held up his phone, and pointed it in the direction of the officer.

A reporter from the local paper. That was all they needed. It would be all over the media before they'd had a chance to make a start on the case.

'Nothing to do with you,' she said, glaring down at him.

'Says who?' he said.

He clearly hadn't recognised her, or he'd have been pumping her for information. Then again, he could have vouched for her. But who was to say the officer would have believed them, anyway?

She didn't respond to the reporter and instead looked further along the cordon where there were at least twenty other people rubber-necking.

The officer probably thought that she was a nosy tourist, especially the way she was dressed. It was still annoying, though. Especially as she didn't have much time to find out the circumstances surrounding the discovery.

She held up her hand to the side of her mouth, again. 'Is the pathologist here?'

The officer stared at her. 'No.'

He might have been twenty metres away, but the annoyed look on his face was clear for anyone to see.

'Look, he'll tell you who I am. We're wasting time. Please let me through.'

'Sorry, no can do.' He turned and walked away until all she could see was his retreating back.

She'd be having a word with his superior officer, that was for sure.

TWO

Detective Sergeant Matt Price continued walking until he was out of earshot of the woman with the bike, who had insisted she was a police officer. Judging by the way she was dressed, it was most unlikely. He suspected she was with the media – they'd try anything to get an exclusive. Either that or she was one of the many nosy onlookers. He couldn't believe so many people were already aware that human remains had been found on the estate.

The coastal wind, bringing with it the scent of the salty sea air, whistled past and Matt shivered, buttoning up his jacket. Not that it made much difference because it was so thin. He'd need a total wardrobe rethink, if he was going to survive the weather down here. The sky had turned ominously grey. Fingers crossed the forecasted storm held off until after the pathologist had arrived.

He stared at the rugged, undulating countryside, a patchwork quilt of wildflowers blanketing the terrain. Despite the weather, it was beautiful and very different from the landscape he was used to around 275 miles away in the West Midlands.

Matt had arrived in Cornwall four weeks ago, moving to be

with his parents so that they could look after his two-year-old daughter, Dani, while he was at work. His wife, Leigh, had recently died in a car crash and he couldn't manage on his own. He'd been fortunate that a post had come up with Devon and Cornwall Police, based in Penzance, because it was less than a ten-minute walk, or two-minute drive, from his parents' house to the station, which meant he didn't have to leave home too early and most nights he could be back for story-time before Dani went to bed.

And today was his first day on the job.

He was alone at the crime scene, apart from a couple of police constables who had arrived before him and who he'd had to instruct to secure the scene. His previous boss, DCI Whitney Walker from Lenchester CID, would have had something to say about how sloppy it was.

He glanced at the crime scene entrance. A man who looked to be in his early sixties, wearing a brown tweed jacket with leather patches on the elbow and dark corduroy trousers that had to be twenty years old judging by how faded they were, was heading towards it, a large bag in his hand.

He must be the pathologist. *Thank goodness.* Matt walked over. Out the corner of his eye he could see the female cyclist running in their direction. What the hell was she going to do now?

'I'm Henry Carpenter, the forensic pathologist,' the man said in a broad Cornish accent, distracting Matt from the woman.

'DS Matt Price.' Matt took the pathologist's outstretched hand and shook it. 'I'm glad you've arrived. We need to get moving on this. It's turning into a three-ring circus with all these onlookers.' He gestured with an open hand to the crowd of people still staring in their direction.

'It's big news. It's not every day human remains are discovered in this area. There's not much I can do straight away. I just came to take a look and assess the situation. Bones aren't my thing. We'll need to call in a forensic anthropologist and we'll work together on it. I—'

'Henry!' the cyclist called as she reached them. 'Please inform this officer who I am.'

'My pleasure. This is DI Lauren Pengelly from Penzance CID.' He frowned. 'You don't know each other?'

Pengelly?

He had to be kidding.

That was the name of Matt's immediate boss. When he'd reported in earlier at the station, DCI Mistry had informed him that she was on annual leave. Well, that explained the attire. Matt cringed. It certainly wasn't the auspicious start that he'd planned. Even if he'd only been doing his job...

'Sorry... I didn't realise. I'm DS Price. I started this morning. The DCI told me I wouldn't be meeting you until you returned from your holiday.'

'And I wasn't informed that you'd be starting today.' She sighed loudly. 'Well, now you know who I am and we have met, so let's get on. First things first, what are you doing here on your own? Where are the rest of the team?'

'When the report came in I was the only one in the office, so the DCI sent me. I haven't met the others yet.'

'Great. Why is it that as soon as I'm not there the place falls apart? Rhetorical question. I'm assuming that you arrived early for your first day.'

'Yes, I was there at eight. My commencement letter didn't state a time so I thought eight would be okay. The DCI was the only one there and he pointed me in the direction of my desk and said he'd speak to me later. But then the report came in and he directed me out here.'

Pengelly sighed again, clearly frustrated. 'Okay. We'll discuss this later, once we've assessed what's going on. Let's go with the pathologist to take a look. We'll need a forensic dig, in case there are more remains. What have you ascertained so far, DS Price?'

'Not much, guv.' He paused. 'Or do you prefer to be called ma'am?'

Whitney had only ever wanted to be called guv, and woe betide anyone who called her anything else. But he needed to check with Pengelly what she preferred. And he should also stop thinking about Lenchester and how much he'd enjoyed working there, because that wasn't going to help. It wasn't as if it was his most recent job. He'd moved to a much smaller force once Leigh had become pregnant to enable him to take care of Dani while she pursued her career.

Tears filled his eyes and he blinked them away. He had to save thinking about his awful situation until he was alone, or he'd never hack the new job. And that would be even more disastrous.

'Ma'am is fine,' Pengelly said with a vague wave of her hand.

'Yes, ma'am. According to Smith – one of the two police constables who arrived on the scene first – two brothers, aged eleven and thirteen, found a skull in the garden of one of the houses over there.' Matt pointed towards the row of dilapidated Victorian cottages, with no glass in the windows and massive holes in every roof.

'Although this is a private estate, there don't appear to be any gates or fences to stop people from entering, hence the crowds who are watching. The boys' family is renting a holiday cottage down the road, in St Buryan, for the half-term week. I suppose we've had so much rain recently that it must have dislodged the bones from their burial site.'

To say there had been a lot of rain was an understatement. Matt had seen more rain in the last four weeks than they'd had in the whole of the previous year in the West Midlands. He hoped this wasn't a sign of things to come. He'd always known it could be rainy in Cornwall, but was it always this bad?

'Where are the two boys?' Pengelly glanced around the site.

'I assume they're back at home, although I don't know for sure. When I arrived they'd already left the scene. According to PC Smith, she allowed their mother to take them back to the cottage because they were wet and muddy. Smith gave me their address should we wish to question them later.'

'We definitely will. Do you know whether it was just a skull they found or were there other bones?'

'I'm not sure, ma'am. I haven't been to the site. I was waiting for forensics to arrive, assuming they'd want to go in there first. I didn't want to...' His voice fell away. He was about to say *contaminate the scene*, but of course that was ridiculous. Who knew how long the bones had been here?

'Good chap,' Henry said. 'At least you've got your priorities straight. Right, I'll go first and you two can follow.' The pathologist pulled on his white coveralls and strode off in the direction of the properties.

Matt wasn't expecting to be praised, but he'd take it. He had no intention of telling his new boss the real reason he hadn't gone in any further. Unless he was forced to.

Pengelly went first and Matt followed behind, in silence. They trudged through the mud to the rear of the cottages and into the gardens, none of which were separated. Had there been fences there once?

There were cycle tracks all around the site and sitting on top of the mud, in the middle of the garden, was the top two-thirds of a skull with a round hole the size of a two-pound coin in one side. A gunshot wound?

The pathologist took out his camera, crouched down and began taking photos.

'Can you see any other bones there, Henry?' Pengelly asked.

'Definitely, but I'm not going to dislodge them,' the patholo-gist replied. 'We'll wait until the forensic anthropologist arrives. Hopefully that will be soon. Before leaving the office I put a call in to Sue Andrews from St Ives. She wasn't there, but I left a message for her to meet me at the morgue because I don't want to hang around here unnecessarily. We'll then come back here together. You can take a look if you'd like to step forward.'

Pengelly did as suggested and peered down, but Matt held back.

'Come on, Sergeant. Don't you want to see?'

'Yes, ma'am.' He sucked in a breath and took a small step forward and stared at the skull from the side, his whole body tense. He could also see the outline of the other bones Henry had mentioned. He should be grateful that it was only bones and not a body covered in flesh but, even so, nausea pitted in his stomach.

Leigh used to say he was such a wuss. But it was easy for her to say that. Being a nurse, she'd been regularly faced with all sorts of gruesome stuff.

'What's the matter? Do you have an aversion to bones?' Pengelly asked, fixing him with a questioning look.

Oh well, he might as well get it over with – she was bound to find out sooner or later.

'It's not just bones, ma'am. Dead bodies full stop make me squeamish.' He gave a half shrug, hoping she wouldn't think it to be a big deal.

'And you're a copper?' The incredulity in her voice was more than obvious.

'I deal with it. Is that a gunshot wound in the skull?' he asked Henry, anxious to move this discussion forward.

'It's too early to tell at this stage.' Henry stood, and turned to them. 'I'll be back later. Make sure no one disturbs the scene.'

'Right, we'd better get back to the station because we've got work to do,' Pengelly said.

'But I thought you were on annual leave, ma'am?'

'That's up for debate. Is your car large enough to take my bike?'

'Yes, ma'am,' Matt said, forcing back a frustrated sigh. He knew exactly what was going to be said next. Could this day get any worse?

'Good. I'll go with you and we can get this investigation kicked off.'

THREE

MONDAY, 24 OCTOBER

DI Pengelly didn't speak to Matt on their way back to the station. In fact, the only words she had uttered were when her phone rang and she informed the caller that she was unsure whether she'd make it and would let them know soon. Matt had taken that to mean the cycling trip she had planned to go on.

Once they'd arrived at the station, they headed to the room he'd been shown to that morning, only now rather than it being empty there were four others in there, two men and two women.

'Good morning, team,' Pengelly said. 'This is DS Matthew Price, who's joining us as of today.'

He glanced at the team, who were all staring intensely at him. It was a weird atmosphere, that was for sure.

'Please call me Matt.'

'Detective Constable Tamsin Kellow is over there,' Pengelly said, nodding towards an officer who looked to be in her mid-twenties.

'Good morning, sir.'

'I'm happy to go by Matt, not sir.'

'We like to operate more formally,' Pengelly said, turning to him, her brow furrowed.

'Okay then, guv will do,' Matt said, immediately regretting it. He couldn't quite see himself as a *guv*.

'Over there are Detective Constables Clem Roscoe and Jenna Moyle.' Pengelly nodded at the other two officers who were older, possibly mid-to-late forties or early fifties. 'And next to you is Detective Constable Billy Ward.' Another young officer, who Matt spied rolling his eyes in Tamsin's direction.

He'd have to get to the bottom of why, if this was going to work out.

'Morning, guv,' they said in unison.

He already hated the formality, but he'd have to go along with what Pengelly wanted. At least when she was around. He'd sort it out with the others himself. No doubt he'd soon learn the politics.

'Aren't you meant to be on annual leave, ma'am?' Jenna asked.

'Yes, but as I'm sure you're all aware, there have been some human remains found at the Trenowden Estate. DS Price was sent there by the DCI in the absence of any of you being in the office at that time.' She paused, and her gaze swept the room, but no one gave any reason for not being there early.

'I was on my way to join a cycling trip, but have taken a detour to come here. I'm going to see the DCI and when I come back we can sort out how the operation is going to proceed. With or without me.'

'Fingers crossed, without,' Billy muttered, but it appeared that only Matt heard.

Pengelly left the room and Matt wandered over to the desk that had been allocated to him. The tension in the room immediately lifted.

'You don't come from round here then, guv, judging by your accent,' Billy said.

'Actually... you know what, I'd rather Sarge, not guv. And you're right. I've recently moved down to Cornwall. I'm from the West Midlands.'

He could live with Sarge, even though at Lenchester and his other force he'd always been known as Matt.

'You'll find it very different here.' Clem spoke up. 'A much slower pace, and a lot fewer people. Almost three million people live in the West Midlands, compared with only half a mill here in Cornwall and—'

'Don't start boring Sarge already with your stats,' Billy said, laughing. 'Clem's a walking Wikipedia. Or as we like to call him, *Clemipedia*. We keep telling him to go on that TV quiz show, but so far he won't agree.'

'Because under pressure my mind will go blank. I don't want to make an arse of myself. And, FYI, it's only Billy who calls me by that nickname.'

Matt laughed. This was the sort of banter he was used to, not the frosty seriousness he'd so far witnessed.

'Had you visited Cornwall before moving here, Sarge?' Tamsin asked.

'Not since I was a child with my parents. They're actually living here now.'

'And have you done much sightseeing since you arrived?' the officer added.

'We haven't had much time, although we did go for a lovely meal at a restaurant in Mousehole at the weekend.'

The four of them erupted and laughter echoed around the room.

'*Mouse hole*,' Billy imitated, smirking.

'What have I said?'

'A rookie mistake. We can tell that you're new to the area and haven't quite got used to the Cornish pronunciation. It's *mowzle*,' Jenna said, pronouncing it phonetically and emphasising both syllables.

Matt joined in with their laughter. He'd thought it was a strange name for a place, but no different from villages or roads where he came from, like The Butts in Walsall, or Lickey End in Bromsgrove.

'Well, thanks for correcting me. I'm sure there'll be plenty of other words that I'll get wrong.'

'Have you got any family?' Tamsin asked.

'Don't be personal, Tams. The sarge will tell us when he's good and ready. And he might never be,' Jenna said, shaking her head and shrugging in his direction.

He was already getting the measure of the team.

'I don't mind. I'm here with my small daughter, Dani. We're living with my parents in a house not far from the station.'

He wasn't prepared to tell them about Leigh. At least, not yet. He wanted them to treat him normally and not feel they had to tread on eggshells when certain topics came up.

'Sarge, what can you tell us about the remains? What could you see? How many bodies were there?' Tamsin asked, excitement shining in her eyes.

It was so different from what he'd been used to. Lenchester was affectionately known as Murder Central because they had so many bodies. It was more a case of *not another one* than the exhilaration Tamsin's look expressed.

'We could only see one skull but—'

He was interrupted by the door opening. Pengelly marched in and stood at the front of the room, beside the whiteboard.

Every member of the team stiffened slightly and it was as if the relaxed atmosphere had been a figment of his imagination.

What on earth was going on here? He hoped it wouldn't interfere with him being able to do his job.

'I've spoken to the DCI and we've agreed that this is important enough for my leave to be postponed for now. I need to be here to lead the investigation. It can't be left to DS Price because he's new to both our team and the area.' She paused, looking around as if expecting a response, but none was forthcoming.

'What we know so far is that some human remains were found by boys on holiday. We don't know yet if there's more than one body or how long the body has been there. The pathologist has contacted a forensic anthropologist to work with him, and a forensic dig will be set up. The bones were discovered in the garden area of some empty cottages on the estate. Our first task is to identify the victim and a good place to start will be speaking to the owner of the land.'

'That's Hector Voyle,' Clem said. 'It's his family estate. They've been there for over one hundred years. The farm is still operational, although it's changed over that time and has downsized a lot. Which most likely accounts for some of the properties being left in a state of disrepair.'

'Matt, you take Clem and go out there.'

'We should phone first to find out if he's there, so we don't waste our time,' Matt said.

'Of course,' Pengelly agreed.

'I'll contact him now, Sarge,' Clem said, reaching to pick up the phone on his desk.

'The DCI is planning a press conference to inform the public and media that remains have been found, although judging by the number of people loitering around the site this morning, probably the whole area knows by now. It does mean the phones must be staffed at all times, between the hours of seven thirty in the morning and ten at night. Jenna, work out a rota between you, Clem, Tamsin and Billy.'

Interesting that she hadn't included Matt in that, though he was pleased because he didn't want the job to interfere too much with Dani's routines, initially. Once they were all settled it would be different.

'Yes, ma'am,' Jenna said.

'Ma'am. I've just spoken to the housekeeper and Hector

Voyle is upcountry and won't be back until tomorrow evening,' Clem said.

'Does he know what's been discovered?'

'I didn't ask. But the housekeeper said they'd been expecting our call, so I'm assuming yes.'

'You'd have thought that it might have brought him back home. Never mind, we'll work around him.'

'When will we hear back from forensics?' Matt asked, glancing at his watch. Surely by now they'd have had some indication of what had happened?

'You've got to remember, Sergeant Price, that things don't move as fast here as you're probably used to in the city. We'll hear when we hear and not before. In the meantime, you and I are going to visit the boys who found the bones.'

They left the station, driving under a sky heavy with the impending storm. Pengelly directed him along the winding roads and through rolling countryside, eventually reaching the picturesque village of St Buryan. They drove past the imposing church in the centre, stopping at the double-fronted stone cottage where the boys' family was staying.

Pengelly banged on the door several times and they walked around the back, but there was no one to be seen.

'Do you think they've packed up and gone home, considering they were here on holiday, ma'am?'

The DI peered into one of the front windows. 'It doesn't look like it. The house is a mess and there are toys and clothes strewn all over the place.' She walked to the other front-facing window and looked in. 'Same in here, too.'

'Maybe they've gone out for the day?'

'Were they asked to stay at the cottage until the boys could be interviewed?'

'I don't know, ma'am. I didn't ask PC Smith.'

He could've kicked himself. It was basic procedure and it had totally slipped his mind.

'Well perhaps you should have done and then we wouldn't have had this wasted journey.' Pengelly's mouth was set in a flat line.

No need to wonder what she was thinking at this precise moment.

'Yes, with hindsight, I should have, ma'am, but I'm sure we can speak to the boys another time.'

His stomach rumbled and he checked his watch. It was already past lunchtime and he hadn't eaten since his breakfast cereal and toast at six thirty that morning. No wonder he was flagging.

'We'll have to. I'll have a word with Smith when we're back at the station and ask to check her notes. She might have taken down a mobile number.'

They returned to Matt's car and, again in silence, they drove back to the station.

If this was an indication of how working with DI Pengelly was going to be, he suspected that he'd made a huge mistake taking the job.

FOUR

TUESDAY, 25 OCTOBER

'Come in,' Lauren called out when there was a knock at her door, shortly after she'd arrived for work the next morning.

There were two entrances into her office, one from the room where the team sat and the other coming off the corridor. The knock came from the latter.

A uniformed officer came in.

'You wanted to see me, ma'am?' PC Smith said, standing in front of the desk, her hands by her side.

'*Yesterday* I asked for you to see me. What happened?' Lauren's tone was deliberately cold. The delay might have cost them valuable time, especially if the family left Cornwall before the boys were interviewed.

'Sorry, ma'am. After leaving Trenowden Estate, I was tied up policing at the Penzance gymkhana until the end of my shift.'

And heaven forbid she might actually have stayed late and reported in.

'I see.'

'I had an emergency dentist appointment straight after work

and so couldn't stop by to speak to you,' Smith added, as if she'd read Lauren's mind.

A valid reason, rather than simple forgetfulness, Lauren could accept. She gestured to the seat opposite her and the officer sat down.

'Okay, at least you're here now,' she said, taking care to make her voice more congenial. 'We weren't able to contact the boys who found the remains because they were out when we visited. What information do you have so we can continue with our enquiries?'

Smith pulled out a notebook from her pocket. 'What exactly would you like to know?'

'Everything. From the moment you were notified about the incident.'

'The 999 call came in at seven-fifty-seven, and PC French and I were sent to the scene to investigate. The two boys were with their mother, standing about fifty metres from where they'd discovered the skull. The mother did most of the talking. She was cross with her sons for disappearing so early in the morning without telling her.'

'How did she find out? Did they go home to tell her?'

'No. The older boy used his mobile to phone her.'

'Did the boys say whether the skull was on show or did they actually dig it up?'

'It seems that they were riding their bikes doing wheelies in the mud...' Smith glanced up from her notebook. 'That's when the bike is on the back wheel with—'

'I do know what a wheelie is.' How old did the PC think she was?

'Sorry, ma'am. They were riding round in circles over the site and must have dislodged it.' The officer looked down again at her notebook.

'Did they mention seeing other bones?'

'No. They only saw the skull.'

'Did they touch it?'

'When I asked, they said they didn't and that as soon as they saw it in the mud they phoned their mum, who came straight away. She contacted us and was told to wait for officers to arrive. Once I'd spoken to the boys, and had taken a contact number and address for where they're staying, I allowed them to go back to the cottage to change out of their wet clothes.'

'Did you ask them to stay there in case we wanted to interview them further?'

The officer flushed. 'No, ma'am. I didn't think it was necessary because we had the mother's mobile number.'

Would Lauren have done the same thing? Maybe. But that was beside the point now because it had caused a delay.

'Except you didn't give me the number and I had a wasted journey out to the cottage where they're staying. With hindsight, you should have passed on their details to one of my team.'

Not that Lauren thought it necessary to question the boys, now. PC Smith had collected sufficient information for them to work with.

'Sorry, ma'am.'

The phone on her desk rang, and she held up her hand to ensure the officer didn't speak. 'Pengelly.'

'I'd like an update on the human remains case. Please come to my office,' her boss, DCI Mistry, said.

'I'll be with you shortly, sir.' She replaced the phone and looked at Smith, who was staring down at her hands. 'Do you have anything else in your notes that will help, Constable, because I have to report on the case to the DCI.'

'No, ma'am. I'll make sure to let CID know the phone number of the boys' mother.'

Lauren waited for Smith to leave before heading down the

corridor to the DCI's office. They were both situated on the first floor of the 1960s grey-brick building, the ground floor of the station comprising the reception, custody suite and interview rooms.

The DCI's door was slightly open so she tapped gently on it and walked in.

'Good morning, sir.'

Her boss was sitting behind his desk, which was empty apart from a laptop and a single photo of his family to one side. He was exceptionally tidy and, as usual, he was dressed immaculately in an obviously expensive dark navy suit, with pale blue shirt and a navy and red paisley tie. He looked more like a city banker than a police officer. He'd been at Penzance only a few months longer than Lauren and she suspected that he, too, was using it as a stepping stone. But he was a good officer and she respected his opinions. Their interactions had always been brief and formal, which was fine by her. She didn't go to work to socialise.

'Come in, and sit down.' He indicated to the seat in front of his desk. 'What sort of response did we have from the press conference yesterday?'

'Not as much as I'd expected, considering how tight the community is. I believe we only had two phone calls yesterday and they were from people wanting to *know* more information rather than to give us any. The estate owner is out of town, due back this evening, and we'll interview him on his return. That should give us more to work with. We're also waiting to hear from forensics. It will be much easier to investigate once we know how long the body's been there. We'll then have parameters on which to base a missing person's search. Currently, it's pretty much a stab in the dark.'

It was impossible to read his face. Was he thinking that they should have done more?

'We need this solving quickly. It's unsettling for the whole community. Be sure to use your best resources. Especially now you have a full team. Which reminds me, how is the new DS settling in? I appreciate it's only his second day and he was thrown in at the deep end yesterday when he had to go to the scene. Oh, and by the way, I wasn't impressed by the lack of staff in the office when DS Price arrived. I know you were meant to be on leave, but didn't you leave instructions for any of them to be in early?'

'Their start times vary. I didn't ask anyone to arrive early because no one informed me that Price was starting yesterday.'

'That's down to HR. Maybe because you were on leave they didn't want to bother you. So back to Price, how is he doing?'

'It's early days. So far all I can tell you is he walks with a limp and has an aversion to dead bodies, and that includes those minus the flesh.'

Damn. Why did she say all that? It was hardly professional. Then again, considering Price had been appointed to Lauren's team without her having been consulted or been part of the interview panel, it was no wonder she felt aggrieved.

Mistry's dark eyes narrowed. 'I can assure you he comes with excellent references. I have no idea why he limps, and frankly it's nothing that should concern us. We adhere to the Equality Act as I'm sure you're aware.'

Great. Now he believed that she had an ableist attitude. That couldn't have been further from the truth.

'I apologise. It was a description of him and in no way did I mean to imply that he was in any way inferior. If you say that he has good references then I'll withhold judgement on his performance until I can assess it for myself. I'm not—'

The DCI's phone rang and he answered, without even acknowledging to Lauren he was going to do so. 'Mistry.' He paused for a moment. 'I see. And where is this?' He glanced at Lauren, worry flickering in his eyes. 'Yes. Thank you. We'll be there straight away.' He replaced the handset. 'A three-year-old child has gone missing from the Acorn Childcare Centre in Penzance. Take a team and get over there, now.'

Lauren swallowed hard. A missing child. The crime every detective dreaded. Most often it was a false alarm – the child had hidden somewhere, or they'd run outside, soon to be discovered. But sometimes... sometimes... No, she wasn't going to go there yet.

'Yes, sir. Do we know anything else? Boy or girl?'

'They didn't say. Report back to me as soon as you can. Let's hope this is a false alarm that can be resolved quickly.'

Lauren hurried out of his office and back to the team.

'Everyone pay attention, please,' she said in a loud voice the moment she entered the room. The sound of chatter immediately ceased. 'A child has gone missing from Acorn Childcare, a nursery in Penzance, and we need to get there immediately. The only information I have is that the child is aged three. Sergeant Price, you come with me in my car because I know the short cuts. The rest of you can meet us there – apart from you, Tamsin. I want you to stay here.'

Lauren glanced at her new sergeant, who had quickly stood up and was putting on his jacket. His face was devoid of colour. If he had a thing about missing children as well as dead bodies, that didn't bode well.

'Why do I have to stay?' Tamsin said, distracting Lauren from wondering about Price.

'Someone needs to be here to take any calls resulting from the press conference yesterday, and follow up on them. While you're waiting for calls to come in you can do some background research into the nursery.'

'Okay, ma'am.' Tamsin slumped back in her chair.

Lauren could see by the look on Tamsin's face that she was disappointed, and no doubt the officer would think it was because she was the youngest member of the team. It wasn't that at all – Tamsin had a good manner when dealing with the public. But Lauren didn't have time to go into that now. She'd mention it soon, though. In the meantime, they had to get going, and pray that the DCI was correct and it was nothing more than a false alarm.

FIVE

TUESDAY, 25 OCTOBER

Matt's fists were tightly balled and resting in his lap while he sat beside the DI. She had the siren blaring and traffic pulled into the side of the road well in advance of them approaching. How different it was from the city.

How could a nursery *lose* a child? Surely they had protocols in place to stop that from happening? Thank goodness Acorn nursery wasn't where Dani went two days a week, although it was one they'd considered. Hopefully there was a logical reason for what had happened. Maybe the child had run away, although presumably the staff would have found them by now.

Pengelly drove fast along the narrow roads and they arrived at the nursery within ten minutes. It was a 1930s, single-storey, grey pebble-dashed building – the last property in the residential street. Running alongside the nursery was a walkway which presumably connected with the road behind.

Jenna and Clem pulled in behind them and followed Matt and Pengelly into the building. A woman in her mid-forties, wearing a navy skirt and pink polo shirt with the nursery name and logo on the front, was waiting for them at the door, an anxious expression on her face.

'Hello. I'm Valerie Archer, the head of the nursery,' she said to Pengelly and Matt, all the time looking over their shoulders. 'Hello, Jenna, I was hoping you'd come.'

Matt and Pengelly turned around.

'Valerie and I are neighbours,' Jenna explained, walking over and standing beside them. 'How are you?'

Valerie Archer shook her head. 'It's so hard to believe,' she said, her voice trembling. 'It's like my worst nightmare come true.' She gestured helplessly with her hands, her expression one of bewilderment and distress.

'Tell us exactly what happened,' Pengelly requested, calmly.

Valerie indicated for them to stand over to the side in the outdoor area, which had swings and slides and other play equipment, so they weren't blocking the front entrance. She sucked in a breath. 'A three-year-old girl, Isla Hopkins, has gone missing from the Orange Room. One of the nursery nurses noticed shortly after some of the children had taken their morning nap.'

'Don't all the children take a nap?' Lauren asked.

'Not in the Orange Room. It's mainly the three-year-olds who do. By the time they reach four, they don't generally need one.'

'I assume you've searched the building to make sure she hasn't wandered off somewhere here?' Pengelly probed, visibly scanning the area.

Valerie tensed. 'Yes of course. I've looked everywhere, mainly on my own because we still have other children to care for and all the staff are in their relevant rooms. I telephoned the child's mother and asked her to come in, but didn't explain why. She should arrive soon. Her workplace is twenty-five minutes away in Helston.'

'Have you searched anywhere in the surrounding areas?' Matt asked.

He glanced at the DI. There was no indication on her face

that he should have waited for her permission before asking questions. When he'd first started at Lenchester, DCI Walker was a stickler for wanting to ask all of the questions. She had a rule that she spoke and whoever she was with observed and listened. That didn't appear to be the case here.

'I've had a thorough search around the perimeter of the nursery, but couldn't find anything and I wanted to be here when you and the child's mother arrived. I couldn't spare any staff to go outside.'

'Clem, I need you to investigate every inch of the outside and everywhere inside the building apart from the children's rooms,' Pengelly barked. 'Jenna, contact uniform and ask them to send as many officers as possible to join the search.'

'Yes, ma'am. Are you going to alert all of the parents and ask them to collect their children?' Clem asked.

'No. We don't want to cause panic.'

Jenna and Clem quickly left, leaving a charged atmosphere behind them.

'How many children do you have here and what's the system?' Matt asked.

'We have three different rooms. Children aged from six weeks to two years are placed in the Green Room. Children aged two years to three years are in the Blue Room. Those aged three to four years go in the Orange Room. Isla had recently moved into the Orange Room because she was more advanced than some of the children in the Blue. We thought it would be good for her,' Valerie explained.

'How many children in each room, and what's the staff to child ratio?' Matt continued.

'We stick to government guidelines. In the Orange Room there's a ratio of one staff member to eight children, with up to sixteen children in there at any one time. Each day varies because not every child is full-time but the maximum number of children on the premises at any one time is thirty-seven.'

'Does Isla attend every day?' Pengelly asked.

'Yes. She's been full-time since she first came to us at age nine months,' Valerie said.

'Didn't Isla miss her friends when you moved her up to the next room?' Matt probed.

Perhaps there was another reason for the child being moved?

'She was a little sad but, like I said, it was for her development. We pride ourselves on the children being ready for school and demonstrating their full potential when they leave.'

'And moving her was nothing to do with needing the space in the Blue Room for another child?' Pengelly asked, pointedly.

Valerie Archer, flushed and averted her gaze, avoiding Pengelly's scrutiny. 'Okay, I admit that did factor in our decision, but she wouldn't have been moved up if she wasn't ready.'

'If she was unhappy, and a bright child, then she could have easily run away, don't you think? Especially as, having been here for so long, she'd be very familiar with the layout,' Matt said.

Valerie cleared her throat. 'Theoretically, yes. But I can assure you that she didn't show any signs of being unhappy. In fact, when she arrived this morning she was full of beans.'

'But with only two staff supervising sixteen children she could have left the room without being seen, couldn't she?' Matt said.

Valerie nervously plucked at the hem of her jacket. 'Possibly.'

'Where are your CCTV cameras?' Matt asked, glancing up at the doorway and seeing one there.

'We have them covering the outside of the building. But none inside,' Valerie said, her voice calmer.

'Why not?'

'We consulted the parents regarding having cameras in every room and they voted against it. They were happy for them to be on the front and back exits, but that's it. I'm not sure how to access the footage, but I can ask Dee when she comes in this afternoon. She's responsible for all the IT.'

'Contact her now to see if she can be here sooner,' Matt said, surprised that the woman hadn't already done so. Then again, when someone's in shock their mind sometimes goes blank. Or was he making excuses for bad management?

'Yes. Okay.'

'Before you do so, what can you tell us about the family? Is there anything we should know that might help in our search?' Matt asked.

'There's been a rather nasty divorce and custody battle concerning Isla,' Valerie said, lowering her voice. 'She's an only child and Mrs Hopkins has sole custody. The father is only allowed supervised visits.'

Matt went on alert, and glanced across at Pengelly, whose face had darkened. Supervised visits weren't something the courts insisted on unless there was good reason. 'Was there violence in the family?'

'Not that I'm aware of. Mr Hopkins was in prison and has only been out for a few months. The court ruled that, for now, he can only have supervised visits with Isla. It might have been because he's on parole. I'm not sure. Since he was released we haven't seen him here at the nursery. Mrs Hopkins always brings Isla every morning before she goes to work and collects her later.'

'Would you recognise him if you saw him?' Pengelly asked.

Valerie turned to face her. 'Yes, because the case was well-publicised when it happened and occasionally, before he was sent to prison, he'd collect Isla. He also attended our parent/teacher consultations last year when Isla first went into the Blue Room.'

He was Matt's first choice of suspect, should the child not be found nearby.

'And you're sure you haven't seen him hanging around? Maybe keeping out of sight by standing beside a tree. Or perhaps walking past?'

'I don't recall seeing him. I doubt any of the staff would've seen him either because they tell me when there's anything suspicious. It's been business as usual here.'

Except it wasn't.

Now they had a missing child and a parent who hadn't yet been informed. The next time his mother took Dani to nursery, Matt was going to ask her to check their security procedures. If they weren't top-notch, then he'd move his daughter somewhere else.

'Ma'am,' Jenna said, walking over to them. 'Uniform should be here soon. Shall I wait for them in the street and instruct them where to go?'

'No. I'd like to speak to them first. I want you to join Clem. We must make doubly sure the child hasn't got stuck somewhere. In a drain, or up a tree. I want everywhere searched.'

'Yes, ma'am,' Jenna said, marching away.

'What's Isla like?' Matt asked.

'She's a quiet little girl. Enjoys her own company and isn't any trouble at all,' Valerie said.

'Do you have any photos of her?'

'Yes, in the admin office in her individual folder. We also have a class photo on the wall in each room.'

'We need to interview all staff who are working today, in particular the two in the Orange Room,' Pengelly said.

'Yes, of course. I'll arrange that. They're in shock, but have had to carry on with their normal duties. I'll take you to the office and show you Isla's photo.'

Before they entered the building, Valerie Archer glanced to the left across the play area. 'There's Mrs Hopkins.' She nodded towards the road. 'When my admin officer phoned her all she said was that there had been an issue and for her to get here as soon as possible. When Mrs Hopkins pressed her, my assistant said she didn't know what it was. I didn't want Mrs Hopkins to know in advance in case it affected her ability to drive here safely. I'll update her first, and then bring her over to you.' She sucked in a breath, and walked away.

'Well?' Pengelly asked, turning to Matt.

'If Isla Hopkins isn't found on site or close by then we need to speak to the husband. He's the one with most to gain by taking her.'

'I agree. But first we need to exhaust every possibility here.'

SIX

TUESDAY, 25 OCTOBER

'I'm not familiar with nursery schools. How come there's no proper security here? No cameras inside because the parents don't want it. Don't you find that strange? Or is it normal?' Lauren asked her new sergeant while they were waiting for Valerie Archer to speak to Isla's mother and bring her over to them.

Lauren had never wanted children or to get married, for that matter. She'd had relationships over the years, but nothing long-term and she'd usually been the one to end things when the other person had started to monopolise her time. She'd always been more concerned with building her career.

Now, at the age of thirty-six, if she did suddenly decide she wanted a child... but seriously, why should she? Her dogs, Tia and Ben, were more than enough for her. She'd never been big on family. Her parents had died in a road traffic accident when she was eight and she'd been brought up by her mother's younger sister and her husband, Julia and Roy Cave, in Bodmin, further inland than Penzance.

They hadn't wanted her to live with them – her uncle had made that perfectly clear from the start. On the day of the funeral, when she'd been sitting alone in a corner crying, he'd come over and told her to stop being so pathetic. He didn't want a cry baby in the house.

From that moment on, she'd resolved to never let him see her upset again, however difficult things became. And it was hard. Her aunt and uncle were the total opposite to what she was used to. She'd learnt to hide her vulnerable side. To not show her feelings. It had also made her determined to make something of her life. She wasn't going to end up like them.

Aunt Julia's family had always skirted on the wrong side of the law and both of her sons, Connor and Clint – Lauren's cousins – had been in prison. Roy, too. Fortunately Lauren didn't have the same surname, so no one in the force could link them to her. They hadn't spoken in years, but she'd be lying if she said that knowing their close proximity hadn't impacted her decision-making process after being offered the job at Penzance. In fact, she'd almost turned it down in case they made a surprise appearance. But at the time it was the best career opportunity she'd been given. Luckily, in the eighteen months she'd been at Penzance she hadn't seen them, so she assumed that they didn't yet know she was there.

The only contact she ever had with her family was the Christmas card she sent each year. But she never gave her address, so they couldn't send one in return. Because her cousins had criminal records, it had been easy for her to keep up to date with what they were doing. Not that she checked often. Occasionally, Lauren felt guilty about isolating herself from Aunt Julia, who had always been kind to her, and who was the only one who hadn't broken the law. Julia had a lot to put up with, but she'd made her own choices and it wasn't as if she didn't know what was going on in front of her.

'My daughter's enrolled in a different nursery for two days a week,' Price said, cutting across her thoughts. 'I've no idea what their CCTV policy is. To be honest it's not something I'd

considered because I'd assumed there would be adequate security. I do need to check, though.'

Price had a young daughter? He hadn't shared that. At least
not with her. What else didn't she know about him? Not that
his private life was her concern.

'But now you're thinking about it, how do you feel? Surely
if there are cameras in a classroom then it acts as a deterrent for
any inappropriate behaviour.'

'Well... it's tricky. I expect most parents think it might lead
to the cameras being hacked. Giving paedophiles a chance to
access the footage. It's happened before. And don't forget that
nurseries are required to stick to staff/children ratios. You'd
think that would be enough security. It's not like we're in a big
city. I get that they might need heavier security in certain areas
of London or Birmingham, but surely not here. Not that I've
any idea how city nurseries operate because Dani's only two
and was at home until we arrived here. She only goes now to
give my parents a break from looking after her full-time.
They're retired and childcare isn't for the faint-hearted.' He
gave a dry smile.

No mention of the child's mother.

'I understand what you're saying, but we now have a
missing child so that might cause parents to reassess their
views.' She glanced across to the play area. 'Valerie Archer's on
her way over with the mother.'

'This is Mrs Hopkins... Bev,' Valerie Archer said when they
reached Lauren and Matt, 'this is DI Pengelly and DS Price.'

'I can't believe she's gone. Where can she be? She wouldn't
go off on her own, she's not like that. You've got to find her. She
—' Bev's voice broke and a loud sob erupted from her. Lauren
placed her hand on the woman's shoulder to reassure her.

'Bev, we're doing everything we can to find Isla, I promise.
More officers will be joining us shortly. I know this is difficult,
but we need to ask you a few questions.' Lauren glanced at

Valerie Archer. 'Is there somewhere quiet we can talk? That's more private?'

It was difficult enough for the woman as it was, without her grief being on full view for everyone to see.

'You can use my office. It's this way,' Valerie said, her voice firm and resolute.

Lauren, Price, and Bev followed the head into the building, along a short corridor. The office had a light oak desk with a computer on top. To the side of the desk was a matching small round table with four chairs around it. Children's artwork covered the walls.

'Please could you leave us, Mrs Archer? And could you send a photo of Isla to my phone? Here's my card.' Lauren pulled one from her pocket and handed it over. The woman then left, closing the door behind her.

Lauren gestured to the chairs and the three of them sat down.

Bev was shaking, her hands wrapped around her knees.

'Would you like a glass of water? Or a cup of tea?' Lauren asked.

The woman sniffed and shook her head. 'No, thank you. We can't waste any time. W-what do you want to know?'

Lauren slid her chair a little closer to the woman. 'Please could you tell us what Isla was wearing today?'

Price pulled out his notebook and pen, poised ready to take some notes. Lauren nodded her approval.

'She has on a pair of dark blue leggings and a pink jumper with a bear on the front. It's her favourite. She'd wear it every day if she could.' Bev gave a watery smile. 'On her feet she had some black patent leather boots and she had a dusky pink puffer jacket. She's also wearing a pink headband and her hair is tied up in two bunches with ties that also have bears on them. She loves bears.'

'Thank you. Tell me, is Isla a friendly child? Would she go

off with someone she doesn't know?' Lauren steeled herself for Bev realising the meaning behind the question.

'She usually sticks close to me when meeting strangers. But she can be quite a chatterbox with people she knows well.' The woman's eyes widened in horror as it dawned on her. 'Do you think someone took her? Could it be Luke?'

Lauren tensed. 'We don't know, but please don't start imaging the worst. We understand there's been a custody battle with your ex-husband – Luke Hopkins. Is it likely that he could have taken Isla without asking permission?'

In Lauren's experience, cases like these often involved someone known to the victim.

The woman grimaced. 'It would be typical of the bastard to do whatever he wanted, no matter the consequences. He hated that he wasn't allowed to see Isla on his own because of his parole and moaned about it all the time to whoever would listen. He's been in prison for fraud, but now he's out he thinks he's entitled to pick up where he left off as far as Isla's concerned. But he's not allowed to – at least not for a while. What he did was inexcusable. He stole money from his clients, and even took some from my family, without any thought of the position it left them in. I bet it's him. It makes total sense. And of course Isla would have gone if he'd asked her. When I get my hands on him I'll—'

'Bev, we don't know yet if it is him,' Lauren said, resting her hand on the woman's arm. 'But we'll contact him straight away, while continuing our search here and in surrounding areas. Do you know where Luke is?'

'He lives in Marazion, with his parents. He's been there ever since he came out of prison. I don't have his mobile number – I blocked him and deleted it. All the visits he has with Isla are arranged through a social worker. I take Isla to the social services office in Heamoor for the visit and collect her once it's over.'

'Do you know his parents' address?'

'They're in Trevenner Lane, beside the turn into Church-way. I've always got on well with them and, when Luke was inside, Isla and I saw them regularly. But since he's been out I haven't been back. He probably wouldn't let them see her anyway. They're lovely people, but I think they're frightened of making Luke angry.'

'We're going to speak to them now, and I'll arrange for our family liaison officer to take you home and stay with you until we have some news. They'll be your link person and will answer any questions you have about the search for Isla. I know it's hard, but try not to worry. We'll do our best to find your daughter soon.'

'Thank you. If anything's happened t-to her... I-I...' Her voice cracked.

What could Lauren say? No amount of platitudes would change the situation. The woman's child was missing. Of course she was going to be beside herself with worry.

'Bev, I'm going to ask the FLO to drive you home because it's not advisable for you to drive right now. I'll arrange for another officer to return your car to you later.'

There was a light tap on the door and Jenna came in.

'Ma'am, uniform have arrived. What would you like me to tell them?'

'I'll give them their instructions. Contact the station and arrange for the family liaison officer to come here and take Mrs Hopkins home.' She turned to her sergeant. 'Sergeant Price, stay here with Mrs Hopkins until the FLO arrives while I sort out the wider search.'

'Yes, ma'am. After that shall I join the search?'

'No. I want you with me at Isla's grandparents' house.'

Lauren left the nursery and headed to the road where there were ten officers standing beside three police cars.

'Good morning, Sergeant Ford,' she said when reaching

them. 'We have a missing three-year-old girl. Isla Hopkins. Here's a photo of her.' She showed her phone to the officer. 'She's wearing blue leggings and a pink jumper with a bear on the front. We have no idea how, or when, she left because no one saw anything. Search all the surrounding areas.'

'Yes, ma'am. I'll send two officers in each direction so we can make sure we cover everywhere. What about a house-to-house?'

'I'll ask two of my officers to do that and if you could spare some to go with them that will speed up the process. I want you to report back to me throughout. I'm going to see the child's grandparents. There's a possibility the child has been taken by her father, but we don't want to assume anything. She could be on her own or she could have left with someone.'

'Are we expecting other parents to arrive and collect their children because of this?' the sergeant asked.

'No. At the moment we're keeping it quiet. The children are still in their classes.'

'Well, let's hope that she's wandered off accidentally. You know what young kids are like. I've got three of my own. They can never stay in one place.'

Sergeant Ford returned to the other officers and began instructing them.

Lauren turned and headed back to the nursery. On her way, Clem and Jenna came up to her.

'We've searched everywhere other than the classrooms as you requested, ma'am. No sign of the child,' Jenna said.

'Uniform are about to search the surrounding areas. I'd like you to go door to door and find out if anybody saw anything. But don't alert them to the fact there's a missing child at this stage. Ask if they've seen anyone acting suspiciously in the area. Any strange cars or people hanging around. It's not like this is a busy town centre so someone should have noticed anything suspicious. The main thing is we don't panic the community unnecessarily. At least, not until we've eliminated the father. He could have been the one to take Isla. Although how he could have done that without being seen remains a mystery to me.'

'Yes, ma'am. Would you like us to return here after?' Jenna asked.

'Yes. We'll need to coordinate questioning all of the staff and possibly parents, but first I'm taking DS Price with me to visit the child's grandparents. If any parents or caregivers arrive to collect their children, have a quiet word with them and ask if they've seen anything suspicious. That's as much as we can do at the moment. As I've said, the main thing is we don't let this get out of control until we are sure she was taken.'

SEVEN

TUESDAY, 25 OCTOBER

'Let's hope the child's here and we can avoid the panic that's bound to come with her disappearance,' Pengelly said to Matt as they were driving towards the grandparents' home in Marazion.

Seriously, was *that* her main concern? What about the safety of the child? Okay, he got that they could end up with public panic if someone had been able to take a child from what should have been a place of safety. But Matt was more worried about little Isla and what horrors she might be going through, especially if it wasn't her father who'd taken her.

'Yes, ma'am. Although Mr Hopkins is on parole and could end up back inside. Surely taking Isla for a day out or something isn't worth that? And as her father, surely the little girl's health and happiness should be paramount so, again, *why* would he do it? And he would know that his parents' house would be the first place we'd visit.'

Pengelly tossed a glance in his direction, and clicked her tongue in disapproval.

'You surprise me, Sergeant. You should know by now that people are very unpredictable and often do things that we think

are totally ridiculous because they're blinded by their own
desires. In this case, taking the child because he wants to see her
more, and taking her somewhere he feels is safe. I'm not saying
that's definitely what has happened, but surely you can see that
it is most likely.'

So this is what his new DI was going to be like? Agree with
her or you'll be viewed with derision. Okay, not derision, but
clearly she believed that her view was the only correct one.

Was that why the rest of the team seemed not to like her?
Then again, did it matter? As DI she wasn't there to be liked but
to make sure the team was effective. And if she wanted to be a
stickler for the rules and have a regimented way of approaching
things, then he'd have to learn to accept it. She wasn't going to
change on his account.

And yet... could she be any different from his old boss,
Whitney, who wore her heart on her sleeve and would do whatever it took to solve a case? Although, the fact that Pengelly had
cancelled her leave after learning about the human remains
showed a huge dedication to her work, which was similar.

Anyway, he shouldn't be comparing the two of them – it
wasn't like he was ever going back to Lenchester to work. Not
only that, he was probably over-analysing the whole thing,
considering that he'd only been on her team for two days.

Pengelly pulled up outside Isla's grandparents' house, a
semi-detached red-brick building with a small rectangular patch
of grass at the front which had a neatly trimmed low hedge
around it. It was very well maintained, as was the house from
the outside. There were net curtains on the windows, making it
impossible to see inside.

After knocking, the door was opened by a tall man, dressed
in beige trousers with a brown V-necked jumper and a pale-
blue open-necked shirt. He had a slight stoop and looked to be
in his early seventies. His grey hair was cropped close to his
head.

Pengelly held out her warrant card. 'Good morning, I'm Detective Inspector Pengelly from Penzance CID and this is Detective Sergeant Price. Are you Mr Hopkins?'

'Yes, why?'

'We'd like to have a word with you and your wife, if she's there.'

'What's it about? What's happened?' he asked frantically.

'We'd rather talk inside,' Pengelly said, gently.

'Has someone been hurt?' His voice wobbled and his eyes darted from Pengelly to Matt.

They couldn't reassure him because they had no idea yet what had happened to his granddaughter. But he'd know soon enough. Unless they already knew and had been expecting the visit. Matt would make sure to scrutinise their reactions when they were informed about Isla's disappearance.

'Please, Mr Hopkins, if you could let us in we will discuss everything then. Is your wife at home?'

'Yes, she's in the front room.' The man opened the door and ushered them inside the small square hall which had stairs going up the right-hand side.

'Good. We'll speak to you both together.'

They followed him into the room and sitting beside the open fireplace was a woman, with short grey hair, wearing a floral print dress, who looked around the same age as her husband.

'Ivy, it's the police.'

She jumped up from her chair, her eyes wide. 'Who's hurt? What is it? Has Luke had an accident?'

Certainly a genuine response, so far.

'Please sit down, both of you,' Pengelly said gently. She also nodded for Matt to do the same. He sat on the upright chair under the window and Pengelly sat beside Mr Hopkins on the sofa. 'I do have some worrying news. We've just come from the nursery where Isla, your granddaughter, attends. She's missing and we'd like to speak to her father. We believe it's possible he may have taken her from there.'

Mrs Hopkins' jaw dropped and she looked at her husband, her face ashen. He appeared as shocked as his wife. If they had any knowledge of this they were bloody good actors.

'Isla's missing. Oh no. Where is she? Who took her? What are you doing about it?' The words tumbled out of the woman's mouth.

'That's why we wish to speak to your son. We hope it's all been a misunderstanding and we can find the child.'

'Luke's at work,' Mrs Hopkins said. 'He's not going to take Isla. No way. It's hard that he can only see her at certain times and in a particular place, because then we don't get to see her either. At least, not at the moment. We know that's how it is and have to accept it. It won't be forever. That's why I'm sure he hasn't taken her. He wouldn't risk it.'

Matt hoped that they were wrong. The best outcome would be for Isla to be with her dad. Because if she wasn't... he didn't want to go there just yet.

'We'll need to talk to him about this,' Pengelly said. 'And if he hasn't taken her, then we can exclude him from our enquires. I must warn you that if you were involved in Isla's disappearance in any way you could be subject to prosecution for aiding and abetting.'

The grandparents exchanged a knowing glance. What was that about? Had Matt missed something? They'd appeared genuine to him and he was usually good at judging people in this type of situation.

'Look, we have nothing to do with Isla's disappearance. And I'm sure Luke hasn't either,' Mr Hopkins said, leaning forward and staring at Pengelly. 'He wouldn't be so stupid. He might've said sometimes that he should take her and go off somewhere to start a new life, but I know he didn't mean it. It was said in frustration because of the situation he was in. And he definitely went to work this morning. I saw him leave at his usual time.'

'Cliff,' Mrs Hopkins said. 'Why did you say that? It makes Luke look guilty and we both know he isn't. The police are wasting their time here with us. They should be out looking for Isla.'

'But...' Mr Hopkins' voice fell away.

'Mr Hopkins. Mrs Hopkins. If you do know anything that's going to help, then please tell us now. Our main concern is for Isla's wellbeing and that should be yours, too. If Luke has taken her, then we have to find them. Kidnapping is a crime, not to mention the effect it would have on Isla herself and her mother.'

'Exactly, and that's why we know he hasn't done it,' Mr Hopkins said, with a nod.

'Cliff's right. We know our son. Yes, he did something wrong in the past, but underneath he's a good boy. He's sorry for what he did and he's paid the price. All he wants to do now is put it all behind him and get on with his life.'

A very different story from what his ex-wife had told them. But if, as they'd been told, the divorce was acrimonious, then they wouldn't expect to hear anything less from her. Plus they were his parents, so of course they would take his side. Then again, if Luke Hopkins was guilty, it would mean he'd broken his parole and could end up back inside where he wouldn't see Isla at all.

'I understand why you think it might be him but you'll find out soon enough that it wasn't,' Mr Hopkins added. 'It's not fair that he can't see Isla when he wants to and that it's always at the social services office. How can he be a proper father to her in those circumstances? Okay he did something wrong and he's paid the price but he's always been a good father to Isla, and was a good husband to Bev.'

They had begun going round in circles and this was getting them nowhere.

'Well, that's what we need to find out. And we need Isla back with her mother. What's the name and address of the place where Luke works? We'll see if he's there,' Matt said.

'He works for Generate, a call centre in Helston. A ridiculous job for someone with his qualifications. It was all he could get. No one wants to employ someone with a prison record,' Mr Hopkins said.

'Thank you.'

'Is there anything we can do to help? We love Isla. We wouldn't want any harm to come to her. Shall we go out looking and help with the search?'

'Thanks for the offer, but we'd rather you stay here. If Luke contacts you before we've interviewed him then please let me know. I don't want you getting in touch with him first. If he does have Isla, we don't want him to be alerted.' Pengelly handed her card over to Mrs Hopkins, who took it and placed it on the coffee table. 'We're working very hard to find Isla, so try not to worry.'

'Easy for you to say. She's not your granddaughter,' Mrs Hopkins said.

Matt and Pengelly saw themselves out of the house.

'What do you think?' Pengelly asked him.

'From their reactions, it's doubtful they know anything. Whether Luke Hopkins did it without telling them, though, remains to be seen. We need to get to Helston straight away. Let's hope that they do as you've asked and don't warn him.'

EIGHT

TUESDAY, 25 OCTOBER

Lauren walked up to the reception of Generate and held out her warrant card. 'I'd like to speak to Luke Hopkins please.'

'I'm new here, do you know the department he works in by any chance?' the receptionist asked, a sheepish expression on her face.

'Sorry, I've no idea.'

'No problem. I'll check the staff list.'

Lauren waited with Price beside the desk watching while the receptionist stared at the screen, her fingers hovering over the keyboard and pressing the occasional key.

'I've found him. He's situated on the third floor in the complaints section. I'll call and ask him to come down to reception.'

'Don't say we're from the police,' Price said.

Her sergeant had made a good call. They didn't want Hopkins to do a runner before they had time to speak to him. She had to admit she was impressed with him so far. Hopefully it would continue.

The receptionist pressed several numbers on her phone keypad. 'Hello, it's Sadie on reception. Please could you ask

Luke Hopkins to come down? He has a visitor.' She paused for a moment and then glanced up at Lauren. 'He's not at work today. He called in sick.'

The hairs rose on the back of Lauren's neck. He wasn't at home. His parents believed he was at work. It was pointing to one thing. That he'd taken his daughter somewhere. But where? They had to find them both before he got too far away. He might have even planned to go overseas, which would mean there'd be very little chance of locating them.

'Ask his supervisor to come down here straight away.'

'Please send Wanda down to reception, now. The police are here and they need to speak to her, urgently.' The receptionist ended the call and stared at Lauren. 'What's happened? Is it serious?'

'We can't discuss police inquiries, as I'm sure you appreciate.' Lauren held back an exasperated sigh. Surely the woman didn't expect them to tell her what they were doing there?

'Sorry. I understand.'

The phone rang, distracting her, and Lauren and Price stepped to the side to wait for Hopkins' supervisor. Within less than a minute there was a ping and the lift door opened. A short woman in her thirties, dressed in a business suit, walked out. They were the only people in reception and she headed directly to them.

'Hello, I'm Wanda Dawson. Are you the police?'

'Yes. Is there somewhere more private where we can talk?' Lauren asked.

'We can go to our meeting room, providing it's free.'

They followed her down the corridor and into the first room on the left, which had a rectangular dark wood table with eight matching chairs situated around it and a whiteboard at one end of the room.

'This is fine, thanks.' Lauren pulled out a chair and sat down. Price and Wanda followed suit. 'I understand Luke

Hopkins called in sick, today. Can you tell me what time that was?'

'It was quite late, maybe around nine fifteen, which I wasn't pleased about because of reallocating his work. He was due at work by eight thirty and we ask employees to contact us first thing if they're going to be off sick. He sounded very croaky on the phone and said he wasn't feeling well, but he was hoping to be back tomorrow.'

'Did it sound put on at all?' Lauren asked, drumming her fingers on the table.

'I had to strain to hear him and it didn't seem fake. Are you saying that it was?'

'We don't know, so can't answer that.'

'Does he often call in sick?' Price asked.

'He hasn't worked here long and this was the first time. Why are you asking?'

'We wish to speak to him regarding one of our inquiries, and we were informed that he was at work.'

With hindsight Lauren should have said that they'd come to his workplace first. If Hopkins wasn't guilty of taking his daughter, she may well have got him in trouble. But really that was the least of her worries. And if he had bunked off for the day then he deserved whatever he had coming. The main thing was to find out what had happened to Isla and if he was involved in any way.

'Oh, I see. Are you saying that he's not at home today?' She narrowed her eyes.

Lauren wasn't going to get herself involved in company politics.

'We're just looking for him at the moment. We can't comment on his whereabouts if he's not here. What can you tell me about his performance at work?' She wasn't prepared to spend any longer debating whether or not Hopkins was sick; they didn't have time.

'So far, I have no complaints. To date he's been reliable. Always on time and will stay late if necessary.'

'How does he get on with his co-workers?'

'He's very quiet and keeps to himself. He'll ask if he has any queries relating to the work, which isn't often because he picked it up very quickly. Other than that he doesn't engage in conversation. From what I've observed, he doesn't appear to have made friends with anyone here. Call centre work is high pressured, especially on the complaints side, which is where he's stationed. Dealing non-stop with customer complaints is draining and can take it out of you. But he seems to be coping well and his colleagues speak highly of him.'

They had enough information from the woman and needed to leave – to head straight back to see his parents.

'Well, if you do hear anything from him please let us know because we are anxious to speak to him.'

Lauren and Price left and returned to the grandparents' house.

Mr Hopkins answered the door. His face was pale and his eyes flickered with worry.

'You're back. Have you found Isla?'

'No. I'm sorry we haven't yet. May we come in?' Lauren asked.

'We're still in the lounge.'

They followed him in. Mrs Hopkins was sitting in the exact same place she was before. Her eyes were red, as if she'd been crying. She looked up hopefully, but her husband shook his head and she slumped back into the chair.

'Luke wasn't at work. He phoned in sick at nine fifteen this morning. Why do you think that was?' Lauren asked.

'That's impossible. He definitely went. I saw him leave at eight, and he was carrying his packed lunch. His mum always makes it for him the night before and leaves it in the fridge.' Mr

Hopkins pressed his lips together, the bottom one trembling slightly from the pressure.

'Did he actually say that he was going to work?' Lauren asked.

Mr Hopkins shook his head. 'All he said was "Bye, Dad. See you later." I stood by the door and waved when he drove away. Nothing was out of the ordinary. Except... well, he did seem more cheerful than usual.'

Because he thought he'd be seeing his daughter, no doubt.

'In what way?'

'Singing to himself. Smiling. Being chatty. You know. Just happy. I thought maybe he'd got used to his situation and he'd decided to make the best of it. But...' His voice fell away, and he let out a long sigh.

'Could you try his mobile for us, please,' Lauren asked.

Mr Hopkins headed over to the sideboard and picked up a phone and keyed in a number.

'Put it on speaker,' Price said.

Mr Hopkins did as instructed, and it rang for a few times before going to voicemail.

'Ask him to phone you,' Lauren hurriedly said, before the beep signalled for a message to be left.

'It's me, Luke. Dad. Give us a call when you get this. Thanks.' Mr Hopkins ended the call.

'Thank you. If he does contact you then let us know,' Lauren said.

'Yes.' Mr Hopkins nodded.

'Since we were here earlier, have you checked his room to see if anything is missing?' Price asked.

'No. We haven't moved,' Mrs Hopkins said.

'Please will you take me upstairs and we can have a look together?' Price said, looking directly at the older woman.

Good move. That would leave Lauren with Mr Hopkins,

who seemed more realistic than his wife and might be prepared to tell her more when they were alone.

'I'll go,' Mr Hopkins said.

'No, let me,' his wife replied. 'You don't know what clothes he has, or what other things he has up there.'

Lauren waited until they'd left the room before addressing Mr Hopkins. 'Knowing that Luke called in sick today, do you think he might have gone to the nursery and taken Isla?'

She stared intently at him, taking in the despair in his eyes.

He sighed. 'I don't know. I really don't know. I thought that everything was working out okay. We're all unhappy about the visiting restrictions, but that's not going to last forever. Why would he take her? Where would he go? It makes no sense. Unless... unless... If he has got Isla, do you think he might bring her back here?'

'I think that highly unlikely because he'd know this is where we'd look first,' she said, having changed her mind from earlier when she admonished Price. With hindsight, she shouldn't have been so dogmatic.

'I don't know what to say.' He averted his gaze, unable to meet her eyes as a guilty flush crept up his neck and onto his cheeks.

What wasn't he telling her?

'Mr Hopkins, you've already told us that Luke had made comments about going off somewhere with Isla. Is there anything else that's alerted you? Because you're acting as if there is. What else has Luke said to you?'

Lauren's attention was diverted when Matt and Mrs Hopkins walked back into the room.

'There's nothing missing,' Price said.

'Okay. Mr Hopkins was just about to tell me something about Luke.'

Mrs Hopkins' brow furrowed. 'What is it, Cliff?'

The old man lowered his head. 'I'm sorry, Ivy.' He turned to

Lauren. 'I should have mentioned this before, but I thought Luke was at work so didn't think it mattered. I overheard him on the phone yesterday. I don't know who he was talking to but he did say "I'm putting a lot at risk, so no one must know what we're doing." I wasn't sure what he meant and didn't think it was about Isla, but that he was thinking of doing something illegal again. But—'

'But it could be about your granddaughter's disappearance,' Lauren said, before he could continue.

'If that's the case then it means he wasn't working alone,' Price said. 'Can you tell us the names and contact details of his friends?'

'He doesn't go out much, not really,' Mrs Hopkins said. 'Usually he goes to work each day and stays at home in the evening. He doesn't want to get himself into any trouble in case he breaks the conditions of his parole and ends up back in prison. I don't know who he could have been talking to on the phone.'

'We have to find Isla before any harm comes to her,' Price said. 'It might not be Luke who has her and if that's the case we have to concentrate our investigation elsewhere. We need to know, urgently, if Luke has anything to do with this. Remember, if he gets in touch you must let us know straight away.'

'Yes, we understand. We promise to tell you if he contacts us,' Mrs Hopkins said, resolutely. 'You have to know that we had nothing to do with this. Isla's our main concern. She's just a small child and all we want is for her to be found. Bev must be beside herself with worry.'

'Make sure you stay near the phone. We may want to talk to you again,' Price said.

After leaving the house, Lauren turned to her sergeant.

'Right. We'll head back to the nursery. Radio in and request a BOLO for Luke Hopkins right away. I want everyone to be on the lookout for him. We have to find him. And fast.'

NINE

'Ma'am, Tamsin's sent me the car registration details for Luke Hopkins,' Matt said, checking his phone as they were driving back to the nursery. Matt also saw that he had a message from his mum asking how his day was going and telling him what was for dinner. He'd have to reply later. 'We can look at the nursery's CCTV to see if his car was in the vicinity at the time Isla disappeared.'

It might all be pointing to Hopkins being the guilty party, but Matt didn't think they should be narrowing down the suspect pool just yet. There could be something else going on here.

As the minutes ticked by with no sign of Isla, the worry and dread were growing ever more intense. With every corner of the nursery searched and no trace of her disappearance, it seemed like it had to be someone with regular access to the nursery, someone who wouldn't be suspected. Perhaps the CCTV footage would come up with something. Although Matt had a sneaking suspicion that it wouldn't.

'Good. We'll look at the footage as soon as we're there,'

Pengelly said, glancing quickly in his direction before going back to focusing on the road ahead.

When they arrived, several police officers in uniform were stationed outside. Pengelly strode towards them, and Matt followed.

'Any luck?' Pengelly asked the sergeant.

'No, ma'am. There's been no sighting of the child at all.' He sighed in frustration. 'We'll continue with the search, but we're running out of options round here.'

'Keep me informed.' Pengelly turned to Matt. 'Let's find Valerie Archer.'

They hurriedly made their way to the head's office. Valerie was sitting at her desk, her face etched with worry. 'Have you had any success?'

'Not yet,' Pengelly said with an air of urgency. 'We're chasing up Isla's father, who called in sick to work this morning. His parents were in the dark about it because he'd left the house first thing, as usual. Is your IT person here yet? We need to take a look at the CCTV footage.'

'Yes. Dee's in the next office; I'll take you through. It will be good to do something other than sit here worrying and trying to act like everything's fine when parents call, or if someone visits. When can we announce what's happened? Because surely that would help.'

'We don't wish to cause widespread alarm. If we discover that Isla isn't with her father, then we'll revisit whether or not to make it public knowledge.'

'I understand. But I can't help worrying about the poor child.'

That made two of them. But at least if she was with her father it wouldn't be so hard for her.

The head led them to the next-door office where an older woman in her fifties was seated behind a desk. She looked up, anxiety shimmering in her eyes. They approached her desk and stood to the side.

'Dee, this is DI Pengelly and DS Price. They're here to see the CCTV footage. What have you found so far?'

The woman spun around in her chair. 'I've gone over it several times, even slowing it down, but there's no sign of anyone leaving the nursery with Isla. There was no evidence of anyone unfamiliar entering the building, through the front or back, either. How could the child have vanished without a trace?'

'We're looking for this car.' Matt showed Dee his phone with registration details for Luke Hopkins' car. 'It's a white Ford Focus. Can we look through the footage to see if we can locate it? Start from when Isla arrived at nursery this morning.'

'Yes, of course.' Dee spun back her chair and rewound the footage until reaching the time when Isla was dropped off. 'Okay. There she is.'

Pengelly and Matt peered over Dee's shoulder as she scrolled slowly through the footage. There was no sighting of the car anywhere.

'He could have been in a different car, to make sure we didn't spot him,' Matt suggested. 'Or he could have parked further up the road out of the camera's range.'

Were they clutching at straws? With no other clues, they had to.

'But then we would have seen him walking down the street,' Dee said, shaking her head sadly.

'Not if he was working with someone else and that person headed this way towards the nursery,' Matt said.

'It's impossible to identify all the people who have walked past,' Pengelly said.

Matt's fists balled. They were getting nowhere.

'Okay. Let's look at the footage from over the last two or three days. We might be able to identify a car that's been here on a regular basis, other than those belonging to parents dropping off and collecting their children,' Pengelly said.

They again stared over Dee's shoulder but there was nothing out of the ordinary. No suspicious cars visiting. It was only parents who Dee identified, and staff cars which were parked in a separate section of the car park. And one time there was a courier delivery.

'This is ridiculous,' Pengelly said, banging her fist on Dee's table and making the woman visibly jump. 'How can the child disappear without there being any sign of it happening? Is there any way someone can come in and out of the building and avoid the cameras? Is it possible for someone to stick close to the side of the building and come in and out via the rear exit?'

Valerie Archer sighed. 'It could be done in theory, but it would be far from simple.'

'Well, we should check,' Pengelly said, turning to Matt.

Matt and the DI left Dee's office and made their way down the hallway, exiting the building through a door at the rear. They peered around the corner to an area where the refuse bins were standing.

Matt turned and pointed to a camera that was situated above the back door and angled slightly to the right. 'Providing the person wasn't too big, I think they could possibly creep around the corner to the refuse area and avoid being seen. There's no camera focused on that small section.' He frowned. 'I wonder how they put the bins out?'

'It looks like they have to be wheeled all the way down the back and then through the car park,' Pengelly said. 'Does that mean someone could walk along the back and then through to the bin area, undetected? With a child in tow?'

'No,' Matt said, shaking his head. 'Because they'd have been caught on camera by the back door. A more likely scenario would be them exiting through the rear entrance, going to the bin area, crossing that small grassed area to the hedge and climbing over to the open field behind.' He pointed to the hedge which was only a few metres away from where they were standing.

'But how would they climb over the hedge without being spotted if they had Isla with them? It doesn't seem possible,' Pengelly said.

'What about if the person who took Isla came into the nursery this way, without being caught on camera. And then walked out of the front door with Isla hidden in a bag or under a coat?' Matt suggested.

'No. That wouldn't work because we'd have seen them leave on the CCTV footage.'

No matter what they thought of, they had a logical explanation. Even if Luke Hopkins was guilty, they still had no idea how he could have actually got Isla out of there.

'In that case, all I can think of is that someone came over the hedge and went into the nursery. From there, they went to the Orange Room, took Isla and then went back out the way they came,' Matt said.

'Without being seen?' Pengelly said, frowning. 'Is that even possible?'

'Well, it's not impossible,' Matt said, but not really believing it. 'Let's see if there are any footprints or signs of the area having been disturbed.' He left the bin area and made his way over to the hedge. He got within six feet, and noticed muddy footprints and the hedge squashed down. 'Don't come any closer,' he shouted over his shoulder. 'Someone's been here.'

'Are there footprints? How many can you see?' Pengelly called from behind him.

'On the mud between the grass and the hedge. It looks like several sets. Facing both forwards and backwards.'

'Arriving and leaving. Are there any small enough for a child?'

'No. But she could have been carried. This looks like two adults.'

'Bloody hell. We can't even account for one adult coming into the nursery without being seen and now you're suggesting there are two?' Pengelly said, a helpless tone in her voice.

'Are you okay? Do you need my help at all?'

Matt and Pengelly turned at the sound of Valerie's voice.

'We believe there have been people jumping over the hedge and coming onto the nursery grounds,' Pengelly said.

'I know,' Valerie said, sighing. 'We often find graffiti on the walls. In fact, only this past weekend we had to re-paint them because of it. The footprints could have been from the culprits.'

'Have you checked the CCTV to see who's doing it and when?' Matt asked.

Valerie shook her head in response. 'We only have the cameras on while the nursery is open.'

'What?' Pengelly spluttered. 'Why on earth would you do that?'

'We've always done it. People don't realise. They're still a deterrent.'

'I suggest that you rethink your policy and have them operating all of the time,' Pengelly snapped, shaking her head in disbelief. 'At least then you could identify the graffiti artists.'

Matt agreed. It was a crazy policy.

'So we still have no idea whether or not the damage to the hedge and the footprints are from the person, or persons, who took Isla,' Matt said, turning back to Pengelly.

'In the absence of any other evidence, I suggest that we assume this was the route taken. I'll call forensics. Where does the field lead to?' Pengelly asked Valerie.

'It's actually surrounded by houses. If you head straight over you'll come to a pathway into an estate.'

'A field in the middle of a housing estate is unusual,' Matt said.

'It was originally part of this property, but when the owner sold the building he donated some of the land to the council for use by locals. But there's never been anything put on the field. No play equipment, or sporting nets. Kids sometimes congregate on there. Well, teens, mainly.'

'For drinking, smoking and drugs, no doubt,' Pengelly said.

'Yes. But the police patrol regularly and move them on.'

'Right, let's find some officers and send them over there. They can go through the field and then do a house-to-house in the area close to the path.'

'Shall I co-ordinate that, ma'am?'

At least now they had a lead. However tenuous. One thing was certain. Whatever had happened to Isla had taken a great deal of planning and wasn't a spur of the moment thing.

'Yes. You do that while I contact forensics. After that, we need to speak to the staff individually. In particular those in the Orange Room that Isla was in. Also, any staff in rooms that overlook the rear of the property, in case they saw someone coming over the hedge.'

TEN

'What are the logistics for interviewing the staff?' Lauren asked Valerie Archer once they'd all returned to her office. For legal reasons they couldn't take them out of their classes at the same time because it would leave the children unattended. They also couldn't barge in and expect the staff to give their full attention while at the same time keeping an eye on their charges.

Crime scene investigators weren't due to arrive for a while because they were busy down at the human remains site – which she hadn't even given thought to since she'd arrived. Lauren had requested that two investigators be sent over to the nursery as soon as possible, but how long that would take was anyone's guess.

She'd suggested to the forensics manager that he call in investigators from another station, but his response was that they would have to manage because it could take ages to requisition staff. It was one of the cons of working in a small rural area. She imagined that Detective Sergeant Price was already comparing them with his beloved Lenchester and finding them wanting.

To be honest – and she'd be keeping this thought to herself – in this case, she'd agree with him. But she also realised that she'd be on a path to nowhere if she didn't accept the situation down here and make the best of it. Moaning about lack of resources wasn't going to alter a thing, other than undermine her reputation. And that she wasn't prepared to do.

'I'll relieve them one at a time and you can use my office for the interviews,' Valerie said. 'This morning there were two staff in the Orange Room, Tina and Sean.'

'If you're going to be there, then we'd rather speak to the staff inside the room because it will make it easier to ascertain the logistics of exactly what happened.'

'Um... I suppose that would work. As long as you don't disrupt the children.'

There was a knock at the door and Jenna and Clem walked in.

'What would you like us to do now, ma'am? Everything has been checked and double-checked. Uniform have almost finished speaking to people in the area and nobody has seen anything,' Jenna said.

'What about the houses across the field?'

'Officers are still there. Billy's with them.'

'Where's Isla's mother?'

'She went back with the FLO, if you remember, ma'am?' Price said, frowning.

Of course she remembered. She was preoccupied, that was all. 'We should conduct a more in-depth interview with her after we've finished questioning the staff in the Orange Room. Jenna, you and Clem can interview the staff from the Green and Blue rooms.' She turned to Valerie Archer. 'Is there someone else who can stand in there?'

'I'll ask Dee.'

'Can we use her office? It's not necessary for us to take a look around the Green and Blue rooms.'

'Of course. I'll get her now.'

After Valerie left, Lauren turned to Jenna. 'After you've questioned the staff, go back to the station and help Tamsin check out CCTV footage for roads heading in this direction. See if you can spot any cars arriving and leaving around the time Isla went missing. I also want someone to do further research into the father.' She glanced at Clem. 'You can make a start on that. Contact Billy and ask him to go back to the station once he's finished.'

'Yes, ma'am,' Clem said, his voice flat.

None of the team showed any emotion whenever she was around and if she hadn't overheard them discussing cases in their office, she'd be convinced that they never interacted with each other at all. She suspected they were close and it was more a case of *her* and *them*. Well, as long as they got the job done...

Dee, Clem and Jenna departed for the Green Room while Lauren, Price and Valerie left for the Orange.

'Sean,' Valerie called over to a man when they entered the room. He was in his early thirties, wearing light chinos and a white nursery polo shirt, and was on a stool with the children sitting on the floor around him. He glanced across. 'I'll take over; you're needed here.'

When Valerie reached him, he passed her the book he was reading to the children. He then headed towards Lauren and Price.

'I'm DI Pengelly and this is DS Price,' Lauren said once he'd reached them. 'We'd like to ask you about this morning. Who discovered Isla was missing?'

'Me. I was stunned. The children had been asleep in our designated sleeping section, which is partitioned off from the main area and when I went to wake them, she'd vanished. I called out to Tina and we both searched everywhere in here to make sure she wasn't hiding anywhere. Then I ran to Valerie's office and alerted her and we both came back here and searched again.'

'Are you always responsible for waking the children after their naps?' Price asked.

'Tina and I share the job, but she'd taken one of the older children to the toilet so I was waking the rest of them.'

'Where are the toilets?'

'Over there.' He pointed to a door going off the room. 'We have a cloakroom with pegs for the children's coats and a place for their shoes. There are also two low-level toilets and basins suitable for the children to use.'

'Can you show us?' Lauren asked.

They followed him through the door into the cloakroom and looked around. The window was small and up high. An average-sized adult would be unable to squeeze through, even if they could reach it.

'Impossible for anyone to use this as the exit point,' Lauren mused, more to herself than the other two. 'Was Isla's coat left behind?'

'Yes, it's over here,' Sean said, leading them over to a hook where a pink puffer jacket was hanging. There was also a pair of patent boots underneath it.

'Does she have anything on her feet?' Lauren asked, nodding at the shoes.

'The children all have indoor shoes which they change into when they arrive. Isla would have been wearing hers.'

'Where do the children have their naps?'

'I'll show you.' They followed Sean out of the cloakroom and into the main room, stopping at some screens which were adjacent to the door. 'This is the sleeping area. Each child has their own sleep mat, with their own sheet and a blanket, which we store away after they've woken up.'

'And Isla was taken from the sleeping area?'

'Yes.'

'Looking at the layout,' Lauren said, gesturing to the screens, 'would you say it would have been possible for someone to enter the room and walk into the sleeping area, take Isla, and not be noticed?'

Sean lowered his head, and nodded. 'Yes. I suppose it would.'

'Where were you and Tina during nap time?' Price asked.

'Tina was taking care of the children who weren't sleeping and I was cleaning down all the surfaces with bacterial wipes. We do that regularly.'

'Do many children choose not to nap?'

'It depends on the day and which children are here. Tuesday we have more three- than four-year-olds with us and most of them will have a sleep.'

Lauren exchanged a glance with Price, who was nodding and clearly thinking along the same lines that she was. Someone knew very well what went on in the nursery if they chose today to take Isla. Was it still pointing to Luke Hopkins? She wasn't so sure. But she certainly wasn't eliminating him either.

'Did you or Tina leave the room at all during this time?' Lauren asked.

'I went to the bathroom, and so did Tina. But separately, obviously, because of being with the older children. Also Tina made us both a cup of coffee which she brought in here. But other than that, no we didn't.'

'Did anyone else come into the room at all during the morning?'

'Valerie was in and out, as usual. One of the parents came in to drop off her child's asthma inhaler. Other than that, I don't think so. Maybe another member staff if they wanted to borrow something? I don't remember seeing anyone, but I might have missed it.'

'Well, clearly you did, because Isla was taken,' Lauren said, her voice more accusatory than she'd intended.

Sean coloured and bit down on his lip. 'I know,' he muttered.

'How long is nap time?' Price asked.

'Up to an hour, but most of the children stir after forty-five minutes.'

'What can you tell us about Isla?' Lauren asked.

'She's a lovely little girl. Very quiet and never boisterous like so many of them. She's changed a bit recently.'

'In what way?'

'I used to work in the Blue Room when Isla was there. In fact, we moved in here together. Even though she didn't understand everything about her father going to prison and then her parents getting divorced, I could see it made a difference to her. She became even more timid. That's why I can't understand what's happened because she wouldn't go off with just anyone. She's not that sort of child.'

'Unless she had no choice, and there was something placed over her mouth to stop from her from calling out,' Lauren suggested.

'Yes.' His eyes were wet. 'But then surely someone would have noticed? It makes no sense at all. Unless it was someone she knew.'

He was voicing Lauren's thoughts. What other answer could there be?

'Thanks, Sean. Please send Tina over now.'

'What do you reckon, ma'am?' Price asked when they were alone.

'Like Sean said, it had to be someone Isla knew. Someone who was aware of nursery procedures.'

'Not Sean or Tina themselves?'

'I don't think there would have been enough time. And why would they want to?'

'The dad, then?'

'He could have made it his business to find out. And if he came through the rear he could have taken her without being seen. But he would have needed a huge amount of luck not to have been spotted and—'

Tina walked over, interrupting Lauren.

'Is there any news?' Tina asked, her face ashen.

'Sorry, not yet.'

'I feel like it's our fault, somehow. That we should have seen something. But we didn't. Everything was fine until we went to wake Isla from her nap and—'

'You mustn't blame yourself, Tina,' Price interrupted. 'We'll find out what happened. But in the meantime, Sean told us how much Isla had changed after her parents divorced and her father went into prison. Do you have anything to add?'

'Isla's such a lovely child. It broke my heart to see the changes in her. She had started to get a little better, but when her father was released from prison and there was the divorce custody battle, which was in the media, it made her withdraw. She's a very intelligent child and that's why I think it affected her so much. But no... I'm not sure I have much else to add to that.'

'Have you seen anyone hanging around the nursery recently. Or has anything unusual happened?' Price asked.

Tina shook her head. 'No. Everything's been the same. There's been nothing out of the ordinary.'

'If you do think of anything that might assist us please let us know. Mrs Archer has our details,' Lauren said.

Tina returned to the children and they left the room.

'It's useful to have seen where Isla was taken from. But it's bizarre that no one noticed anything,' Price said, grimacing.

'What we do know is that whoever took Isla had an intimate knowledge of the nursery and its procedures,' Lauren said.

'Someone on the inside?'

'Or a parent. It wouldn't be beyond the realms of possibility for Luke Hopkins to have discovered all he needed to know so he could take his daughter. Let's speak to Beverley Hopkins again. The more we learn about her ex-husband, the easier it will be to locate him.'

ELEVEN

TUESDAY, 25 OCTOBER

Bev Hopkins lived in an upmarket area of Penzance, her home having glimpses of the crystal-clear turquoise waters so typical of Cornwall. When Lauren and Price knocked on the door, it was opened by Tracie, the family liaison officer.

Although Lauren hadn't struck up a close friendship with Tracie, she was one of the few officers that she'd actually spent some time with away from the office. They'd been on a two-day Health and Wellbeing training in Newquay and had travelled together and ended up in the same working group. Tracie was a few years older than Lauren, and had been at Penzance a little longer, having moved from Croydon, in London, with her family to Cornwall. Tracie originally came from Australia and still had a noticeable accent. Lauren liked her, not least because what you saw was what you got. The woman was upfront and direct.

'Hello, Tracie. This is Sergeant Price; he joined the team yesterday. Tracie Nichols is our FLO. How's Mrs Hopkins doing?'

'Not good, ma'am. Understandably,' Tracie said, shaking her head. 'I asked if she wanted me to call a family member or friend to be with her, but she said no. Her parents are on holiday in Spain and she didn't want to alarm any of her friends. I made her a cup of tea but it's still sitting where I left it. She just keeps pacing and doesn't know what to do with herself. She wanted to drive around looking for Isla, but I persuaded her that it wasn't a good idea and to leave it to us. Is there any news?'

'I wish there was.'

Tracie clasped her hands together and gave a heavy sigh. 'Bev's in the front room. Would you like something to drink? A coffee or tea?'

'Thanks for the offer, but we really don't have time. We're not going to stay long.'

Lauren and Price followed Tracie into the large front room with modern furnishings. The sofa and two easy chairs pointed at the TV screen on the wall. There was a pale-wood sideboard situated along the opposite wall, with photos of a child, presumably Isla, though Lauren couldn't see them clearly. Bev Hopkins was sitting on the edge of one of the easy chairs staring into space. Her arms were wrapped around her knees and she was rocking backwards and forwards.

'Hello, Bev,' Lauren said softly.

The woman started, and jumped up from the seat. 'Have you found her? Have you found my Isla?' Hope flickered in her eyes.

'No, not yet. I'm sorry. We have officers searching everywhere, and we won't give up. We're now working on the assumption that your ex-husband might have taken Isla.'

'That's exactly what I told you. This has Luke written all over it.'

'I know, but we can't jump to conclusions without first weighing up the evidence we have. We went to interview Luke at work and discovered that he'd phoned in sick. His parents had no idea that he hadn't gone to work this morning, because he left home first thing as usual and didn't mention to his father that he was going anywhere else. At the moment, we don't know where he is but we've got police out there looking for him. He won't escape us.'

Lauren didn't want to give the woman false hope. She believed it was still possible for them to locate him before he vanished from the area. He certainly wouldn't be able to leave the country because his photo and details had been circulated.

'I hate him. Okay, there were problems between us but why would he put his daughter through this? Isla must be so confused.' A sob erupted from Bev and she dropped back down onto the chair. Lauren and Price sat quietly on the sofa while Tracie comforted her.

After a couple of minutes, Lauren knew they could no longer stay quiet. Every minute they were seated there was a minute they were away from the hub of the investigation.

'I know this is hard for you, Bev. But we need to know everything we can about Luke. If we can get inside of his head, it will help our search. Work out where he's gone and why.'

'I-I get it.' Bev nodded, sniffing. 'What do you want to know?'

'First of all, can you give us some background on how Luke ended up in prison?'

They knew the outcome, and that he'd stolen some money, but not what had led up to it.

'H-he used to be a financial adviser and had his own company. You might have heard of it. HFS, short for Hopkins Financial Services. He advertised on the buses, and all the different media outlets, including radio. Everyone knew his jingle and would sing it to him. He was very successful and we weren't short of money.'

She paused, and sucked in a breath. 'But then one of his investments went sour and instead of admitting it to anyone, not even me, he started borrowing money from his clients to pay off other clients and it got out of hand. He borrowed money from my parents without me knowing. He swore them to secrecy. I'll never forgive him for that. He told them it was a tax issue and that once it was sorted he'd pay them back. But he'd no intention of doing so. He also spent all of our savings...' Her voice fell away.

'How did he get caught?' Lauren asked.

'It was quite by chance. His secretary had to take six weeks off following an operation and he brought in a temp. This temp had studied commerce at university and started to dig around. She then reported him to the police and they investigated. He was prosecuted and sent to prison for eighteen months. After nine months he was let out on licence and one of the conditions was supervised visits with Isla. In six months it will be over and after that he can see Isla on his own. He might be annoyed about not having joint custody, but to take her... What was he thinking?'

Quite.

'Was this the family home?' Lauren asked, frowning. If it was, then why hadn't it been seized?

'Yes. But it's in my name, which meant I could keep it. Before we lost everything, my parents gave us some money to pay off the mortgage and in the divorce settlement it became mine.'

'Did your parents pay off the mortgage after Luke had borrowed money from them?' Lauren asked.

'No. They gave us the money a couple of months before.'

'So, they weren't doing it because they foresaw what might happen in the future,' Lauren clarified.

'Not at all. They were as shocked as I was when it all blew up. They were questioned by the police, too. They wanted to make sure none of us knew what he'd been doing.'

Lauren was already getting a picture of the man they were dealing with. A risk taker, and that may very well predispose him to kidnap his daughter. Not only that, a planner too. The two things required to have taken Isla.

'Before Luke went to prison, was your marriage in good shape?' Price asked.

It was a good question, because if it wasn't then Bev could be painting the situation in a worse light than it actually was.

She shrugged. 'It was okay, but once the proverbial hit the fan and I found out how much he owed and what he'd done to everyone, including my parents, that was it. I couldn't stay with him.'

'What's he like as a father?' Price asked.

'That's probably the one area where I don't have any complaints. He idolises Isla. She was only two when he went into prison, but up to that point he'd been the perfect dad. That's what doesn't add up. I know he hates having his visits restricted, but it's not forever. That's why this whole thing is so horrible.'

'People often act out of character when faced with a situation they can't handle,' Lauren said. 'Can you think of anywhere he could have taken Isla? A friend's place maybe? It's possible that he might have been helped.'

'I've no idea who he keeps in touch with these days. I don't see him at all, apart from when I take Isla to social services and he's sitting in his car waiting for the appointment. Sometimes he's still there, sitting in his car watching, when I collect Isla. I don't speak to him. In fact, I deliberately look the other way because if we did talk I might have a lot to say about what he did to everyone.' Bev's eyes narrowed.

'Does Isla tell you about her visits with her dad?' Price asked.

'She enjoys seeing him. When I ask if she's had a good time, she always says yes. When it's visit time she never holds back or tells me she doesn't want to go.'

At least if Luke Hopkins did have his daughter, it sounded like she would be looked after. That was a huge relief. Massive.

If it is him.

The thought that it might not be kept pushing its way to the forefront of her mind.

'How well would you say he knows the nursery? If he was the person who took Isla, he would have to know where the cameras were situated to avoid being seen. There are very few of those spots.'

'Isla's been going since she was three months old, though I was usually the one who did pick-up and drop-off. But he's very smart. He could have found a way to take her without anybody seeing, I have no doubts about that. But surely he'd phone to let me know she's safe? He's not that callous.'

'If he's so dead set on taking Isla, he might not have even thought about it. Or he might believe that if he did call we could track his phone and find him,' Price said.

'We're going back to the station now,' Lauren said. 'If you do think of anything that might help, tell Tracie and she'll get in touch straight away. I know it's hard, but please try not to worry. You have my word that we won't rest until Isla, and Luke, are found.'

TWELVE

TUESDAY, 25 OCTOBER

Pengelly strode into the room, with Matt close behind. Each member of the team was staring at their own computer screen, concentration etched across their faces.

'Right,' Pengelly said, calling the team to attention. 'Let's go through all the evidence we've collected so far.'

Matt moved forward and stood next to the DI. 'Before we start, ma'am – Tamsin, has there been any new information regarding the human remains?'

He realised that finding Isla was paramount, but they still had a possible murder case on their hands and it couldn't be neglected. The two inquiries had to be worked alongside one another.

'No, Sarge. The lines have been unusually quiet considering we're usually inundated with calls when we ask for help. It's weird.'

It was, he agreed. In a small community like this, it was rare that someone could be missing without anyone noticing.

'Thanks,' Matt said. 'It could mean that the person didn't come from around here. But once we know exactly how long they've been dead, it will give us more to work with.'

'Yes, Sarge. On the Isla case – I've done some research into Isla's parents after Jenna told me Luke Hopkins is your number-one suspect,' Tamsin added. 'Apart from him having a record, which I'm guessing you already know, when he was in his late teens he was brought in for questioning regarding an incident which occurred at the Newquay shopping centre. He was seen hanging around the play area talking to the children, and one of the parents was worried so she called the police. No further action was taken, other than he was given a warning and told his behaviour was inappropriate.'

Matt raised his eyebrows. It could be nothing, but then again every little thing helped when piecing together a person's behaviour and what they might and might not do when under pressure.

'And the mother, Beverley Hopkins. Was there anything on her?' Pengelly asked.

'Nothing on record for her, ma'am. I was planning on checking her social media platforms next.'

'I didn't expect there to be because I don't believe that she has anything to do with this. Park that line of inquiry for now. It's all pointing towards the father, so we'll concentrate our efforts on him. Have you checked his social media pages?'

'No, ma'am. I'll do that now, and—'

'Ma'am!' Clem called out. 'A call's come in from uniform. Luke Hopkins has been found on St Michael's Mount. He was with a woman. He's being brought to the station as we speak. Luckily they caught him before the tide turned or it could have been much more difficult.'

Matt had heard of the place from his parents, who had talked about going there during one of his days off, but he had no clue about its location or what it was. 'St Michael's Mount?'

'It's an island linked to Marazion by a causeway. Definitely worth a visit,' Clem said. 'It has a medieval church and castle and lovely gardens to wander around. It's one of the area's most popular tourist attractions. It has more than three-hundred-and-fifty-thousand visitors each year. Lord and Lady St Levan live there, and—'

'Was Isla with him, Clem?' Pengelly interrupted.

'Not as far as I'm aware. I was told he was with a woman, who's also being brought in for questioning in a separate vehicle,' the officer said.

'Why would he take his daughter there?' Matt mused. 'Unless it was to get lost among the crowds.'

Pengelly drummed her fingers on the desk beside where she stood. 'Also, if he did take Isla, then where is she? He'd hardly kidnap her then leave her to go sight-seeing, or whatever it was he was doing there. Clem, call uniform and make sure officers search the Mount in case Isla accidentally slipped away when he was caught, or if she was there with someone else we haven't yet identified. We don't know how many people were involved in this abduction.'

'Yes, ma'am. I'm onto it,' Clem said, picking up the phone on his desk.

'Where are we on the CCTV footage in the vicinity of roads leading to the nursery? Have you spotted Hopkins' car anywhere close?'

'No, ma'am,' Tamsin said. 'But if he took the back roads he could avoid being seen. It's relatively easy to do providing you know the area.'

'Keep on looking. Also check from a few days leading up to today, in case he was driving around working out where the cameras are and which would be the best route for him to take on the day. Jenna and Clem, did you learn anything useful from the staff you interviewed at the nursery?'

'Only that no one saw anything. It's crazy. How can a child disappear so easily,' Jenna said.

'It only takes a few seconds. I'll tell you what, though. They definitely need to review their security systems,' Clem said.

'Once Health and Safety get wind of this they'll be on to them big time. And that could mean huge fines or other penalties.'

'When Sergeant Price and I spoke with staff involved in caring for Isla in the Orange Room, we heard the same answer: no one saw an intruder,' Pengelly said. 'Some of the children had been taking their morning nap in the designated sleeping area. A member of staff was present in the room at all times, although they were occupied with taking care of the children who weren't sleeping and occasionally one or other of them left the room. We have no proof, but it's likely that it was one of the times when only one member of staff was in the room that the child was taken. I want background checks into all staff working there. Billy, you can start on that,' Pengelly said.

'Ma'am, how do we even know that Isla was the intended victim? Could she have just been unlucky?' Billy asked.

Matt shook his head. 'If someone wanted to abduct any child, then there are far easier places to take them from. A busy play area in a park, for instance. When I've been at the park with my daughter, who's a bit younger than Isla, you need eyes in the back of your head if you want to know where your child is every single second. What happened at the nursery was meticulously planned. How could it not be? So, we have to assume that Isla was the child the kidnapper wanted. And—' The phone on the desk beside him rang and he picked it up. 'DS Price.'

'Sarge, it's PC Smith here. We've arrived with Hopkins and he's in interview room one. They're not far behind with the woman he was with. She'll be put in interview room four.'

'Thanks, Constable,' he said to the officer who he remembered as the PC on duty the day before at the scene where the bones had been found. He replaced the handset and turned to the DI. 'Hopkins is here. The woman he was with will arrive shortly.'

'Thanks. We'll speak to him now. If we leave him alone for

too long he might ask for a solicitor and we don't have time to waste.'

'Yes, ma'am.'

'Has Hopkins been told why he's here?' Pengelly asked, as they took the stairs to the interview rooms.

'I've no idea, ma'am, PC Smith didn't say. How do you wish to proceed in the interview?'

'What do you mean?' Her brow furrowed.

'Regarding the questioning. Do you want to lead and I'll observe?'

'I'll lead, but feel free to ask questions, should you wish. How else would we run it? This isn't a dictatorship.' She paused a moment. 'Despite what some people think.'

So she had noticed how much her team held back when she was around.

Not that he was agreeing with it being a dictatorship. It was far too early to say. Still, he thought it prudent not to mention that in Lenchester, Whitney always asked the questions, so he could monitor suspects' behaviour and gauge if they were being honest. Even if the words coming out of their mouths appeared truthful, body language would often tell a different story. The way they worked together had been effective. It had helped them spot the smallest indications of guilt in a suspect's story. He doubted Pengelly would take kindly to being compared with his previous boss. It would probably annoy her.

They walked into the interview room, and were faced with a slim man who was in his late thirties, had short, dark blond hair, and a long pointed nose with a twist in the middle from having been broken at some time.

'Why am I here?' He banged his hands on the table.

'To discuss the disappearance of your daughter, Isla.'

The man gasped. 'What? Why didn't anyone tell me? What's happened?' His eyes darted from Pengelly to Matt and back again.

'We'll be recording this interview.' Pengelly pressed the button on the equipment. 'Interview on Tuesday, twenty-fifth October. Those present: DI Pengelly, DS Price and...' She nodded at the man.

'Luke Hopkins. Now tell me what's going on.'

'Isla disappeared from nursery a few hours ago.'

'How? What happened? She can't just disappear.'

'We don't know how it happened. That's what we're investigating.'

'Why am I only being told this now? What is it with you lot? Just because I have a record doesn't mean I shouldn't—'

'Nobody could find you. We went to your workplace to speak to you and they informed us that you'd phoned in sick,' Pengelly interrupted. 'Your parents also believed that you'd gone to work. And your dad left you a message on your phone. So perhaps you can tell us what you were doing?'

The man lowered his head, his cheeks pink. 'I was with someone,' he muttered.

'Yes, we gathered that. You were found with a woman. Where's Isla?'

'I don't know. How many times do I have to tell you?' Hopkins said, his voice agitated. 'You've got to believe me. Who would take her? Does Bev know? She'll tell you that I wouldn't do anything like that.'

'When was the last time you saw Isla?' Matt asked, ignoring Hopkins' reference to his ex-wife.

'At my fortnightly Friday visit.'

'Ah, yes. You hate having your visits restricted, don't you?' Pengelly said, leaning forward, her palms flat on the table.

'What do you think? I'm her father. It's not like I'm a convicted paedophile. She's not at risk when she's with me.'

'Which is why you took her?'

'No. I didn't. Leave me alone and concentrate on finding my little girl. Do you have any idea who took her? And don't say *me* because I didn't. I was out with Josie. That was why I phoned in sick. We wanted to spend the day together. Ask her if you don't believe me. Or ask at the ticket office on St Michael's Mount. We paid for a tour of the garden.'

'Believe me, we will check. And speak to Josie. But our prime concern is Isla and if you know anything that will help us find her then we need to know it now. Her wellbeing is paramount,' Pengelly said in a no-nonsense tone.

'Look, I do want to help but I know nothing.' A tear formed in his eye and ran down his cheek. He brushed it away with the back of his hand. 'She's the only good thing in my life. I didn't take her. Please find her.' He slumped in his chair.

Matt glanced at Pengelly, who ended the recording. There was nothing in Hopkins' demeanour that indicated he was lying.

'Stay here while we speak to Josie to confirm your story.'

* * *

Pengelly's phone rang as they left the interview room.

'Pengelly.' She paused a moment. 'Yes. I'm convinced that either he's an excellent actor or he knows nothing about it, most likely the latter. We're about to question the woman he was with to confirm his alibi.'

Pengelly ended the call and put the phone back in her pocket. 'CCTV has been checked and Isla's nowhere to be seen on St Michael's Mount. Hopkins and the woman were seen together, from ten thirty, which is before Isla was taken, and there was no sign of the child. It doesn't look like he was the one to take her.' She let out a sigh.

'I'm assuming we'll still confirm that with Josie?' Matt said.
'Yes.'

They headed into the interview room and sitting at the table was a young woman who looked to be in her twenties, petite with short dark hair, appearing very anxious.

'Why am I here? I don't understand.'

'We are investigating the disappearance of Isla Hopkins, Luke's three-year-old daughter. Was the child with you today?' Pengelly asked.

'No. It was only the two of us.'

'How much do you know about Luke?'

'Not much. This is only the second time we've been out together and we haven't really talked about our pasts. I do know that he's divorced and he has a little girl.'

'And you took time off work today to be with him? Or do you not work?'

'I work evenings at a pub in Penzance. That was where we first met. Luke took a day off work so we could go out.'

'He actually phoned in sick, did you know that?'

'No. But I didn't ask. Anyway, lots of companies allow you to have sick days.' She shrugged.

'To be taken when you're actually sick, not just because you fancy a day out,' Pengelly said, glaring at the woman.

'So you think that Luke has taken Isla?'

'It's important that we eliminate from our enquiries anyone who has a connection with the child. That means finding out where someone was and what they were doing at the time she disappeared.'

'Well, all I can tell you from being with Luke is that he loves Isla and would never do anything to harm her. He even mentioned that I could meet her one day, but it's too early in our relationship to do that.'

'Do you know how often he sees his daughter?'

'His wife has full custody, but whenever he can. We haven't really discussed it in detail. But I can tell you that he's been with me since first thing this morning and we've definitely not seen Isla. If you need an alibi for him then I'll give it. I don't want you wasting your time questioning him when someone else has her.'

'Thank you for your assistance. You're welcome to leave now. We may wish to speak to you again, so please leave your details at reception and also don't leave the area without contacting us first.' Pengelly picked up the folder she had placed on the table.

'Why? I haven't done anything.'

'I've just told you that we may wish to discuss matters further. My concern is finding Isla. Please don't make this any more difficult for us.'

They escorted Josie to reception and left her giving her contact details to the sergeant on duty. Pengelly also gave instructions to release Hopkins. They turned and headed back towards the main office.

'I'm going to instruct uniform to put some surveillance on Hopkins just to make sure,' Pengelly said. 'He may well have orchestrated something and put himself in the clear by taking Josie out. I'm also going to speak to the DCI regarding a press conference. We have no choice but to alert the public that a child has gone missing.'

THIRTEEN

TUESDAY, 25 OCTOBER

As Matt opened the door to his parents' house he glanced at his watch. It was way past Dani's bedtime. But he had to see her. All day long, while they'd been desperately searching for Isla, his mind had been flooded with terrifying images of what it would be like if it was his daughter who'd gone missing. A chill ran down his spine as he realised how totally devastating the thought was.

Before telling his parents he'd arrived home, he rushed upstairs to see Dani. The door to her room was slightly ajar, and the hall was bathed in a golden glow from her nightlight. Matt crept into the bedroom and stared at his beautiful daughter. She was fast asleep, thumb in mouth and dark curls framing her face. Her favourite cuddly toy, an elephant called Edna that she'd had since she was six months old, was in its usual place tucked up beside her.

Tears filled Matt's eyes and he quickly blinked them away. If only Leigh could be by his side to witness how much their daughter had changed in the past few months. She had suddenly grown up in so many ways. People often talked about the 'terrible twos', but Dani was nothing like that. She was a demanding child, always questioning everything. But that's what made her so special. It always amazed people when they heard Dani talking. Most children her age could only speak a few words, but Dani had spoken her first word at nine months and hadn't stopped chatting since. It had to be seen to be believed.

Recently, Dani had stopped asking where her mummy was, but it clearly still affected her. She was more introverted than she used to be and always stayed close to Matt whenever he was around. When he was out, she'd follow her grandma around. It was one of the reasons they thought going to nursery two days a week was a good idea. It meant she was interacting with children her own age, and also being in the company of different adults. It had been the right decision. She loved going.

'Hello, Daddy.' Dani half-opened a sleepy eye and beamed with delight.

An overwhelming wave of emotion crashed through him, leaving him breathless.

'Hello, sweetheart.' Matt sat on the edge of her small bed, and stroked the top of her head.

She sat up, Edna clutched tightly to her chest. 'Can I come downstairs with you? I promise to be good.'

He knew she should really stick to her regular bedtime, but he wanted to be with her.

Had to be with her.

And how could he resist those wide and innocent dark brown eyes, that reminded him so much of his beloved Leigh? He swallowed hard, determined not to break down. He had to stay strong. For Dani.

'Okay. But just this once or I'll be in trouble with your grandma. And we don't want that to happen, do we?'

'No.' She sombrely shook her head from side to side.

He picked her up and she wrapped her arms around his neck and snuggled into him. He carried her downstairs and into the kitchen where his mum was preparing the evening meal. It was later than they usually ate dinner, but when he'd phoned to say he was going to be late, his mum had said they'd wait and all eat together.

'Hi, Mum.'

'I didn't hear you come in, love,' his mother said, looking up from peeling the carrots.

'Daddy said I could come downstairs,' Dani piped up, now fully awake.

'So I see, young lady. I hope that doesn't mean you're going to be a little sleepyhead in the morning. Because we've got a very busy day ahead.'

'It won't. I promise.' Dani looked at him and giggled.

'And it's just this once,' Matt said.

'Just this once,' Dani repeated.

Matt and his mum exchanged a glance and both laughed. Dani was so cute. He wished this stage would last forever. Well, not forever – of course she had to grow up, but he wanted to hold on to these precious moments for as long as he possibly could.

'Where's Dad?'

'Where he always is at this time of night, sitting in front of the telly, watching the news. Or so he says. He's probably fallen asleep.' His mum chuckled. 'How was work?'

'A very busy day and a very difficult case.' Over the top of Dani's head he mouthed, 'I'll tell you about it later.'

His mum nodded.

'Do you like the people at your work?' Dani asked.

A good question. Two days in and he was very much unde-cided. The atmosphere was interesting, to say the least. But he couldn't fault the work ethic, especially from Pengelly. He doubted he'd be forging any long-term friendships with them, though. Was he being harsh? It didn't matter. It was a job and one that he'd hoped would give him the chance to spend as much time as he could with Dani. Although, considering that since he'd arrived they'd had a possible murder and a missing child, it wasn't boding well. Then again, if the comments the team had made were anything to go by, it was an unusual state of affairs.

'Yes, they're very nice.' He wasn't going to voice his concerns out loud, especially not to Dani. Or his parents, for that matter. He didn't want them worrying even more about him than they already did.

His phone pinged and he pulled it out of his pocket. It was a message from the DI:

Make sure to be at work early. Time's running out in the hunt for Isla.

Seriously, she felt she had to tell him that? Didn't she know that he was fully aware of the situation? She should. It was obvious enough. Okay, she didn't know him or his work ethic, but even so... He tapped out a reply.

Yes, ma'am.

'Who's that from?' Dani asked, peering down at his phone.

'My new boss. She wants me to go to work early in the morning because we're very busy.'

'Ohhhh. What's her name?'

'Lauren Pengelly.'

'That sounds like *jelly*.'

'Yes, you're right, it does. You're very clever. Isn't she, Grandma?' He glanced at his mum.

'Too clever by half,' his mum said, shaking her head.

'What does that mean?' Dani asked.

'It's something old people say,' Matt said, grinning at his mum, who responded by swatting him away with her open hand.

'Is your jelly boss nice?'

Matt forced back a smile. If Dani saw that he was amused then she'd continue with the jelly analogy and that wasn't good, in case she met Pengelly one day and she called her jelly. He couldn't imagine her taking kindly to that.

'I've only just met her, but I think so. She works very hard and that's the main thing.'

'Does she tell you what to do?'

'Sometimes. You have to have someone in charge to make sure the work gets done properly.'

'Is she as nice as Nelly?'

'Who's she?' He glanced at his mum.

'She's at Dani's nursery.' His mum put water in the saucepan, placed it on the hob and turned on the heat.

'Well, I don't know your friend Nelly so I can't compare. But I'm sure they're both nice.' Dani giggled. 'What's funny?'

'Nelly isn't one of the children at nursery, Daddy. That's silly. Nelly reads stories to us and she tells us what to do and she takes us to the toilet. So she's like your boss at work.'

Matt laughed, imagining Pengelly escorting him to the toilet. 'Oh, I see. Yes, they sound very similar. Come on, I'm taking you back to bed or Grandma will never be able to get you up in the morning.'

'Am I going to nursery tomorrow? I really like it there.'

'Not tomorrow, sweetheart. Your days are Tuesday and Friday,' Matt's mum said. 'But we are going out tomorrow. I need a few bits and pieces in town and I don't want you to be all miserable because you're tired. Off you go. I've got to dish up dinner for Daddy and Grandpa.' Matt's mum walked over and gave Dani a kiss on the head.

'Ne-night, Grandma. Love you.' Dani yawned and rested her head on Matt's shoulder.

'Love you, too, chicken. See you in the morning.'

'I won't be long.'

Matt headed out of the kitchen and took Dani back up to bed. She fell asleep the moment her head touched the pillow.

He stared at her for a few seconds and then went downstairs and sat at the table. His dad was already there.

'Hello, son. Good day?' His dad had retired a year ago from the bank where he'd worked for forty years, and his parents had planned a world cruise with the money he'd received from his pension. But everything changed the day of Leigh's crash. His parents never mentioned their disappointment, but Matt knew that deep down they must regret not being able to travel.

'Not bad, Dad. I guess.'

'Now tell us the truth,' his mum said, as she dished up the dinner and put it on the table in front of them.

'About what?' He frowned. He hadn't misled them about anything.

'Your new boss. What's she really like? You were saying nice things about her in front of Dani, but I could tell by the expression on your face that you've got reservations. Am I right?'

'Not reservations exactly, but let's say that she's going to be interesting to work with,' he admitted.

'Meaning?'

'From what I've seen so far, her work ethic is second to none, and clearly the rest of the team respect her for that. But there's a tension when she's in the main office. I'm sure I'll get to the bottom of it. They're not close to her and she doesn't give off a friendly vibe. I think for DI Pengelly it's work, work, work.'

'Well, you're not there to socialise,' his father said. 'That's the trouble with young people, today. They think that work is simply an extension of their social life.'

'I think you're being a little unfair, Dad. Anyway, at the moment she's the right person to lead the inquiry. I didn't say this in front of Dani, obviously, but we have a missing child. She was taken from a local nursery. Thank goodness it wasn't the one Dani attends. We've worked very hard on this today, but so far with no luck. It's like she's disappeared into thin air. I'll be leaving early tomorrow morning probably before Dani's awake.'

'We heard it on the telly a while before you came home,' his mum said. 'The police mentioned a child had gone missing, but didn't say her name or where she was taken from. It's dreadful that it was from a nursery. You know we're always here for Dani, so don't worry about having to go to work early. Finding the child is the most important thing.'

FOURTEEN

WEDNESDAY, 26 OCTOBER

'Good morning, ma'am,' Matt said, greeting Pengelly, who was parked next to him and had just stepped out of her car.

He'd left home at seven fifteen, armed with a travel mug of coffee and a croissant that his mum had handed to him on his way out. Dani had still been asleep – normally she was a good sleeper and woke around six thirty to seven, but being up the previous night had tired her out, even if it was for less than half an hour.

'I'm glad you managed to get here early. I was in constant contact during the night with officers on patrol and searching, but Isla Hopkins is still nowhere to be found.'

'Did you get any sleep at all?'

'Fits and starts. It didn't help that one of my dogs insisted on sleeping on the bed next to me, instead of in her basket.'

So, there was a softer side to her. *Interesting.*

'And you didn't mind her in your bed?'

'Usually, yes. Last night, no. I had a lot on my mind and I think she could sense it. I'd hoped that the TV coverage might have brought in some useful information, but it didn't.'

'I understand there's been no mention of the nursery Isla was taken from, or her name. Is that wise?'

'DCI Mistry made the call because he didn't want to cause a mass panic. I wasn't convinced, but we'll revisit the decision if we have no luck today.'

'Yes, ma'am. How wide did the search teams go last night?'

'We kept them to within a three-mile radius of the nursery. Including door knocking until ten p.m. We couldn't do that any later. If Isla had been wandering the streets, or in a park area, we'd have found her by now. Someone has her, there's no other explanation. But who, where and why is anyone's guess,' Pengelly said, her brows knitted together in frustration.

'I agree, ma'am. What shall we get the team working on today?'

'Once everyone's arrived I'll assign the tasks.'

'Which are...?' He wanted her to realise that he was capable of running a team, even if she did want to micro-manage everything.

'More scrutiny of everyone who visited the nursery over the last week. Re-checking of CCTV. A continuation of looking into staff backgrounds, and more information about both of Isla's parents and their relatives. We'll go as wide as is necessary. My fear is that the longer this goes on, the less likely it is we'll find the child alive.'

Her words hung in the air.

Matt's insides clenched. The situation was hopeless. Was whoever had Isla looking after her? Reassuring her? Making sure she wasn't hungry or scared?

They walked into the station, both in sombre moods, and Pengelly strode past the reception desk, not even stopping to acknowledge the desk sergeant.

Matt glanced over at him and nodded.

When they reached the main office, Matt headed to his desk and Pengelly walked through to her office, closing the door behind her. He pulled up on his screen details of the calls that had been logged regarding both appeals. Pengelly had been correct. Nothing of any use had come in.

Within the next half hour, the rest of the team arrived in dribs and drabs, and by eight they were all there. Pengelly must have been keeping a lookout because the moment Billy turned up, the last to arrive, she came out of her office and stood in front of the whiteboard, her hands on her hips. One by one, the team members glanced up from their screens and stared at her.

'Any news about Isla, ma'am?' Clem asked, a half-hopeful expression on his face.

'I'm afraid not. Nothing at all.'

'That's not good. It means—'

'I'm fully aware of what it means, Detective. But we can't dwell on that. We have to divorce ourselves from our feelings and concentrate on working as hard as possible to find the child.'

'Yes, ma'am. But as a father, it's hard to pretend it's not affecting me.'

'Me, too,' Jenna added. 'I didn't sleep all night worrying about Isla and imagining all the awful things that could have happened to her.'

And me, Matt said to himself, thinking better of voicing his concerns out loud.

'I understand,' Pengelly said, her voice softening a little. 'But we have to remain focused. It's our only hope if we're to discover where Isla is. We also have another case that needs our attention. I've just heard from the pathologist regarding the human remains that were found on Trenowden Estate and he's asked me to go over there as soon as possible. Sergeant Price will come with me. The rest of you, continue researching. No one should be missed. Nursery staff and their partners. Regular visitors to the nursery. The Hopkins family, including their extended family. Someone can look again at the CCTV footage.

I also want the sex offenders register checked to see if there's anyone locally whose MO is very young children.' Pengelly grimaced. 'I'm available by mobile if you need me. We shouldn't be more than an hour.'

Matt had been about to mention looking at the register. Although how an offender could have got into the nursery, known the routines and taken a child was certainly a puzzle, considering the limitations placed on them when out in the community. But it didn't mean they shouldn't check it out. He'd learnt many times over the years to expect the unexpected.

'My car or yours, ma'am?' he asked as they left the room and headed towards the car park.

'We'll take mine,' she said.

That was a refreshing change. Whitney had hated her car and always insisted on being driven.

Pengelly stared straight ahead during the drive to the morgue, not encouraging conversation. Matt didn't mind because clearly his boss was deep in thought, most likely regarding the case. The drive took less than fifteen minutes. The morgue, which was part of the hospital, was much smaller than any he'd visited before, but as soon as he walked through the double doors, that familiar antiseptic smell hit him and he gulped, hoping that they'd only be viewing bones and nothing else.

He followed Pengelly over to the main area where, side by side, there were two stainless steel tables. Foolishly, he glanced over at them. On one was bones, and on the other a body. At least, what remained of one. Two of the limbs had been detached, and were lying beside the torso.

Bile shot up into Matt's mouth and he swallowed it back down. It stung his insides.

Pengelly turned round. 'You okay, Sergeant? You've gone green.'

'I'm fine thank you, ma'am,' he managed to say, turning his head to block the body from view.

'Good morning, DI Pengelly,' Henry Carpenter, the pathologist, said, striding over to them. 'And DS Price. Judging by your pallor, you're not keen on corpses.' He laughed. 'Don't worry, the body you've seen is about to be moved to the mortuary cabinet until we work on it later. It's a particularly gruesome case. The poor chap lost an arm and leg when he was in the way of an overturning tractor. Keep your eyes right and focus on the table with the bones. I'll introduce you to Sue, the forensic anthropologist who's been working here with me.'

'Thanks,' Matt managed to mutter as they headed to the table where the bones were set out.

Matt winced, and pretended to look at the bones, but really he focused his attention on the wall behind the body. He seriously needed to do something about this problem of his. It seemed to be getting worse. Maybe he should try a course of hypnotherapy? That's what Dr Cavendish, the forensic psychologist who worked at Lenchester, had done. She used to have an aversion to blood that was so bad she had to give up training as a doctor. After a series of hypnotherapy sessions she was able to deal with any blood when faced with it. Maybe he *should* consider therapy. He'd look into finding a hypnotherapist once he was more settled.

'Sergeant?'

He glanced up at Pengelly, who was frowning in his direction. 'Yes?'

'You weren't paying attention when you were introduced to Sue Andrews.'

'Sorry.' He diverted his attention to the small woman standing next to Henry Carpenter, who was smiling at him.

Carpenter was a big, thickset man, and made her seem even more petite. 'I'm Matt Price.'

'Pleased to meet you, Matt. We've made some progress with the body. It's definitely a woman, as determined by the pelvis, which is broader in a female, and the sciatic notch, which is also broader.' She pointed to the area and Matt held his breath while peering over to take a look. 'The fluorescence from the ultraviolet light indicates that she's been dead for between fifteen and twenty years. We can be more specific once we receive the chemical analysis of the bones. Assessing age at the time of death isn't an exact science, especially once the maturation process is complete, but judging by the pitting and sharpness of the ribs, I would say she was between forty and forty-five.'

'Thank you. That's given us more to go on, and should help in her identification,' Pengelly said.

'Wait,' Sue said, a half-smile on her face. 'I haven't told you our most interesting discovery. This woman didn't die of natural causes. She was shot, hence the partial entry and exit holes in the ribs. There was also a large hole in the skull that was caused either by a blunt instrument or from a fall. See here.' She pointed to the ribs and then the head.

Matt could just make out a slight, jagged half circle on one of the right-hand ribs.

'So, the victim was shot and then fell? Or hit over the head and then shot? Or fell, hit and then shot. Can we narrow it down at all?' Pengelly asked.

'It's not possible to ascertain the order in which it all happened. But certainly this is a suspicious death. No question about that.'

'Great. So now we have an old murder case on top of everything else.' Pengelly turned to Matt. 'Go back to the place where the remains were found and speak to the owner of the estate. We need to know exactly who was living in the cottages between 2003 and 2008.'

FIFTEEN

WEDNESDAY, 26 OCTOBER

After Pengelly dropped Matt at the station to get his car, he drove to Trenowden Estate along the coastal road, along Cornwall's imposing granite cliffs. He headed straight to the large farmhouse. It felt so much longer than two days since the bones had been discovered. Hardly surprising considering what else had happened.

The door was opened by a man in his mid-seventies, wearing jeans and a tatty brown jumper that had seen better days. He was tall and had a shock of unruly, thick, white hair that came to below his ears. His nose was veined and red. A drinker?

'Is Mr Hector Voyle here?'

'That's me.'

'I'm DS Price from Penzance station.' Matt held out his warrant card. 'We tried to contact you on Monday when the human remains were found on your land, but were informed that you were away. May I come inside to discuss this with you, please?'

Matt found the soft approach worked much better when wanting to interview someone in their home. If Voyle refused to be questioned, then Matt would up the ante, but until then getting the man on side was a much better way to ensure his cooperation.

'Of course. Come on in.' Voyle held open the door.

Matt stepped into a large rectangular hall with flagstones on the floor. He shivered, pulling his jacket around him. Didn't Voyle believe in central heating?

'It's cold in here,' Matt said, his breath fogging the air.

'Sorry, the heating's on the blink and until it's fixed we're all wearing plenty of layers. Even when it's warm outside it's freezing inside. It's warmer in the kitchen because of the range; we'll talk in there. I apologise for having been away when you first called. I was attending a family funeral and it wasn't possible for me to return straight away. Would you like a cup of tea, or coffee? I was just contemplating making one. Or something stronger, perhaps?' Voyle glanced at his watch. 'Or perhaps you think it's a little early in the day for that?'

For Matt, yes. For Voyle... well, it did confirm his earlier suspicion.

'Thanks for the offer, but I won't be staying long, so nothing to drink for me.'

He didn't want to be there any longer than necessary. Yes, this was now an important case, but a missing child took priority in his book.

Matt followed the man into a large farmhouse-style kitchen with terracotta tiles on the floor and a large oak table in the centre. There was a range at the far end. It was much warmer than the rest of the house.

Voyle took a mug from a glass-fronted kitchen cabinet and headed to the coffee machine. 'Are you sure you don't want anything?'

'Quite, thanks,' Matt said, standing in the middle of the room facing him.

'Okay, what do you need to know?' Voyle asked, once he'd

poured his coffee. He leant against the kitchen unit, a relaxed expression on his face.

'I've just returned from seeing the pathologist and forensic anthropologist and, following their report, we're now treating this as a murder investigation.'

The man's mouth fell open in astonishment and he grabbed the edge of the worktop with his empty hand. 'Murder? I hadn't even thought of that.'

Really? What had he thought? That it was a crude burial site from ancient times?

Although he could be pretending to be shocked because he knew more than he was letting on.

'We believe that the murder took place between fifteen and twenty years ago and the victim was female.'

'How did she die?'

'We're awaiting confirmation on that. How long have the cottages where the remains were found been derelict?'

Voyle frowned. 'The last time we had people living there would have been around twenty years ago, maybe a little more, I'm not sure.'

Which fitted with the timeline. If the murder took place after the houses were abandoned there would have been no one to discover the body.

'Why did people stop living there?' Because of the murder? Or was it a coincidence?

'The cottages were rented by estate employees who worked on the farm. But our farm has struggled over the last two decades. To stop from going under, we had to diversify. We mostly shut down the farm and, nowadays, our main source of income is from the sale of our own honey and the many products that contain honey.'

'Do you have a shop on site where people can purchase the goods?'

'People buy from us at the local farmers' markets, but the

majority of our business is done online. We also make and sell our own cheese using milk from the few cows that we have.'

'What was the farm like before it all started to go downhill?'

'The estate comprises fifteen hundred acres and this house was actually built in the 1300s, although there have been additions over the years and it's hardly recognisable from how it was initially. My family has been here for over one hundred years and for most of that time the land was successfully farmed. But times changed and we were no longer able to make a profit. Before things turned sour, we had many cottages for the farmworkers to live in. At least twenty-five, possibly more, I don't remember. Nowadays we only have five houses rented by workers who help with making the honey and the cheese. We sold off many of the other houses to finance the estate. The majority are used as second homes by people from outside of the area, mainly London.'

'Why didn't you sell the row of cottages where the bones were found?'

'Because they were the closest to the main house. The others were further away so having people in them didn't impinge on our privacy. We've discussed pulling them down to build a new dwelling, or extend our current operations there. We'd even considered renovating them and offering holiday rentals. But I changed my mind. I'm not getting any younger and don't have the energy to start a brand new business. Although my son did offer to do the work. He can do what he likes when I'm gone and he inherits the estate. For now, nothing changes.'

'I understand. Starting a new business is a difficult undertaking at any age. Do you have a list of all the people who were renting the cottages between fifteen and twenty years ago?' Matt leant against the back of one of the chairs.

'Yes. They were all farmworkers. The records will be somewhere, we just have to find them.'

Voyle took a sip of coffee, not appearing to make a move anytime soon.

'May we do that now? I'm needed back at the station.'

'Of course. We'll go to the farm offices.'

Matt followed Voyle out of the back door, across the yard and into an old barn that had been converted into an office. Inside, there were two desks and several filing cabinets. Behind one of the desks, staring at a computer screen, was an older woman.

'Gwen, this is DS Price from the police. He's here about the bones found. Please could you fish out a list of tenants who rented the cottages between 2003 and 2008 because the pathologist believes the remains have been there since then. The police think it was murder.'

Gwen's hand flew up to her mouth. 'Murder? Oh my giddy aunt. Have you identified the body?' Far from being shocked, the woman appeared to be excited at the thought.

'That's what we're investigating. Do you remember the people who lived there back then?'

As she answered, Matt checked her facial expressions for any sign that she might be lying or hiding something from them. 'No, I wasn't working here then. I've only been in Cornwall for ten years and have worked here for the same amount of time. I've always thought it was a bit creepy round where the cottages are so I try not to go near them.'

'What do you mean by creepy?'

'It's difficult to put into words, but I always get a cold chill running down my spine when I'm close by. It's probably me. Luckily I don't have cause to go there often, only if we're walking round checking the farm or if I'm looking for Hector and know he's somewhere on the farm.'

She went to one of the filing cabinets and pulled open a drawer. It was jammed full of paper. After a couple of minutes sifting through she pulled out a large notebook. 'Here you are.

This book has details of tenants going back fifty years and the rent they paid each week. Nothing was computerised when I arrived ten years ago. Sorting everything out was a nightmare and it took me ages to implement all the systems we now have in place. Hector's very old-fashioned like that.' She nodded in her boss's direction.

'And I'd still do everything by hand given the choice. You can't beat writing things down. But we can't do that now, because everyone we do business with uses computers.'

'Is it just you and Gwen running the business, or do you have people to help?' Matt asked. Surely he couldn't manage alone?

'Bloody hell, no. I'm far too old to shoulder the responsibility of it all. My son does all of our marketing and sales. Most of it online, as I explained.'

'And does he work from here?'

'No, his office is in his own home twenty miles away. He comes here maybe once or twice a week to check on the honey production and to make sure everything is running smoothly.'

'You mentioned selling cheese? Where do you do that?'

'At the local farmers' markets with the honey products. My wife runs that operation, apart from going to the markets. She leaves that to Melanie, my son's wife, because it's too long a day for her to cope with. That's what happens when you get old. And I don't recommend it.' He gave a hollow laugh.

'Do you have any other children?'

A shadow crossed the old man's face. 'I did have a daughter, but she drowned when she was four in a pond on the farm.'

'I'm sorry to hear that. But thank you very much for giving me this list of tenants. We may need to come back to discuss matters further with you.'

'Of course, anything I can do to help. When will you have confirmation of who the victim is?'

This was Cornwall. He had no idea.

SIXTEEN

WEDNESDAY, 26 OCTOBER

'Right, where are we on the missing child?' Lauren asked the moment she arrived back from the morgue.

She had a good team, but at times they needed direction. She was never one hundred per cent confident that they were fully focused on a task unless she was there to check on them. She'd hoped that her new sergeant would be her eyes and ears, but it was too early to tell whether that was going to happen. For now, she was going to make sure he spent his time with her so she could train him in the correct way of doing things.

To be fair, he was already proving to be competent. Apart from their visit to the morgue where he had been totally useless. But how often would he have to go there? More had occurred in the last three days than they usually had to deal with in six months. Although the more time he did spend there, the more desensitised he ought to become. That was certainly an avenue to pursue in the future. But not now. Their primary focus was finding Isla Hopkins. Followed closely by investigating the murder.

'I've gone through the sexual offenders register and discovered that a Terry Lipton was recently released from prison after serving a six-year sentence for having child pornography on his computer and for attempting to abduct a child from a local park, in Torquay,' Jenna said. 'He's forty-eight and is renting a flat in the centre of Penzance, close to the Quay.'

'How recently was he released?' Lauren asked.

'Two months ago, ma'am.'

'Okay, text me his details. We need to speak to him, pronto. Especially as he lives within walking distance of the nursery. What else do we have? This child's been missing for almost twenty-four hours and I'm sure you are all of the same mind as me and beginning to fear for her safety.'

Lauren scrutinised her team. The expressions on their faces were difficult to read. She knew they didn't like her, but she wasn't there to be their friend. She was there to solve cases. She'd heard them referring to her as the Ice Queen when they thought she couldn't hear. Again, that didn't matter. She couldn't care less whether they liked her or not. She'd no intention of staying in Cornwall for the remainder of her career. But, more to the point, she wasn't prepared to have a dead child on her watch.

'Yes, ma'am. That thought is with us all, constantly,' Clem said, glancing at the rest of the team, who all nodded. 'But what else can we do? We've gone through the CCTV footage again and still found nothing out of the ordinary.'

'I appreciate your hard work, but maybe you should start looking at what appears to be the mundane.' For goodness' sake, it wasn't rocket science. 'Check again and look at the days leading up to yesterday. There's got to be a clue, we're just not spotting it yet. Nobody disappears into thin air. It's impossible. What else do we know about the father and mother? Is there anything new to report there?'

She looked over at Tamsin, who was the team member most efficient at research and who she trusted to find anything that needed finding. The others had their individual strengths.

Clem, the peacemaker and font of all knowledge, especially in the Cornwall area. Jenna, the most reliable and shrewd about people. Billy... well, the less said about him the better. If they were in London he'd be known as a typical wide-boy – he used his wits and was quick thinking, even if sometimes it was misguided. Lauren suspected he was the one who'd come up with her nickname.

'No, ma'am. Beverley Hopkins is a regular social media user. Luke Hopkins, less so. Obviously while in prison he wasn't on there, but before and since he's only posted occasionally. Nothing in their accounts points to anything murky. I've looked into their finances. Because Luke Hopkins was bankrupt, he doesn't have a credit card. He earns minimum wage at Generate where he works but that appears to suffice because he doesn't spend much. There are no regular payments made to his parents, so I suspect he doesn't pay them any rent. There are no strange incoming or outgoing amounts from either account. They're both normal people,' Tamsin said.

'Normal?' Billy piped up. 'That should be a red flag in itself. No one is normal.'

'Speak for yourself,' Tamsin said, smirking in his direction.

'Well—'

'And the nursery staff, Billy?' Lauren said, wanting to stop them going off track.

'Everything checks out and I'm—'

The door opened and Price marched in, holding up a tatty notebook in his hand. 'I have a list of people who lived in the farm cottages during the time we believe our victim was murdered.'

'Wait... did you say murder?' Jenna said.

'Yes. We also have a murder inquiry on our hands, which I'm sure we'd all suspected,' Lauren said. 'So we now have two important cases demanding our attention.'

'It's like buses. Never one when you want one, and then two

come along at once. Will we be asking another station to help?'
Clem asked.

'Not at this stage. I'm confident that we can manage. If
there is an issue, then I'll discuss it with the DCI. According to
pathology, the murder victim is female and has been dead for
between fifteen and twenty years. She had a gunshot wound
which may or may not have killed her. She also had blunt force
trauma to her head, hence the hole in the top of the skull. We'll
work the two cases together, although if we have to prioritise,
then the missing child comes first. Sergeant Price – we're going
to see Terry Lipton, who's recently been released from prison
and is on the sex offenders register.'

They arrived at the flat, which was above a small craft shop,
within a few minutes. Lauren rang the bell and not long after,
heard the sound of footsteps coming down the stairs. The door
was answered by a small man, five-foot-five at the most, with a
wiry build and small eyes set close together. He had thinning
straight light-brown hair and looked younger than his age.

Lauren shuddered. There was something intangibly
revolting about him.

She held out her warrant card. 'Terry Lipton?'

Panic crossed his face and he glanced to either side of them.
Was he planning to make a run for it?

'Yes. What do you want?'

On the defensive straight away. What was he hiding?

'We'd like to come in to ask you some questions.'

'You can ask here.' He folded his arms and blocked the
entrance.

Lauren placed her hand on the door and pushed it open. He
gave no resistance and moved out of the way. Clearly it had
been all bravado.

'No. We'll speak to you inside. After you.' She followed him up the stairs until they were standing in a small hallway. Lauren marched into the room on the left. His lounge. 'We'll talk in here,' she called over her shoulder.

The room was sparsely furnished, with two aged chairs facing a small TV standing on an old table. She noticed an open laptop on the dining table at the opposite side of the room. What had he been looking at? She marched over to check. On the screen was a news article about the Hopkins' custody case.

'Don't touch my things,' Lipton said from behind her, his voice weak.

Lauren glanced at Price and nodded for him to stand by the door. No way was Lipton going to get away.

She spun around to face the man. 'I see you're reading about the Hopkins family. Why's that?'

He bit down on his bottom lip. 'I heard about it on the news and was looking into it. I'm allowed. It's not breaking my parole. Reading the news isn't a crime, you know.'

'Except this isn't *news*, as you put it. This case happened a few months ago. So why are you looking at it now?'

'Because I am. That's all. Are you here about the missing girl? I was expecting you. Typical – I make one mistake and I'm the first suspect.' His eyes narrowed.

That was the first time she'd heard any real antagonism in his voice. Were they getting close to the truth?

'We're speaking to everyone in the area.'

'Yeah, right. Is the missing girl the one from the custody case?'

'We haven't yet announced the name of the girl. What were you doing yesterday morning between the hours of nine and twelve?' Lauren asked, ignoring his question.

'I was here all day. It was my day off.'

'On a Tuesday? Where do you work?'

'I'm sure you already know that I work in a warehouse. My days off are Monday and Tuesday.'

'Can anyone vouch for you being here?'

'No. I was on my own.'

'How convenient. Did you go out at all?'

'No.' He averted his eyes. 'I mean... yes. I might have done.'

Now they were getting somewhere.

'Did you or didn't you go out? It's not a hard question. I'm sure even you can manage to answer that one.'

She sucked in a calming breath. She didn't want to go in too insistently and have him clam up.

'Okay. I went out for a walk.'

'At what time?'

'I don't remember.'

'Try.'

'Maybe between ten and eleven? I hate being stuck at home. I needed some fresh air.'

'Where did you go?' Price asked, walking over to them, but still keeping the way to the room's exit blocked.

'I just walked around.'

'Did you go anywhere near Acorn Childcare Centre?'

His cheeks turned pink. 'I don't think so.'

'You don't think so? Well, your body language is telling me otherwise. Now, let's try again. Did you go anywhere near the nursery? I assume you know the nursery I'm talking about?' Lauren demanded.

'Yes, I know it.'

'Good. I'm glad we've established that. Now, I'll ask you again. Did you go anywhere near there when you were out walking yesterday morning?'

Lipton shrugged. 'I don't remember.'

That was enough for her. The laptop, and him likely to have been in the nursery's vicinity was sufficient for him to be taken to the station.

'Mr Lipton, we're taking you to the station for further questioning. We'd like to search your flat before we leave. Do we have your permission?'

'No. Not without a search warrant.'

'Why not? What do you have to hide?'

'No comment. And I'm not going to speak to you without my solicitor present.'

SEVENTEEN

WEDNESDAY, 26 OCTOBER

'The search warrant has come through,' Lauren said, leaving her room and stepping into the main office. 'Lipton's solicitor isn't due for another hour. Sergeant Price, Tamsin, Billy and Clem, you come with me to the flat. Jenna, you stay here and check to see if Lipton can be seen on any of the security cameras close to Acorn nursery. If he's on foot, it would take him at least half an hour to get there from his flat. This is the first real lead that we have. Let's hope we can put him in the vicinity.'

'Yes, ma'am.'

They left together, and Lauren parked a little down the road from the flat.

'Billy,' she said, once they'd all arrived. 'Go into the craft shop and find out what you can about Lipton's comings and goings. Tamsin, you take the shops on the opposite side of the road. See if they've noticed Lipton acting suspiciously, or if anyone has seen him with a child. Then come upstairs to the flat. It's only small and shouldn't take long to search.'

Using the key that she'd obtained from Lipton after explaining that it would be much better to let themselves in than to break down the door, Lauren, Price and Clem headed up the stairs and into the flat. They came to a standstill in the narrow hallway.

'It smells musty,' Clem said, wrinkling his nose. 'That's the trouble with these old buildings.'

Lauren hadn't noticed when they were there before, but now it had been pointed out she could smell it. She pulled on some disposable gloves and the others did the same.

'I'll take the lounge. Sergeant, you search the bedroom and bathroom. Clem, you do the kitchen. Call out if you find anything.'

Lauren entered the lounge and made a beeline for his laptop, which was where they'd left it. It was still open and she pressed one of the keys but it was locked. Damn.

She slammed the laptop shut and put it in an evidence bag. She'd get forensics to go through it.

'Ma'am,' Clem said, coming into the room. 'I found his phone in the kitchen. It's locked, but I'll take it with us.'

'Was there anything else of interest?'

'No, ma'am. There's very little food and nothing indicating that he's had a child in here.'

'Ma'am.' Price hurried into the lounge holding a small cream leather jewellery box. 'I found this in his bedroom.' He opened the lid. 'Look, these are ribbons, hair ties and hair bands that young girls would wear.'

The items had fairies, unicorns and little animals on them.

'Do any belong to Isla?' Lauren asked.

'She was reported as wearing a pink headband, but there isn't one here, nor are there any ties with bears on them,' Price said.

'If he does have her then he hasn't yet taken a souvenir. That's a good sign. Put the box in an evidence bag and I'll question him about it.'

'Did you have any luck?' Price asked.

'I'm taking his laptop in for forensics to go through, along with the phone that Clem found in the kitchen.'

'Do you have a mobile phone data extraction device that we can use, so we can get into the phone straight away rather than having to wait for forensics?'

She wished they did, but this was southwest Cornwall.

'I'll have to check to see if there is one somewhere within the Devon and Cornwall police force area. We don't have one in our team but they might have one elsewhere at another station. Possibly in Torquay or somewhere larger.'

'So annoying,' Price muttered.

'Yeah, I get it. Not what you're used to.' She scrunched up her face in annoyance.

'I didn't mean—'

'Whatever,' she interrupted. 'We'd better get back because Lipton's solicitor will be arriving shortly.'

* * *

'Right, let's begin,' Pengelly said the moment she and Matt walked into the interview room. She'd been off with him ever since his comment about the phone extraction device. But he hadn't meant her to think he was moaning about the station. It was an off-the-cuff remark. Hopefully she wouldn't hold it over him.

They sat at the table opposite Lipton and his solicitor, a woman in her late thirties, wearing a navy jacket with a white blouse, who looked decidedly bored.

Matt leant over and pressed the recording button. 'Wednesday twenty-sixth October, interview with DI Pengelly, DS Price and—'

'Nola Dunbar-Boothe, solicitor.'

'Terry Lipton,' the man muttered, keeping his eyes focused on the table and not looking at any of them.

'Mr Lipton, you've been brought in for questioning concerning the disappearance of a three-year-old girl. When we visited you at your flat, on your laptop you had details of a court case from several months ago concerning the child's parents.'

'So, I was right. It was her,' Lipton said, appearing smug.

'Why were you reading about the case?' Lauren continued.

He glanced up and stared at Pengelly. 'I've already told you. No reason. I'm allowed – there's no law against it.'

'Would you say it's a bit of a coincidence that we're looking for their little girl and you're interested in the family? Bearing in mind your history.'

The man remained silent, but shot a furtive glance at his solicitor.

'I fail to see how that's relevant at this point,' Dunbar-Boothe said.

Matt looked at her, fully aware that he had an incredulous expression on his face. How could the woman say that? It had everything to do with it.

'We'll decide what's relevant,' Pengelly said. 'Mr Lipton, how did you know that Isla Hopkins had gone missing considering her name wasn't announced at the press conference?'

Matt scrutinised the man for any tell-tale sign of his guilt, or that he was about to lie. But there was none.

'I don't know.' Lipton shrugged.

'That's not good enough. How did you know?' Pengelly placed both hands on the table and leant forward, staring directly at Lipton. 'I think it's because you were the person who took her. Where is she?'

Panic flickered in Lipton's eyes as he returned the DI's stare. 'I don't know. I didn't take her. It was just chance that I was looking at the custody case.'

'And you expect us to believe that convenient story, do you? Well, forget it. Either you tell us the truth or we'll charge you now.'

'Look, Terry,' Matt said, softly. 'All we care about is Isla's safety. She's a small child. She'll be wanting her mum. Please, tell us what you know.'

Matt wasn't usually into the good cop, bad cop routine, but they had to do something. Clearly Pengelly was getting nowhere, and Lipton would most likely clam up.

Lipton lowered his head. 'I didn't take her,' he muttered. 'I didn't.'

'Where were you yesterday morning between the hours of nine and twelve?' Pengelly asked, her voice cold.

Lipton raised his head. 'I've already told you. I was at home and during that time went out for a walk.'

'Where did you go?'

'Just around and about.'

'And can anyone vouch for you?'

'You know that, too. I'm not answering any more questions. Because you're just trying to trip me up.'

'But surely you're concerned about the child? You want us to find her, don't you? We're only doing our job,' Matt said.

'No comment.'

'Don't be ridiculous. Just answer our questions. All we want to know is what happened to Isla. Where is she? Where did you take her?' Pengelly said.

'No comment.'

'Is that no comment because you're not going to tell us where you took her?' Pengelly goaded.

Matt nodded his head in approval; she was good.

'I've just told you that I didn't take her but—' He paused.

'But what?' Pengelly said. 'You definitely know something. Why don't you tell us and then we can concentrate on finding the child.'

'Look, I knew which child had gone missing because when I went out for my walk I was close to the nursery and I saw Mrs Hopkins talking to you. I recognised her because of the court case and after the press conference I realised who it was.'

'So you're saying that you have nothing to do with Isla's disappearance, but you knew it was her because you happened to be walking past the nursery and recognised her mother. That's a very convenient story. Do you make a point of walking so close to the nursery? It's not like it's a place where most people would go to. Why didn't you go for a walk in town? Why choose the place where you knew there would be young children?'

'I didn't mean to go there; it just happened. I didn't take her. And okay, so I like to watch the children playing, but you can't do me for that. I kept my distance.'

'When we were searching your place we found a box and inside there were lots of little girls' headbands, and hair ties.'

The man went bright red and lowered his head.

'Are they yours?' Matt asked after a few seconds of silence.

'No comment.'

'For goodness' sake, man. You tell us you're innocent, but why should we believe you? You're not exactly helping. What are you doing with a box full of hair things belonging to little girls?' Matt demanded. 'Did you steal them? Did you buy them? Why do you have them?'

'If I find any lying around I take them. It's nothing to do with what's happened to Isla Hopkins. I've already told you it wasn't me. You're picking on me because of what happened in the past. I can't change that, but I'm trying to live a normal life now... if you'll let me.'

A loud knock on the door interrupted them and Clem poked his head around.

'Ma'am, I'd like a word. It's important.'

'Interview suspended,' Matt said.

He left the room with Pengelly.

'Another child's gone missing, but this time from Redwood,

the nursery in Penare Road. Same MO,' Clem said the moment the door was shut.

'What? When?' Pengelly said.

'About half an hour ago, I believe.'

'We had Lipton in custody at the time. It couldn't have been him,' Matt said.

'I don't believe this is happening. Clem, sort out Lipton. Release him for now, but make sure he doesn't leave town. Sergeant, you and I are going to Redwood nursery. You can drive.'

EIGHTEEN

WEDNESDAY, 26 OCTOBER

Lauren drummed her fingers on her leg while Price drove them to the nursery. How the hell could she have got it so wrong? She'd truly believed that Lipton was their man and they'd lost valuable working hours focusing on him. Had she automatically assumed he was guilty because of his history and not the facts?

Another child missing put a whole different complexion on the case. For a start, it highlighted the fact that Isla having been taken was not personal.

She groaned.

'Ma'am?' Price said, tossing a glance in her direction.

'A second missing child changes everything. Was Isla specifically targeted, or just an unlucky victim?'

'I've been thinking about that, too. There's definitely something personal about this. But is it the specific child, or just nurseries in general? And if the latter, then why take Isla, because there were other, more accessible children. Another consideration is that this second missing child is also a girl. That could be relevant, too.'

He was right, of course. Nothing about this screamed

random child abduction. And equally, nothing else really made sense. No logic behind it that she could fathom.

'Do you think there's any chance this second kidnapping could be a copycat?' she muttered, more to herself than to her sergeant, although his view would be welcomed.

'No. How can it be? We haven't released sufficient details of Isla's disappearance for anyone to have copied it. Unless...' His voice fell away.

'Unless what?'

'Well, unless it was an inside job. But we looked into all of Acorn's workers, and these are two independent nurseries with completely different staff.'

She nodded slowly. Then a thought hit her.

'What if it's someone from a government agency with responsibility for overseeing both?' She pulled out her phone and pressed speed dial for the station.

'CID. DC Moyle speaking.'

'Jenna, it's the DI. I want you to do some research into any agencies who have responsibility for childcare centres in the area, and check for anyone who visits them on a regular basis. If these kidnappings are linked, we suspect it's someone with an intimate knowledge of both places.'

'Yes, ma'am. Are you at the nursery already?'

'We're pulling up now. If you discover anything of use, act on it. Don't wait for my approval.'

'Oh. Okay. I'll see you later, ma'am.'

Lauren frowned. Jenna's surprise at being given some responsibility to act on her own accord was obvious. Maybe she should trust her team more often... Now wasn't the time to be ruminating on her management skills.

Price parked the car outside a late Victorian, three-storey, end-of-terrace townhouse, and they hurried along the short path and up the three stone steps to the partially glazed green front door, with *Redwood Nursery* in gold lettering. She rang the bell and the door was opened almost immediately by a woman in her fifties. Standing behind her in the entrance hall was another, much younger woman holding the hand of a little boy.

'I'm DI Pengelly and this is DS Price. Who's in charge?'

'I'm Mrs Palmer-Thompson,' the woman said, in a clipped, upper-class accent. 'I own the nursery. Come in.'

They walked into the hall which had a mahogany staircase to the right, leading up to the first floor. The head closed the door behind them.

'This is Mrs Boardman. She collects Violet, the child who's gone missing, each day.'

'So, you're not her mother?' Lauren said, looking at the woman.

'No. When I pick up my son, Eric, I also take Violet and keep her until two o'clock when her dad finishes work. He collects Violet from my house.'

'Which is where?'

'About a five-minute walk away, in St Alban Street.'

'When did you discover Violet was missing?' Lauren asked, returning to Mrs Palmer-Thompson.

'At midday, when Mrs Boardman arrived. Nothing like this has ever happened before. It...' She drew in a breath and visibly attempted to pull herself together, clearly not wanting to lose it in front of one of the parents. '... Sorry.'

'So you don't know the exact time Violet went missing, only the time you realised?' Price asked, an incredulous tone in his voice.

'It couldn't have been much before midday or we would have noticed.'

Another disappearance without a trace. It was impossible.

'How many children do you have here?' Lauren asked.

'We're a small nursery with only twenty children when we're at full capacity. Which we are on some days, and others not. I prefer it that way, because it means we can give quality childcare to each child on an individual basis.'

'But surely if you follow the legal requirements for staff/children ratios then they would get that level of care anyway?' Lauren said, frowning.

Mrs Palmer-Thompson shook her head. 'You'd like to think so, but in the bigger nurseries, which are usually part of a larger company, staff move between rooms and, in my opinion, much of the personal touch is lost.'

Yet, despite this additional care, it hadn't stopped a child from going missing.

'We'd like to take a look at your CCTV footage,' Price said.

'The only camera we have is on the front door. We've discussed having one on the back door, but didn't think it was necessary. It's only staff who use that exit so they can get to the small car park at the rear, which is accessed from around the corner. At one time it was mooted that we have cameras in each of our rooms, but the staff and parents both said no.'

Exactly what they'd said at Acorn, and look where that had got them.

'I'm sorry, but I need to get my little boy home. Is that okay?' Mrs Boardman asked.

'Of course,' Lauren said. 'We may need to speak to you again, though.'

'I understand. Mrs P-T has my details. Come on, Eric, let's get some lunch.'

'Violet?' the little boy said, looking all around him.

'She's not coming with us today. You'll see her another time.' The woman stared over the top of his head at Lauren, panic glistening in her eyes.

'Goodbye, Eric,' Mrs Palmer-Thompson said.

Lauren waited until they had left and then turned to the head. 'We need to speak to Violet's parents. Do you have their work and home details?'

'Yes, I have their address and both of their workplace contact numbers in my office. I didn't want to get in touch with them until I'd spoken to you first. I wasn't sure of the protocol in this situation. My office is down the corridor, if you'd like to come with me.'

Lauren and Price followed Mrs Palmer-Thompson into her office and waited while she found them the details.

'Thanks. Sergeant, contact the station and ask them to send officers to fetch the parents. We'll meet them back at their house and explain what's happened when we get there.'

'Don't you think I should go, ma'am, and tell them on the way? It's not fair to keep the parents in the dark during their journey home.'

He was right.

'Okay, you go.' She glanced at the addresses. They were both in Penzance and not far away. 'On your way, contact the station and get officers out here pronto to start searching for Violet and to undertake a house-to-house enquiry.' She handed him the paper with the parents' details on it.

'Yes, ma'am. How will you get to the parents' house?'

'Call me a lift, please.'

'Will do.'

Price left and Lauren turned to Mrs Palmer-Thompson. 'Can you show me the CCTV footage from this morning?'

She had time to look through it before leaving.

'Yes, I can access it from my computer.'

Lauren walked around the desk and peered over the woman's shoulder.

'Run the footage from the moment you opened this morning.'

'That would be seven thirty.'

'Run it at double speed for now, so we can get through it quickly.'

The first child was dropped off at the door at seven thirty-five and there was a regular flow of children after that.

'Here's Mr Dent,' Mrs Palmer-Thompson said, when the footage showed seven forty-five. 'He's parking on the opposite side of the road and taking Violet out of her car seat. Here he is dropping her off at the front door and leaving. Nothing out of the ordinary there.'

Lauren stared at the screen. The man handed his daughter over to a staff member and then left. Interesting he didn't even turn back to wave. He just headed straight down the path, got into his car and drove off. Now, she might not have children, but even Lauren realised that he wasn't being very demonstrative considering his daughter was so young.

'Keep playing the footage until midday when you noticed Violet was missing. To see if she was taken out of the front door,' Lauren said.

The head restarted it and they stared at the screen. But there was no sighting of the missing girl.

'That's it,' Mrs Palmer-Thompson said, stopping the footage. 'She didn't come through here. At least, not that we could see.'

'And the only other exit is the back door, with no camera on it,' Lauren said, unable to hide her frustration.

'Yes,' the head said, her voice low.

'How many staff are on duty today?'

'Five, but they're not all full-time.'

'Who knows that Violet's missing?'

'Everyone working here because we've been looking for her. But no one else, apart from Eric's mother. This is the second one, isn't it? I presume you haven't found Isla Hopkins yet?' Mrs Palmer-Thompson said, swivelling around on her chair and giving Lauren an accusing look.

'How do you know it's Isla? It hasn't been announced.'

'I'm friends with Valerie Archer,' she said, referring to the head of Acorn nursery. 'She told me.'

And who else had been told? That was the trouble with small communities; things spread like wildfire. She would have to speak to the DCI about making an announcement before it was plastered all over social media, making the police look like idiots.

'Please keep that to yourself because we deliberately haven't named Isla. We're not going to announce Violet's name either.'

'I understand. I did actually tell the staff here because I wanted them to take extra care. I'll make sure they know to keep quiet about both little girls. Although these things do have a habit of getting out.'

'We'll need to interview all staff on duty, in particular those in the room when Violet went missing.'

'Yes of course. I'll relieve them. Do you wish to do that now?'

'Not yet. I'll wait until we've interviewed the parents. I assume every part of the building has been searched?'

'Yes. There's no way she is hiding anywhere.'

'What's Violet like?'

Mrs Palmer-Thompson paused for a moment, as if weighing up her words. 'To be honest, she's not the easiest of children. In fact, she can be quite difficult. We had to speak to her parents not long ago because she bit another child.'

'What did you say to them?'

'I explained that biting is a form of communication and gave suggestions regarding how to support Violet in developing empathy for others. I made sure to explain that Violet shouldn't be scolded. We have a policy regarding biting, which staff follow, and we were careful to keep an eye on Violet to see if there was a particular trigger causing a repeat of the behaviour.'

'And what happened after the incident?'

'She didn't bite again. She's a bright child and I think she now understands that it's not an acceptable way to behave. That's not to say it's been plain sailing since. She is prone to throwing a tantrum every now and again. But she's three and that's what we expect from children of her age.'

Another bright child. Had that been a factor in choosing her?

Lauren's phone rang. 'Pengelly.'

'PC French, ma'am. I've been sent to pick you up.'

'Thank you.' She ended the call and turned her attention back to Mrs Palmer-Thompson. 'I'm going to see Mr and Mrs Dent. Officers should be arriving shortly to begin their search. I'll be back soon.'

NINETEEN

WEDNESDAY, 26 OCTOBER

'Let's go inside,' Matt said to Mr and Mrs Dent when they arrived at their modern detached house. 'DI Pengelly should be here shortly and we can discuss what's happening.'

'*Discuss what's happening?* This isn't some office meeting regarding... I don't know... Whatever... This is my daughter we're talking about!' Mrs Dent turned to her husband, who was sitting next to her on the back seat of Matt's car. 'I blame you.'

Mr Dent didn't speak. There was no reassuring contact between them.

'I'm sorry. I didn't mean for you to think we're trivialising this. I can assure you we're not.' A police car pulled up behind them. 'The DI's here. I'll take you to meet her.'

Matt got out of the car and Mr and Mrs Dent did the same. They waited on the pavement while Pengelly got out of the car and came over.

'This is Mr and Mrs Dent, ma'am.'

'Actually, I go by my maiden name, Fletcher,' the woman said.

'Have you found her?' Mr Dent asked.

'Not yet,' Pengelly said, her face grim. 'But we're doing everything in our power to find her.'

'Everything in your power?' Mrs Fletcher said, her voice tight. 'Because it doesn't feel like it.'

Matt kept his voice calm. 'I have explained to Violet's parents that officers will be searching everywhere.'

'Let's go inside,' Pengelly said, her voice gentle.

They walked up the drive and Mr Dent took out a key, opening the front door. They followed him inside and into a large sitting room.

'I don't understand how she can be missing from the nursery,' the child's mother said, once they were all seated. 'What happened? Did someone leave the door open? She's only three. She has asthma and isn't good in the cold air.' The woman stared angrily at her husband. 'This is all your fault, Patrick. Why do you have to go out to work? I earn enough for both of us so there's no need for it. You're a delivery driver, which is hardly going to change the world. I wouldn't mind if you were using your qualifications, but you're not. You hardly need a PhD to sit behind the wheel of a van. If it hadn't been for you, Violet wouldn't be missing. She'd be here at home. Safe.'

Now Matt understood her earlier outburst.

'We agreed that you'd be the main breadwinner, but that doesn't mean I have to be stuck at home all day. My job gives me flexibility and—'

'Yeah, right,' his wife interrupted.

'Please, Mrs Dent— I mean Fletcher,' Pengelly said. 'This isn't helping. We have to do our best to find Violet. The staff have looked everywhere in the nursery and she's definitely not there. Officers are already combing the streets and speaking to neighbours. We'll do our best to locate Violet.'

Mrs Fletcher appeared suitably chastised, although she continued to stare daggers at her husband.

'But another little girl went missing from a nursery yesterday, didn't she?' Mr Dent said, his voice barely above a whisper. 'D-do you think the same person has taken her? Have you found the other child?'

Matt took a sideways glance at Pengelly. What was she going to tell them?

'We can't speculate at the moment. All we do know is that we're doing our best to find Violet. I know this is going to be hard, but we need to ask you some questions. Questions that will assist us in our inquiry.'

'We understand,' Mr Dent said. His wife nodded.

'Does Violet have any brothers or sisters?' Pengelly asked.

'No. She's our only one. I had a difficult pregnancy. Sick every single day. I couldn't go through that again,' Mrs Fletcher said.

Pengelly nodded her understanding. 'I'd like you to think back over the last few days. Did you notice anyone hanging around here? A car maybe. Or someone walking. Anything suspicious and out of the ordinary?'

'No, I don't think so,' the mother said. 'But then I don't spend time looking to see if there's anyone loitering. I mean... I leave for work first thing in the morning and am not back until after six, when it's dark.'

'What do you do?' Matt asked.

'I'm chief accountant for a large agricultural supplier. I work from the satellite office here in Penzance, although I frequently go to our head office in Plymouth.'

'Mr Dent, have you noticed anything? You have Violet in the afternoons after two. Has anything struck you as odd? Maybe when you've been at the park? Has anyone you don't know paid particular attention to you or started talking to Violet?'

'He wouldn't notice even if that did happen. If he goes to the park he spends all his time talking to the other mothers.' Mrs Fletcher glowered at him. 'Don't think I don't know because

Melanie from next door has told me she's seen you *socialising* with all the mums while I'm hard at work.'

'What do you expect me to do? Stay inside and stare at four walls? Of course I'm going to take Violet to the park or to town. And we're bound to see people I know. For goodness' sake, Katie, this isn't the time to discuss what I do when you're at work. It's Violet we should be worried about, not your pathological need to control everything I do.'

Mrs Fletcher flinched. It was the first time her husband had answered her back since Matt had been with them.

'I know this is really difficult for you both, but please try to stay calm and focused on what we have to do. Which is to find Violet.' Matt's words belied his true feelings on the matter, despite him trying to sound calm. They'd made no real progress with Isla, and that didn't bode well for this second missing child.

'I want to go out with your officers to look for Violet,' Mr Dent said. 'I can't just sit here and wait. Not knowing where she is. Or if she's suffering.'

'No. It's best if you stay here in case she turns up,' Pengelly said, her voice kind, but firm.

'Don't be ridiculous. She's three years old,' Katie Fletcher snapped. 'How's she going to know how to get home? She doesn't even know her address. She knows the house b-but—' A sob escaped her mouth and she leant forward, wrapping her arms around her knees.

'I was meaning in case somebody found her and brought her home.'

'Sorry,' the woman mumbled, sniffing.

'Can you tell me what Violet was wearing today?' Matt asked, focusing on Mrs Fletcher.

Her cheeks coloured. 'I don't know. I leave for work before she gets dressed and she's ready for bed when I arrive home. Patrick will know.'

'She's wearing a green gingham long-sleeved cotton dress, with a white broderie anglaise collar. It has a little pocket with a patch and the word *Love* embroidered on it. She was also wearing some white tights. In her hair she had a slide with two ponies on it,' Mr Dent said.

'Do you have a recent photo of Violet on your phone? It will probably be more up to date than the nursery photo,' Pengelly said.

'Yes, I have hundreds. I'll send one to you,' Mr Dent said, pulling his phone out of his denim jacket pocket.

'Here's a card with my email address. Please send it now. It will be a great help.'

'What happens if we don't find Violet?' Mrs Fletcher asked quietly.

'They will,' Mr Dent said, leaning over and resting his arm around his wife's shoulders. 'They have to.'

The woman tensed and pulled away from him. 'You don't know that. You're doing your usual thing of always looking on the bright side. But there is no bright side here. Why can't you act like a normal person for a change?'

There was certainly a lot of tension between the couple, Matt thought. Could the daughter have picked up on that and taken off? No, that was a ridiculous thing to think. Children don't have those sorts of thoughts. Not at three. Plus they had the other child abduction to consider.

But what was the motive?

'You need to be strong for each other. Fighting won't change anything. One of our family liaison officers will come here to be with you while we're searching for Violet and they'll be able to let you know how the operation is going. If you have any questions you can ask them. I'm not sure who the officer will be, but they'll be with you as soon as we can arrange it. You have my card. I'm available any time should you need me. We'll see ourselves out.'

'Which FLO are we going to use? Would you like me to contact them?' Matt asked, once they were outside.

'We only have one attached to our team so I'll need to make a call to the DCI and ask him to find one from another station.'

'Only one? That's crazy. How can we do our job properly under these conditions?' Matt blurted out.

Pengelly stared at him, her eyes narrowed. 'How many times do I have to tell you? This isn't one of your big stations, Sergeant Price. And we don't have all the fancy resources that you're clearly used to. So, deal with it. Someone will be with Violet's parents as soon as it's possible.'

Matt stiffened. He hadn't meant anything by it; the words had left his lips before he had time to consider how Pengelly would react. This was the second time he'd annoyed her recently. He'd try hard not to make that mistake again.

'What did you make of the parents?' he asked, changing the subject.

'Certainly no love lost between them. It can't be a happy environment for a child to live in. We need to go back to the nursery to interview the staff. We'll start with those working in the room Violet was taken from.'

TWENTY

WEDNESDAY, 26 OCTOBER

Lauren let out a frustrated sigh. It was like they were starting from scratch. Two missing kids and no clues. She was in Mrs Palmer-Thompson's office with Price, waiting for the first staff member to come in. She'd been a bit hard on Price when he'd asked about the FLOs, but she needed to nip this constant comparison with his previous force in the bud or he'd drive her insane. It was like he still felt connected to the larger force. If he'd loved Lenchester so much, then why on earth had he left?

There was a gentle tap on the door.

'I'll get it,' Price said, jumping up from his chair, opening the door and ushering a young woman in.

She looked to be in her late twenties, and was wearing black leggings and a turquoise polo shirt with the nursery logo on it. Her face was ashen and red rings circled her eyes.

'I'm Zoe Carpenter. You wanted to speak to me about Violet?' she said softly.

'Yes. Take a seat.' Lauren gestured to the sofa in the corner.

Price returned to his chair.

'How long have you been working here?'

'Almost ten years. I came here on placement during my training, and after qualifying Mrs P-T offered me a job.'

'So you're well aware of all the procedures?' Lauren said.

'Yes.' Zoe nodded.

'We'd like you to go through what happened this morning leading up to when you discovered Violet was missing.'

Zoe sniffed, and wiped her eyes 'I don't get it. Nothing strange happened at all. Nobody came in the room who wasn't working here. The children played as they usually do. We read a story, did some painting and then had our mid-morning snack. After that we played some games as a group and then the children engaged in some free-play time. One minute Violet was there the next she wasn't.' Zoe bit down on her bottom lip and a tear rolled down her cheek.

'Is it possible for Violet to leave the room on her own? Or any child for that matter?' Lauren asked.

'We don't lock the doors because that would be a fire hazard. So, yes, I suppose she could have pushed the door open. But surely we'd have noticed.'

'Can you be certain?'

Zoe bowed her head. 'No.'

'Did you see any strangers in the nursery at all this morning?' Price asked.

'No. I saw no one who shouldn't have been here.' She paused for a moment. 'The problem with this building is there are lots of different rooms and that's why we first thought she'd got out and was hiding somewhere. Or had got lost. But we searched everywhere. In all the rooms. Everywhere.'

'We understand that Violet could be a difficult child and had bitten another child recently. What sort of mood was she in today?' Lauren asked.

'The bite only happened once. It's not unusual behaviour for young children. She was fine this morning. I'm not sure whether I should say this but...'

'But?' Lauren prompted.

'It's not easy at home for her. I've met both of her parents when they've been in for parent/teacher chats and there's always tension. I'm sure Violet's affected by it and that's why she can act up sometimes when she's here.'

That didn't surprise Lauren, if her meeting with the parents was anything to go by.

'Is there anything else you can tell us that might help?'

'No. It was as if Violet disappearing happened by magic. Which sounds ridiculous.'

Lauren agreed. But with both children having vanished into thin air with nobody seeing a thing, it was beginning to sound plausible even to her.

'I'm sure there'll be a logical explanation. If anything else springs to mind, let us know. For now, please ask the other staff member in your room to come to see us.'

'Umm... I don't think there's any point because Ellie's part-time and didn't come on until lunchtime, after Violet had gone missing.'

The hairs rose on the back of Lauren's neck. So whoever was working in the morning must have already left the premises. But why? Surely they would have waited to speak to the police? Had they taken Violet somewhere? It would prove that she was right about it being an inside job... Then again, that didn't answer how Isla had been taken.

'Who was with you before lunch?'

'It was Maddie. She's working in her usual room this after-noon. We had to do some shuffling today because of staff sick-ness which is why she ended up being with me. Mrs P-T has also been working between rooms.'

Lauren exhaled. That made more sense. The woman hadn't disappeared without first speaking to them. It was a shame, because it had almost been a lead.

'Thank you, Zoe. Please could you ask Maddie to come see us. We'll want a word with Ellie after that.'

'I'll have to relieve Mrs P-T first and ask her to send Maddie to you. Or perhaps you could see Ellie first, that would make it easier?'

'Yes, that's a good idea as Mrs Palmer-Thompson is already in your room. Please ask her to hurry, though. We can't afford to waste any time.'

'If this Maddie wasn't used to working in Violet's room then she might not have adhered to correct procedures,' Price said, once Zoe had left. 'That could have made it easier for Violet to get out without being seen.'

That thought had crossed Lauren's mind as well.

'It's something we can ask when she arrives. This place certainly isn't as well-organised as the Acorn Childcare Centre, which would have made it easier for someone to take Violet, for sure.'

'But again, we have the mystery of how it happened,' Price said. 'I've never been on a case so perplexing.'

The door, which had been left slightly ajar, was pushed open and a woman in her mid-thirties walked in. She had shoulder-length, mid-brown hair with blond highlights and a fringe. She was dressed identically to Zoe.

'Hello, I'm Ellie.' She gave a hesitant smile.

'Come in and sit down. We have some questions about Violet.' Lauren stood and gestured to the empty sofa.

'I couldn't believe it when Zoe told me,' Ellie said, as she walked over. 'How did it happen? The poor child must be so distraught. She's such a sweet kid.'

'Really?' Lauren said. 'We'd heard she could be difficult.'

'That's not her fault. It's a matter of how you deal with her. When—'

'I'm sorry, we don't have time to discuss child-care techniques,' Lauren said, interrupting. 'What time did you arrive today?'

'Oh, right. Well... my shift started at twelve thirty, but I was here from around eleven forty-five because I'd been into town shopping and didn't have time to go home first.' She sat on the edge of the sofa, her hands clasped tightly in her lap.

'Where were you for the forty-five minutes before your shift started?'

'In the staff room eating my lunch and reading a magazine.'

'Did anyone see you in there?'

'Um... yes. I think so?' She gave a small shrug.

'*Think*?'

'I mean, no one was in there the whole time. But Mrs P-T popped her head in and said hello.'

'Where is the staff room in relation to the room Violet was in?'

'It's upstairs on the first floor, and Violet's room is on the ground floor.'

'When you came into the building, did you notice anything out of the ordinary? Or anyone who shouldn't have been there?'

'No. I parked my car, walked in through the back and went straight upstairs. I'm sorry, I didn't see anyone.'

'Okay. If you do think of something, please let me know. Here's my card. We'd like to speak to Maddie now. Mrs P-T needs to relieve her.' Lauren stood and gestured for her to leave.

'Is this anything to do with what happened at Acorn?' Ellie asked, stopping at the door. 'Have you found her yet?'

'I'm not at liberty to discuss an ongoing investigation. But, as I've explained to Mrs Palmer-Thompson, please keep to yourself anything about either child. For the sake of the families.'

'Yes, of course. I hope you find them.'

'We're doing our best,' Lauren said, turning away, not wanting to prolong the conversation.

'Well, she wasn't much help,' Price said, once they were alone.

'It's like Acorn nursery all over again. No one can help because they saw nothing. I—' Lauren was about to admit that she felt at a total loss and was panic-stricken in case they couldn't find the children, but thought better of it. She had to stay strong for the team. Or at least give the appearance of being so.

There was a knock at the door and a woman in her fifties, with grey hair tied up in a bun, walked in.

'I'm Madeleine O'Connor – Maddie. You wanted to see me about what happened to Violet? I can't stop thinking about it. Going over in my mind how she could have got out. But I can't think of anything. I'm not saying that we have eyes on all the children all of the time, and obviously there are times when we are busy cleaning and tidying up, especially when they're asleep, but it makes no sense.'

'You don't usually work in the room with children of that age, do you?' Lauren said.

'No, I'm usually with the babies.'

'So obviously that's quite different because they're not moving around, unlike the three- and four-year-olds.'

'That's correct. There are different things we have to deal with for babies, obviously, but that doesn't mean I can't look after the older ones. I'm a fully trained nursery nurse.'

'We not questioning your ability, Maddie,' Price said, gently. 'We're just trying to find out exactly what happened.'

'Do you think it was particularly Violet they wanted, or could it have been any child? It's awful. Especially after it happening at Acorn as well...'

Lauren forced back a frustrated sigh.

'As I've already explained to your colleague, we can't

discuss the case. Other than to say we don't expect anyone from here to talk about the disappearances to people outside of work. It's confidential. In case it jeopardises the investigation.'

'Yes. Of course. I won't say anything. I promise.'

'Thank you. Have you always worked as a nursery nurse?' Lauren asked, moving on.

'Yes. I trained when I was eighteen and worked until I got married and had my own children. Now they're older I've come back to work. I've always lived and worked here in the Penzance area.'

'How long have you been at Redwood?'

'A little under two years.'

'Were you working on Tuesday?'

'Yes.'

'And in terms of efficiency, how's this nursery run? How would you rate Redwood compared with other nurseries?'

'This is a great place to work. The staff are nice and Mrs P-T's a fantastic boss. But...' She hesitated.

'Please continue. This will remain strictly between us,' Lauren said, not wanting to miss out on any information because the woman was worried about her job.

'Well, she's a little old school and maybe not so up to date with developments. We don't have CCTV cameras apart from one on the front of the building and although we pass all of the government inspections, I think it's a bit lax. I do know that a larger company with nurseries all over the county has offered to buy her out and she's thinking about it. She's over retirement age, although she doesn't look it, and working with children can be exhausting at the best of times. Please don't say anything to her; I don't want to lose my job.'

Retirement age? Lauren wouldn't have put Mrs Palmer-Thompson as old enough for that.

'Our concern is to find Violet and we need to know every-thing we can about the nursery in order to do that. If it's possible for someone to walk in without being apprehended and take a child then we need to know,' Lauren said.

'Yes of course. I understand. But I don't think anyone could just walk in. People have to press the bell. Unless... occasionally the door doesn't catch and then it can be pushed open. Mrs P-T knows about it and has mentioned getting someone in to fix it.'

'But it hasn't been repaired yet?' Lauren asked.

'Not as far as I know.'

'Is it likely that Violet would have walked off with a stranger?' Price asked.

'I don't know the child very well because I haven't spent much time with her but she's not easy, that much I can tell you. Whether she'd go off with a stranger or whoever it was that took her, I don't know. Maybe not? When I first spent time with her she was reserved and it took a couple of sessions before she relaxed with me.'

'Do you believe that Violet might have known her abductor in that case?' Lauren asked.

'I don't know. All I can tell you is how she was with me.'

'Thank you for your help,' Lauren said. 'If you think of anything else that might be helpful, please contact us. You can go back to work, now.'

'I hope you find her,' Maddie said, as she left the office.

You and me both.

Lauren released a drawn-out sigh. Every minute mattered, yet despite their efforts progress was elusive. If they didn't find the missing girls soon... she couldn't allow her thoughts to go down that road.

TWENTY-ONE
WEDNESDAY, 26 OCTOBER

Pengelly beckoned for Matt to stand with her beside the whiteboard when they arrived back at the office. Using the red marker pen in her hand, she'd written on the board the names of the two nurseries and underneath each one the name of the child who'd disappeared.

'There's got to be something we're missing,' she said, scanning the team. 'All we know is that two three-year-old girls have vanished from their nursery in what should be very secure environments. Has anyone established a link between the two nurseries?'

The silence was palpable.

'No, ma'am,' Clem finally said.

'Jenna, social services inspections of the nurseries – what have you discovered?'

'It's the government agency Ofsted who registers and inspects childcare providers, not social services. I've contacted them and Acorn was last inspected two years ago, and Redwood five. The inspections were carried out by different people. So definitely no link there, ma'am.' Jenna's shoulders slumped in despair.

'Okay. It was worth a try. What Sergeant Price and I have learnt, having visited both sites, is that Redwood Nursery is less secure than Acorn. Redwood only has one CCTV camera at the front of the building, but after scrutinising footage nothing out of the ordinary appeared to have happened. Exactly like it was at Acorn. Neither sets of parents have identified any suspicious activity in the vicinity of their homes. So, I repeat – what are we missing?'

Pengelly's tone was harsh. Did she believe it was the team's fault they were hitting a brick wall with the inquiry? No. He didn't think so. The case was affecting all of them and they'd been working hard to solve it. If anything, she was probably blaming herself.

'Why don't we ask the parents to give a press conference? It might help to trigger some memories. Because surely someone must have witnessed something, even if at the time they didn't realise it,' Billy suggested.

Several of the team nodded in agreement.

'That's not possible. I've spoken to DCI Mistry and it's been decided that we're not going to announce to the public the names of the girls or their families. We don't want the media harassing them. It's bad enough for them as it is. I'm going to be giving a press conference with the DCI shortly and all we're going to say is that another child has gone missing. That will have to suffice for now.'

Matt observed Billy exchange a glance with Jenna, pulling a face. Clearly they didn't agree with Pengelly but they didn't voice an objection.

'Ma'am, shall we contact all of the nurseries in the Penzance area and ask them to be careful? Or maybe even ask them not to open?' Tamsin suggested.

'Good idea,' Billy said, nodding his agreement.

'It's not practical for them to close their doors,' Jenna said. 'For a start, it would be a nightmare for the parents who have to work and might even end up with them losing their jobs, or worse, children being left alone, or with unsuitable carers.'

'Oh. Okay,' Tamsin said, sighing. 'But we could still warn nurseries to be extra vigilant with their security.'

'That's a good idea, Tamsin. Get on to it straight away. If you need help, Billy can assist,' Pengelly said.

'What about the parents? Surely they should be warned as well?' Clem said.

'That would be a logistical nightmare,' Pengelly said. 'It would mean every childcare provider contacting every parent. If parents see it on the news they'll realise anyway and can make their own decision whether to keep their child at home or continue sending them. We can't have this blowing out of proportion. There are hundreds of children in childcare and only two are missing. Obviously it's imperative that these children are found but what we don't want to do is create total hysteria in the community.'

'Okay, ma'am,' Clem said, the expression on his face one of grudging acceptance.

'I'm going to see the DCI now. Sergeant Price will take over here. We also have the human remains murder case to deal with. We could do with more hours in the day,' Pengelly mumbled as she turned and headed back to her office.

Or more staff.

But Matt certainly wasn't going to say that to the DI, even if he suspected that she might agree with him now.

'Okay,' he said, moving closer to the team and resting against one of the vacant desks. 'Hector Voyle, the owner of the Trenowden Estate, gave me a list of people who lived in the rundown cottages during the time the pathologist has specified the murder took place. I'd like someone to run the names through the database. We need to track them all down and if some aren't traceable... well, we know what that could mean. This is going to be our best way of identifying the remains. Any volunteers?' He scanned the team and they all stared back at him. 'Is there a problem?'

'We're not used to being asked what we'd *like* to do. The Ice Queen— I mean... DI Pengelly tells us,' Billy said.

So, that was her nickname. Had Billy let it slip on purpose? It wouldn't surprise him, already having a handle on what Billy was like. But Matt wasn't going to take the bait and comment. First of all, he was new. And, secondly, he didn't want to undermine his position as their superior officer. Or the DI's for that matter. Although he had to admit, the name was fitting.

'Everybody works differently and we have to learn to adjust. Right, do I have a volunteer?'

'I'll do it,' Tamsin said.

'Yes, she's the best one,' Clem said. 'She's much better than Jenna and me when it comes to the research. It's because she's young and has grown up with computers. Have you ever seen her text? She's so fast my eyes go blurry.'

Matt laughed. It reminded him of when he was at Lenchester. DC Naylor, who was younger than Tamsin by the looks of it, was the best researcher anyone had ever come across. Nobody else could come anywhere near her skills. He wondered how she was getting on. She'd promised to come and visit at some stage with her new boyfriend. Matt hoped she meant it. It would be good to see a familiar face.

'I'm good with IT, too, don't forget,' Billy said.

'Do you want to work on it then?' Matt asked.

'No, thanks. I hate research.'

Laughter echoed around the room. They were so different when Pengelly wasn't around. Relaxed, but still focused.

'If Tamsin works on this then someone else needs to contact all the nurseries in the area, as Pengelly requested,' Matt said.

'I'll do it,' Jenna said.

'Good, that's sorted. I'd like the rest of you to keep working on the missing girls. Check both nurseries again. Find out who visits them on a regular basis, aside from the parents. Are there any companies that make regular deliveries. Check refuse collectors. The time and who does the collection. And if the same people visit both sites. Anything you can think of, however unlikely. Like DI Pengelly said, we've got to be missing something. These children can't just disappear into thin air.'

Matt paused for a moment, deciding whether or not to voice his other concern. Yes. He should. 'Remember, if two girls have already been taken, then unless we solve this crime there's every chance that there'll be a third.'

An eerie silence filled the room. Each one of them contemplating the thought of another child going missing. And whether or not the first two were still alive.

Each member of the team began working on their designated tasks, their concentration unwavering, until the phone on one of the desks rang, interrupting the silence.

Jenna answered it. 'CID. Yes. Will do.' She glanced over at Matt. 'Sarge, there's a call for you.'

He walked over and took the handset from her. 'Price.'

'Graham Lewis here. I'm in charge of the dig at Trenowden. I wanted to give you the heads up that we've recovered more bones.'

His words sunk into the air like a stone.

'Human?' he asked, his mind racing with the implications of the discovery.

'They appear to be a complete set from one body, but obviously Sue, the forensic anthropologist, will confirm that.'

A potential double murder inquiry and two missing children. Could things get any worse?

'Thank you.' He replaced the handset on its base. 'Bloody hell,' he muttered, shaking his head.

'What is it, Sarge?' Jenna asked.

'They've found a second set of remains at the farm. They're on their way to the morgue.'

'You've got to be kidding?' Billy said.

'Is it usually this chaotic? I thought I'd joined a quiet station.' Matt gave a dry smile.

'You have. We've had more excitement this week than we've had in the last twenty years when I joined,' Clem said.

The door opened and Pengelly returned. 'The press conference isn't for another thirty minutes so I thought I'd come back to see how you're getting on. Any progress made?'

'Not the progress you want to hear, ma'am. Another set of remains has been found at the estate.'

'What? That's all we need. What have you put in place to deal with this?'

'I've only just come off the phone to Graham Lewis at the dig so nothing in addition to what we were already doing. Tamsin's currently checking the list of people who lived there to help with the identification of the body – now, bodies. Jenna's taken over contacting the nurseries.'

'Tamsin, how are you getting on?' Pengelly asked.

'Okay, ma'am. Luckily there aren't too many people on the list. It seems that farmworkers stayed a long time. I've already managed to track down four out of the five families of tenants. I haven't spoken to any of them yet, just identified where they are so we can confirm whether or not they're still alive. The only tenant I haven't yet been able to find is the Rundle family. Clive worked on the farm and he had a wife, Olive, and a daughter, Norah. Twenty years ago she was sixteen.'

'Okay, well, carry on with your research. I spoke to the DCI about authorising overtime while we've got these two cases on the go and he's approved it, providing we don't go overboard. We could really do with some further assistance and I asked about borrowing a couple of officers from one of the other stations but he said not yet. So, it's down to us. Don't let me down.'

TWENTY-TWO

THURSDAY, 27 OCTOBER

Lauren was up by five thirty the next morning, and had taken the dogs out for a long walk around some of Cornwall's iconic mining remains, showered, grabbed some breakfast and was sitting in her office by seven fifteen. She'd kept in touch with officers during the night, but there had been no sightings or any new information regarding the two missing children. Were they going to find them alive? She shuddered. For them not to be was unthinkable.

She glanced through the window of her partially glazed office door to the room where the team was based. Price, who'd arrived not long after her, was sitting at his desk staring at his computer screen. She still wasn't sure how to take him. From her observations, the other members of the team appeared to like him and he was settling in well, considering this was only his fourth day. She'd overheard them all laughing about something yesterday. They were relaxed in his company.

There were never any jokes when she was around, but why would there be? She didn't see the need to engage in office banter. In the past, she'd witnessed superiors who'd been over-friendly with their teams, finding themselves being taken advantage of. Well, that wasn't going to happen during her tenure. She ran a tight ship and that was how it was going to stay. It was important for her sergeant to work in the same way she did, to prevent any confusion. Of course she couldn't stop him from having fun and being more involved with the team than she was – if that was what he wanted – providing that it didn't interfere with his responsibilities, which were, in the first instance, to her and the smooth and efficient running of the team.

The phone on her desk rang and she picked up the handset. 'Pengelly.'

'Good morning, Detective Inspector, it's Henry Carpenter here,' the pathologist said. 'We've identified the two sets of remains and have finished our work. Are you able to come over now so we can informally feed back our findings, before submitting the report, which might take a while to reach you? I assume you wish to know everything straight away.'

Of course she did. That went without saying.

'Thank you. Can't we do this over the phone?'

'No. Let's make it more informal, face to face. Plus it's easier to discuss with the bones in front of us.'

'Fine. We'll be with you in fifteen minutes.'

She picked up her coat and bag went into the main office. 'Sergeant, grab your jacket; we're heading to the morgue. They've got names and other info that Henry's going to pass to us before the official report gets sent through.'

Price frowned. Didn't he want to visit the morgue again? Well, this wasn't a pick-n-mix job. He'd do as instructed.

'Shouldn't we wait for one of the others to arrive so any phone call is answered and not left for voicemail?'

Ah. That was the reason. Not his reluctance to go there.

'The rest of the team shouldn't be too far away. Have you gone through the calls that came in after the press conference yesterday?'

'I'd just started. I took several calls myself before leaving last night but there was nothing useful to work with. One caller mentioned Terry Lipton but we know it wasn't him. I did wonder, though, whether we should keep an eye on him and make sure he's not hanging around parks and doing what he shouldn't.'

'Definitely, but not now, there's too much going on.'

'I realise that, ma'am.' He stood, removed his jacket from the back of his chair and slipped it on.

The door opened and in walked Jenna, Clem, Tamsin and Billy. It was too much of a coincidence for them to arrive at the same time. What had they been doing?

'I expected you all in earlier.' She stared at each one in turn but none of them would meet her gaze. Not even Clem. Whatever was going on, she didn't have the time to pursue it. 'Sergeant Price and I are going to the morgue. I want all leads from the press conference followed up and you can report back to me on our return. Any questions?'

'No, ma'am,' they said in unison.

They left the office and no sooner was the door closed, Lauren was able to hear the sound of laughter.

She looked at Price, but he was staring straight ahead. Either he hadn't heard, or was being tactful.

They made the journey to the morgue quickly, thanks to little traffic on the road. As she led the way through the hospital to the morgue, she witnessed the expression on her sergeant's face getting tenser the closer they got. She pushed open the door to the morgue, and the moment they were hit by the smell of embalming agents, the colour drained from his face. He really needed to do something about it.

Harry Carpenter and Sue Andrews were staring at a set of bones laid out on the table. They both glanced up when Lauren and Price reached them.

'Good, you're here. We've got a busy day ahead of us, and

Sue has to get back to the office in St Ives,' Henry said, dispensing with any pleasantries.

That's what Lauren liked about him. He was polite, but got quickly to the point and rarely wanted to engage in chit chat.

'Right. Let's get started then.' Lauren took a step forward until she was standing close to the table. Price remained slightly behind her.

'First of all, we've identified the first set of human remains as being Olive Rundle,' Henry said. 'We discovered this from her dental records. In particular, there's some bridge work and also two missing teeth on the lower left side.' He pointed to the victim's teeth, and Lauren took a closer look.

'Excellent. The Rundle family was the one we couldn't trace,' Price said.

'And now you know why,' Henry said.

'Have you had the chemical analysis back so we can determine more precisely how long the bones have been there?' Lauren asked.

'Yes. Between nineteen and twenty years.'

'Thanks. That gives us more to work with. What can you tell us about the second set of bones discovered?'

'Sue?' Henry said, nodding at his colleague.

'He's male and was also murdered. If you look here you can see the clean hole in the front of the skull.' She picked up the skull and turned it over. 'Here, we can see a slightly larger and more ragged hole. This is where the bullet exited. We've asked for his dental records but have already provisionally identified him as Clive Rundle.'

'Olive's husband. How were you able to identify him?' Lauren asked.

'From hospital records. He had broken his right arm and right leg at different times and the details are in the system. If you look here you can see the callus formations on the ulna in the arm and tibia in the leg.' Sue pointed to each of the bones. 'Callus is new bone that has grown across the fracture site.'

Lauren peered closely and could see both factures and how they'd repaired themselves. 'Was there any other trauma, like on his wife?'

'No. That's why we could determine exact cause of death.'

'Is it possible that Olive was murdered first and the murderer was so anxious about committing their first homicide that they weren't able to get a clean shot and had to finish Olive off with a blow to the head?' Lauren asked.

'I think that's a bit of a mental leap, to be honest. It could have been that the murderer didn't aim well. We don't know because it wasn't possible to establish how the trauma was caused to her skull,' Sue said.

'But if the DI is right, then Clive Rundle couldn't have been killed at the same time, or he would have tried to disarm the killer. Even failing would've meant that the shot wasn't clean, which we know it was,' Price said. 'Unless the killer finished Olive off after both of them were shot.'

'Another interesting theory but, again, not one we can prove,' Henry said.

'Were any bullets found at the site? Or casings?' Price asked.

'Several different bullets, which have been sent off for examination. But these could have been from other guns used on the farm and nothing to do with this shooting.'

'The Rundles had a daughter called Norah. Are you still searching for other remains?' Matt asked.

'The dig is continuing, but so far nothing else has been found. There's still a chance that more remains will be discovered, but it's getting less and less likely,' Sue said.

'We can't stop looking, because it's likely she's there, too,' Price said.

'I'd be surprised if we don't find her. Unless the killer

moved her body, of course,' Lauren said.

'Or she was the one to commit the murders,' Price said. 'As unlikely as that might be.'

'Rest assured, if the bones are there, we'll locate them,' Sue said.

'Henry, why are you submitting your official report before forensics have completed the dig?' Price asked.

'Sergeant, are you suggesting that we shouldn't have the information as it comes in?' Lauren said, glaring at him and then instantly regretting it.

'I was interested in procedure, that's all,' Price replied, smiling, but it didn't reach his eyes.

'It's a good question. And to answer, it's because digs can take a long time, especially if we're hampered by weather. We already have two murder victims; if more remains are discovered then additional reports will be sent to you,' Henry clarified.

That put her in her place.

'Thank you, Henry. When will this current report be forwarded to the DCI?'

'Once the dental records have arrived, and confirmed Clive Rundle is the second victim. Have you announced the discovery of the second set of remains?'

'Not yet. We didn't want to detract from the press conference yesterday which focused on the two missing children. A cold case like this, although imperative to solve, has to come second. Fortunately it's not a situation we would normally find ourselves in.'

'You need more staff,' the pathologist said.

'We certainly do at the moment,' she agreed.

'That's the trouble when budgets are the centre of operations and those at the top are bean counters with no professional expertise,' Henry said.

'Well... quite. Thanks, Henry. Sue. Come on, Sergeant Price, we need to get back.'

TWENTY-THREE

THURSDAY, 27 OCTOBER

'Okay, let's begin.' Lauren stood beside the board, having written up the victims' names. 'The two sets of remains have been identified as Olive and Clive Rundle. We now know that the bodies have been there for between nineteen and twenty years. The dig is still in progress, although nearing the end. In particular they're searching for a third body, belonging to the daughter, Norah.'

'What if she's not there?' Billy asked.

'There are several reasons. She might have been kidnapped. She might be dead but her body was hidden elsewhere. Or she could have committed the murders herself.'

'But chances of that are slim,' Clem said. 'Based on statistical evidence, my guess is that her body's there, but the dig hasn't found it yet.'

'Clemipedia strikes again,' Billy said, laughing.

'Statistics or otherwise, we have to keep investigating. Tamsin, have you discovered anything else about the Rundles?'

Lauren focused her attention on the officer, who was seated towards the rear of the room.

'Actually, ma'am, yes. Norah went to Foxfield High School here in Penzance.'

'Good. With a bit of luck there'll be someone there who remembers her and can give more information about the family.'

'It's half-term week, ma'am. They might not be open, if you were thinking of going now,' Billy said.

'The school office should be and often teachers go in over half-term,' Jenna said. 'One of my friends is a teacher and she often goes into work for meetings and stuff when the kids aren't around. Shall I phone and enquire?'

'Yes, please,' Lauren said.

'Hector Voyle should be able to help now we know who the victims are. Shall I go over?' Price asked.

'Come to the school with me, first, if they're open. We'll go in separate cars and you can go from there.'

'Ma'am,' Jenna called out. 'The school's open.'

'Thanks. Do we have any update following the press conference on the missing girls?' Lauren scanned the room looking for answers from the other team members.

'We've had a phone call from someone reporting a man walking up and down the street several times outside Redwood Nursery recently, but no one else has corroborated it,' Jenna said. 'He can't have gone into the nursery, though, because otherwise he'd have been captured on the camera.'

'Have you looked at any footage from door cams belonging to people who live in the street?' Price asked.

'Uniform questioned people about what they'd seen. I haven't seen any mention of footage. I assume that means there are no houses with door cams in that street,' Jenna said.

'Are you sure? In this day and age lots of people have them. Why would it be any different here?'

'This is Penzance, Sarge. We're a small Cornish town with around twenty thousand people. It's not the same as living in a big city where people feel a lot less secure and the crime rate is so much higher—' Jenna said.

'Actually, Jenna, the population is only that high if you count Newlyn and Mousehole. Contentious as it might seem, some people argue that it's only sixteen-and-a-half thousand—' Clem interrupted.

'Whatever, Clem. It still doesn't alter my point, that having a door cam attached to your house isn't common.'

'I'm happy to stand corrected once we've double checked,' Price said. 'I'd like you to contact the officers who did the house-to-house, and if they didn't check for cameras then please go out and see for yourself.'

Price glanced over at Lauren and she gave what she hoped was an almost imperceptible nod, to indicate that she was perfectly happy with his input. In fact she couldn't have asked him to have handled the situation any better. He had potential. Provided he continued in this vein.

'Yes, Sarge.'

'Billy, you can go with Jenna,' Lauren added. 'Right, everyone knows what they're doing. Contact me if there are any developments concerning Isla and Violet. However minor.' She kept the tone of her voice flat, not wanting to let on that she was panicking.

She was desperate to return the children to their families and couldn't even begin to imagine how the parents were feeling being faced with such a nightmare.

Lauren supposed that the reason she'd never wanted children was because she'd never met anyone she'd remotely wanted to settle down with. Men she'd dated in the past had hated that she put her career first. It was okay for them to be career oriented but for some reason they resented her being like that. Talk about double standards. Hence her longest ever relationship was only twelve months. She didn't care; she much preferred the company of her dogs. They were far more predictable, loved her unconditionally and only ever made reasonable demands on her time.

Lauren pulled into the school car park and waited until Matt arrived and parked next to her. They headed inside together and followed the signs to the office.

'Good afternoon, I'm DI Pengelly and this is DS Price. One of my officers called earlier about Norah Rundle, an ex-pupil of yours,' she said to the woman seated behind the desk.

'Hello, I'm Sylvie the school administrator. I took the call and since then I've spoken to Annie Drake, who's been teaching here for the past twenty-eight years. She remembers Norah and her family. She'll be able to tell you anything you want to know.'

Finally they might actually be getting somewhere.

'Thanks. Is it possible to speak to Annie now? I assume she's not teaching as it's half-term.'

'Actually, we've had students in this week for extra classes. Annie's around and isn't teaching until later this afternoon. I'll give her a call if you'd like to take a seat.' Sylvie gestured with an open hand for them to sit on one of the chairs that were lining the wall opposite her desk.

Several minutes after Sylvie made the call a tall, slim woman walked in. She looked to be in her late fifties, with grey hair pulled back off her face in a headband, and was wearing jeans and a navy blue sweatshirt. She smiled broadly at them.

'Hello, I'm Annie Drake. Are you the police?'

'Is there somewhere quiet we can sit and talk?' Lauren asked, standing to face her.

'You can use Dr Perkin's office if you like, because she's out this morning,' Sylvie said, pointing to the door with *Head-teacher* sign-written on it.

'Thanks,' Annie Drake said.

The large office had a reproduction antique desk beside the window and four easy chairs in the centre.

'What can you tell us about Norah Rundle?' Lauren asked, after they'd sat down.

'I remember her very well. I was Norah's form tutor when she first started here, and also taught her English right up until she left. Her parents weren't particularly involved in her education and I only ever met them a handful of times. They rarely attended parent/teacher consultations or other school functions. Norah was a loner at school and very much an introvert.'

Lauren could relate to that. She'd never had close friends while at school. Mainly because she was too scared to take anyone back to her aunt's house, in case her cousins or uncle did something to embarrass her.

'Was she bullied?' Price asked.

'Goodness, no.'

'No?' Price asked.

'Although Norah was quiet, if anyone got on the wrong side of her she would let them know about it. The other children tended to leave her alone.'

'What type of student was she?'

Annie gave a smile that was tinged with frustration. 'She had a natural ability, but didn't always apply herself, much to my annoyance. I think this innate intelligence was part of the reason she had no time for students of her own age. She often skipped school. We weren't so strict on truancy in those days and didn't follow it up. Sometimes she'd hand in her homework and other times she wouldn't. She enjoyed English and would engage with material, even though she'd seldom speak in class.'

'So how could you tell if she didn't speak?' Lauren asked, frowning.

'From her homework. It was perceptive and insightful. I was sad when she left because she had the ability to go on to one of the good universities. Maybe even Oxford or Cambridge. But it wasn't to be.'

'How old was she when she left?'

'She stopped attending when she was sixteen, after taking her GCSEs, in which she performed very well. After that, we didn't see her again. She didn't return after the summer holidays.'

'Did you get in touch to find out where she was?' Surely they didn't just ignore her absence, even if it was twenty years ago?

'No, because she was at the legal age to leave school. We assumed that she'd chosen to go. There was no obligation on either of our parts to keep in contact.'

'Do you have a school photograph of Norah from those later days?' Price asked.

'I can certainly find one for you from the school records. I'll ask Sylvie, if you'd like to wait a moment.'

Annie left the room, closing the door behind her.

'I'm surprised they didn't follow up on her leaving school if she had so much potential. To try and persuade her to stay on and take her A Levels,' Price said.

'Yes, I agree and—'

The door opened and Annie Drake returned, holding a piece of paper. 'I've printed off a copy of Norah's photo.'

She handed it over to Lauren, who stared at the sullen girl. No hint of a smile, or warmth in her eyes. Was she being a typical teenager, or was she really unhappy? They'd never know.

'Is that a mark on the photo?' Lauren asked, pointing to Norah's forehead and showing it to Annie.

'Norah has a large heart-shaped birthmark. It didn't seem to worry her – she never covered it up with a fringe.'

'Oh yes, now I see.' Lauren held out the piece of paper and showed it to Price. 'Annie, if I give you my email address please could you ask Sylvie to forward me a digital copy of this photo? It's much easier to share than a paper copy.'

'Yes of course. You haven't said why you're looking into her, but is it to do with the bones found at Trenowden? I know that's where the family lived.'

'We're in the process of contacting everyone who resided there fifteen to twenty years ago. We haven't yet been able to find Norah, which is why we wanted more information from you.'

'Okay. What about her parents? Have you located them?'

'That's part of our inquiry. But as I'm sure you'll appreciate, we can't discuss an ongoing investigation. Please will you ask Sylvie to also forward a copy of Norah's academic record and her school file?'

At least now they had a picture to help with their investigation.

TWENTY-FOUR

THURSDAY, 27 OCTOBER

'Hello, Mr Voyle. I have a few more questions for you if you don't mind,' Matt said when the old man opened the door. Interesting that even though he had people working for him he answered himself.

Voyle smiled at Matt, and inclined his head in greeting. 'Of course. Come on in. And please, call me Hector. I was expecting you to call once I'd been informed that more bones had been found on the farm.'

Matt followed Voyle into the kitchen, the warm yellow light of the afternoon sun streaming in through the windows. The strong smell of coffee permeated the air.

'I've just made some coffee; I'll pour us some,' Voyle said, taking two china mugs from the cupboard and heading over to the coffee machine. He pulled the carafe from its warming plate and poured the liquid into the mugs, placing them on the table, along with some sugar and a jug of milk.

'I'd like to talk to you about a family named Rundle. Clive, Olive and their daughter, Norah. Do you remember them?' Matt picked up the jug and poured in some milk.

'Are they the victims?'

Matt had expected him to ask, but didn't want to confirm it in case the news spread and the investigation was jeopardised. The murderer could well be living in the area and might do a runner if he, or she, thought they'd been identified.

'That's one of the theories we're currently working on, but nothing is confirmed. The pathologist hasn't yet sent in his report. But please remember, everything I tell you is confidential. We don't wish to misinform the public.'

'I totally understand. Yes, I do remember the family. Clive was a good worker. He was conscientious and very reliable. But away from work we rarely saw him or his family. They didn't join in any of the social events that we held. They were very private. I recall—' He hesitated briefly.

'You recall what?' Matt probed.

'Very often when walking past their house I would hear shouting.'

'Who was doing the shouting?'

'I remember hearing Olive.'

'And what about Clive?'

'Sometimes him, I think. I didn't hang around to listen.'

'Did you ever go to investigate? To see if anything was wrong?'

Surely he had a duty of care towards his workers?

'No. It wasn't my business. My concern was that he was reliable and worked hard. I assumed that was the way they were. Maybe I should have gone to enquire, but I doubt they'd have told me anything. I was never invited in when I visited. Conversations always took place on the doorstep.'

'What was Olive Rundle like?'

Hector sucked in a breath. 'I don't wish to speak ill of the dead – if it is her you've found – but, to be honest, I never warmed to Olive. She was a cold, unfriendly woman. In all the years they lived here, I didn't ever see a genuine smile on her lips. On the rare occasion she cracked one it would be false and there was no warmth. No kindness. I felt sorry for the daughter. She was a loner. I never saw her with any friends or hanging around the farm like the other teenage kids did. I'd often see her leaving for school in the morning on her bike and returning later in the day but she always kept her head down and wouldn't talk.'

This confirmed what they'd been told by the school. Norah sounded like one unhappy kid.

'Why did Clive Rundle leave if he was such a good worker?'

'You tell me,' Voyle said, shaking his head, appearing confused. 'They gave no notice. Clive didn't turn up for work one day, which was most unlike him. I assumed he was ill.'

'Didn't you check?'

'No because I had to go up country. But when I returned two days later and discovered that he still hadn't been working, I went to the house to find out what was going on. I knocked on the door but there was no answer so I went inside. All their possessions had gone. The furniture belonged to the farm and that was still there, but other than that it was empty. They left the house in a total mess. Furniture was wrecked. The dirt on the kitchen floor was an inch thick, like a carpet of earth. The walls were grimy and scuffed, and the rubbish bins were overflowing. It looked like they hadn't been emptied for weeks.'

'Didn't the neighbours hear them leave?'

'No. They were as taken aback as I was.'

Could it have happened in the middle of the night?

'So they definitely didn't hear any noises around the time the Rundles disappeared?' Matt continued.

'What sort of noises?'

'Gunshots?'

'What? They were shot?' The man placed both hands palms down on the table and stared, unblinking, at Matt.

'We don't know for sure. But would anyone have noticed if that was the case?'

'Gunshots are common on a farm, so it would be like background noise to most people.'

'But what if it was late at night?'

Hector drummed his fingers on the table. 'Thinking back... The time they disappeared we were having dreadful weather. Several thunderstorms, if I remember correctly, so it's possible nobody heard anything.'

That would have made it very easy for the family to be killed and buried without being spotted, especially if it was late into the night.

But who did it? And why?

'Did they own a car?'

'No. They always walked everywhere or took the bus or train. Norah had a bike which she used for school. But I've no idea what happened to it. It certainly wasn't here when they left.'

'Did Clive get on with his fellow workers?'

'In the main he did... although there was one time when I had to break up a fight between him and another worker. Fortunately, I was there before it went too far.'

Matt went on alert. Was it serious enough to be the cause of the Rundles' deaths?

'What happened?'

'It was not long before the family disappeared. I don't know what it was about, other than Clive told me the man deserved it. I pressed for more info, but he refused to say. I can't imagine a situation where Clive would have started a fight. He was very mild-mannered at work.'

'But not at home, if the shouting you regularly overhead was anything to go by.'

Could Clive have shot his wife and daughter and then turned the gun on himself?

No. Because someone had to bury the bodies.

'I can't say what went on behind closed doors. But for him

to snap at work... It must have been something he felt strongly about.'

'Did you question the person he had the fight with?'

'It was Neville Pike and when I asked he clammed up totally and refused to tell me. I didn't want to push it. My main concerns were that they got back to work and the fight was over. Both men continued working and there wasn't another altercation between them.'

'You said the fight wasn't long before the Rundles disappeared. Can you remember how long?'

'Do you think it might have been connected?'

'We have to investigate every possibility.'

'I see. Um... maybe a few weeks, but I can't be totally sure.'

That was close enough for there to be a link. They needed to find out what was behind the fight.

'Did Neville Pike live in the same row of cottages as the Rundles?'

'Yes, with his wife, Erin, and their two children. They moved to a different house on the estate when he started helping with the honey business. It meant he could be closer to the beehives.'

'Is he still here?'

'Not now. He retired two years ago due to ill health. Erin then died less than a year after; it was very sad.'

'Where is he now?'

'He lives at Birchwood Manor, a care home not too far from here.'

'So he didn't move in with either of his children?'

'No, because they're both living overseas with their families. One's in Spain and the other in Hong Kong. As far as I'm aware, they seldom make an appearance. It's such a shame. Nev's a lovely man.'

Was he? That might not be the opinion of everyone.

'He must be lonely.'

'Yes, I'm sure he is. Especially as now he's fallen victim to dementia. He often repeats stories multiple times. I try to visit every couple of weeks but each time is harder than the last. But if I don't go, then who else is there? Life's a lottery. None of us know what's going to happen when we get old. That's why it's important to make the most of the time we have.'

Tears pricked the back of Matt's eyes and he blinked them away. Voyle didn't know how close to the truth he'd been. If only Matt could have his time over, he'd make sure to tell Leigh every day how much he loved her. Now... He'd never get the chance again. He sucked in a breath. This wasn't the time to let his feelings get the better of him.

'How old is he?'

'I'd say around seventy-five. Although I'm not sure when his birthday is. I do remember we had his seventieth birthday party here on the estate.'

'But I thought you said he only retired two years ago,' Matt asked, puzzled.

'Yes, that's right. He refused to retire before then, said he'd be bored. He was fit enough so I was happy for him to continue working.'

'Where is the care home? I'd like to call in to see him. To ask him about this fight.'

Voyle glanced at his watch. 'He's not always good in the afternoon, but you never know. It's worth a try. Head back towards St Buryan and take the road heading south out of the village, past the Merry Maidens stone circle. The home is on the right. You can't miss it. It's a large detached Victorian building. There's a big sign outside.'

'Merry Maidens?' Matt queried.

'Legend has it that there were nineteen maidens who'd been at a wedding on a Saturday who were turned to stone for continuing to dance as the night turned into the Sunday.'

'Oh. I'll look out for them. Before I go, were there any other witnesses to the fight who might know what it was about?'

'No. It happened behind one of the barns. It was by pure chance that I was passing at the time and caught them. Thank goodness, or who knows how it would have ended.'

'Well, thank you very much for your help and for the coffee. Please remember that everything we've discussed is to remain confidential.'

'I won't tell another soul. You have my word on it. I won't even tell the wife.' He laughed.

Matt left the farm and headed back to his car. He was certain there was a connection between Rundle and Pike's fight and the murders. It was too much of a coincidence for there not to be.

All he had to do now was find out what it was. And his first port of call was Birchwood Manor and Neville Pike.

TWENTY-FIVE

THURSDAY, 27 OCTOBER

'Hello, ma'am, it's Matt. I'm going to Birchwood Manor, a care home out the other side of St Buryan, where Neville Pike, one of Clive Rundle's ex-colleagues lives. They had a fight shortly before the family went missing.'

'You think he could have done it?'

'I don't know, but it's worth looking into. I'll head home afterwards, if that's okay, and see you first thing in the morning.'

'Yes, that's fine. Make sure to be here early, we've a lot to do.'

'Yes, ma'am.' He tried to hide his frustration at her comment. Surely she knew by now that he wasn't a slacker. 'Any news on Isla and Violet?'

'Nothing at all. Both sets of parents are beside themselves, understandably, and I've instructed the FLOs not to leave them alone, including staying overnight with them.'

'That seems for the best. I'll see you in the morning.'

No matter how much he wracked his brain, he couldn't get his head around how the children could disappear unseen in such a small community. It was the most puzzling case he'd ever been a part of. And the fact that they'd passed the crucial initial forty-eight hours was heart breaking. The parents must be going through hell. Whatever happened to the children, whether they were found alive or dead, it would change the families' lives forever...

He shuddered. Dani wasn't much younger than the missing children. How on earth would she manage if someone took her? Yes, she was bright, and advanced for her years. But being kidnapped... His teeth dug into his lower lip, making it bleed, as he struggled to comprehend the unfathomable.

And what on earth could be the motive? Were Isla and Violet targeted or were they random? In his view they had to have been targeted, because surely there were other children who were more accessible.

There had to be a connection between the two little girls. But what was it? The team had researched and they couldn't find anything to link them.

Nothing made sense.

He'd love to consult Dr Cavendish, the exceptionally talented forensic psychologist who advised them at Lenchester, but no way would Pengelly agree. It wasn't worth even mentioning.

For now, though, he had to concentrate on the two murders. To solve them quickly so everyone's focus could return to the kidnappings.

He drove past the stone circle Voyle had mentioned, and would loved to have taken a closer look, but didn't have the time. When he reached the care home, he pulled in and parked in one of the three guest spaces. Most of the car park was designated staff parking. That spoke volumes about the number of visitors the residents had.

It was a grand three-storey building but parts of it were in need of attention. The paint around the large windows was flaking and the stonework was cracked in several places.

There was no garden in the front, but he could see some

lawn at the rear when he peered to one side of the house. He walked up the stone steps to the large, maroon-painted double door and, after trying the door, which was locked, pressed the bell. He waited, but no one answered. Peering through the window, he couldn't see anything. He rang again. After a further five minutes he tried one more time, but keeping his finger pressed down. Finally, the door was opened by a woman in a carer's uniform.

'Sorry, I was busy with one of the residents and couldn't get away to answer. Same for everyone else, I expect. I hope you haven't been waiting too long.'

Matt held out his warrant card. 'I'm Detective Sergeant Price from Penzance police. I'm here to speak to Neville Pike.'

'What's it about?' she asked, her voice filled with apprehension.

'An ongoing investigation. That's all I'm at liberty to say.'

'I understand. I was concerned that it was to do with his children or grandchildren. He's very proud of his family and it would break his heart if anything had happened to one of them.'

'No, it's nothing to do with his family,' Matt reassured her.

'Thank goodness. You're lucky that he's fairly lucid today, although that can change very quickly. Before you see him, please sign in using the screen over there.' She pointed to a tablet which was mounted on a stand.

'Where will I find him?' he asked, after signing in.

'Try his room. He's not in the day room and when I last looked there was no one in the garden. He's in room thirteen, which is on the first floor.'

Matt took the stairs two at a time and marched down the hall until reaching thirteen. The door had Neville's name on it. He raised his fist and rapped three times, waiting for a response.

'Come in,' a faint male voice called out.

Matt pushed open the door and smiled at the old man who was seated in one of the dark cream leather chairs beside the window, staring at the football game on the television. He looked much older than seventy-five.

'Hello, Neville. I'm Matt Price from Penzance police. I'd like a quick chat with you, if that's okay.'

'The police? Why do you want to speak to me?' Anxiety flickered in his eyes.

The room was small with a single bed in one corner, and a small table and two upright chairs in the other. Matt sat on the chair next to the old man and reached over to the remote control on the table. 'Would you mind if I turned the television down for now, so we can hear each other?'

It was blaring so loud, it was a miracle that he'd managed to hear when Matt had knocked.

'Yeah. Sure.'

Matt pressed the mute button and then slid his chair around until he was facing the old man.

'Neville, we're investigating the discovery of some human remains at Trenowden Estate where you used to work. You might've heard about it on the news.'

'Yes, I did. Everyone here's talking about it.'

'The remains were found near the old cottages where you lived before moving closer to the beehives. Do you remember living there?'

He nodded slowly. 'Yes.' He gave a low whistle. 'And you found some bodies there... I don't know anything about it.'

Was he being honest?

Matt had no way of knowing because of the dementia. For now he'd have to take the man's words at face value.

'Actually, my interest is in the Rundle family. Clive, Olive and Norah. They were your neighbours.'

'Yes, that's right.' Neville remained motionless, gazing off into the distance as if he was lost in thought. 'They were strange. Very strange. Especially Olive. You know, she gave my Erin the creeps.

It was the way she stared at you with those piercing eyes. Erin said she made Morticia Addams seem like Pollyanna.' He grinned. 'She was funny, my Erin. And very clever. Too clever for me. The children take after her. She died last year. I miss her.' His voice cracked and Matt leant over and rested his hand on top of Neville's.

'I know how you feel.'

'Did your wife die, too?' Neville glanced up at him, a solitary tear sliding down his cheek.

'Yes.' Matt clenched his jaw shut to stop himself from becoming overwhelmed with emotion.

'It's crap, isn't it?'

'Yes. Definitely crap.' Matt reached for a tissue from the box on the table and handed it to Neville. 'Let's talk about the Rundles and then you can get back to watching the football.'

'Is the football on? Who's playing?'

'I don't know. You had it on when I arrived.'

'Did I? Oh. Why are you here? Do I know you?'

Matt's heart sank. The man was rapidly drifting off. 'Neville, do you remember having a fight with Clive Rundle about twenty years ago when you worked at Trenowden? Hector Voyle had to pull you both apart.'

Neville flushed and nodded. 'Yes. Am I in trouble?'

'No, you're not. But I'd like to know what the fight was about.'

'Clive said I went into his house and stole some money.'

'And did you?' Matt kept his voice calm because he didn't want to panic the old man.

Neville averted his eyes. 'No, I didn't.'

It was hard to tell if he was telling the truth. But even if he hadn't stolen from Rundle, something had happened. Matt was sure of it.

'Do you know why the Rundles left? According to Hector it happened all of a sudden and they didn't give any notice.'

Neville scowled. 'Good riddance if you ask me. Life was much better when they'd gone. Everyone agreed about that.'

'But I thought the family kept to themselves and didn't mix with anyone.'

'That didn't matter. No one liked them.' He balled his hand into a tight fist and pounded it against his thigh.

'Neville, I believe that you didn't steal from Clive, but did you go into his house for another reason?'

He blinked furiously. 'Maybe. But I didn't take his money. It was something else.'

'Look, whatever it was, it was a long time ago. Nothing can happen to you so why don't you tell me what happened.'

'I-I went in to see Norah.'

What was he doing seeing a teenage girl?

'Why?'

'She was crying. I wanted to see how she was. Olive and Clive were out. The door was unlocked so I went in.'

'Was Norah cross with you for going in uninvited?'

'No. She was sitting at the kitchen table sobbing. I went over to comfort her. Gave her a hug and then... you know... after, I told her it would be okay.'

Stunned, Matt sat frozen in disbelief. *Surely not...*

'That what would be okay, exactly?'

'Umm... one thing just led to another and... It was legal, she was over sixteen. I didn't do anything wrong. She agreed. If anything, it was her idea.'

Bile shot up into Matt's mouth. What the hell had the man done?

'Is that the real reason for the fight? Did Clive find out about you and Norah?'

'Who's Norah? Who are you? What do you want?'

'I'm from the police. We're talking about what happened between you and Norah Rundle,' Matt said, softly.

'I don't know anyone called Norah. Is it time for dinner yet? I'm really hungry. Are you here to take me to the dining room?'

'I'm not, but I'll ask one of the carers to take you. Thanks for talking to me.'

Matt left the room. He'd got enough from Neville.

Was the man responsible for the deaths?

That was anybody's guess. But it had to be investigated.

TWENTY-SIX
FRIDAY, 28 OCTOBER

Matt's phone vibrated in his pocket and he read, with irritation, the message from Pengelly asking him to undertake the briefing because the meeting she was attending was taking longer than anticipated. Had he known, he'd have started earlier. It was already after ten. They didn't have time to waste. He glanced around the room at the team, who were seated at their desks. The tension in the air was palpable. Today was make or break on so many levels.

He crossed to the whiteboard they'd been using for the Rundle inquiry, removed the cap from the red marker, and wrote Neville Pike's name with an arrow connecting it to Norah's.

'Morning, team. The DI's asked me to take the briefing. First, unfortunately, there's nothing new to report on Isla and Violet, and—'

'We can't hit a dead end! There has to be more we can do. We can't sit back and wait,' Jenna said, her voice wobbling.

'I agree, but teams have been out searching all night. And we still have nothing to link the two abductions. We'll continue researching into the families, and the nurseries. But we also have two murders, and possibly a third, that need investigating. I want to update you on the meetings I had yesterday. One with Hector Voyle and one with the Rundles' neighbour, Neville Pike, who had a fight with Clive back when they were both living there and who's now in a care home with dementia.'

The phone rang on Jenna's desk. 'CID, Detective Moyle speaking.' She glanced at Matt, her brow knitted together. 'Yes, ma'am.' She replaced the phone, confusion etched on her face.

'What is it?' Billy asked.

'Umm... that was the DI. She sounded weird...'

'There's nothing unusual about that,' Billy said, turning to the others and grinning.

'This was different, Billy. It was about Sarge.' Jenna looked at Matt. 'She wants me to make sure you don't go anywhere. But she didn't say why.'

Where did she think he was going to go? And more to the point, why contact Jenna and not him directly? Would he ever get to understand the woman?

'It's just for effect,' Billy said. 'And why did she call you, Jenna? You haven't fallen out with her already, have you, Sarge?'

Matt held up his hand. 'Let's stop this now. I won't be going anywhere and we need to get back to my feedback. I spoke to Pike regarding the fight. Rundle accused him of breaking into his house and stealing money. But he denied it.'

'Do you believe him?' Clem asked.

'Yes. He told me the truth. No one was ever invited into the house – not even Voyle, who was their landlord. But Pike did go in there to *be* with the daughter, Norah.' Matt made quote marks with his fingers and then paused, while the implication of what he'd said registered.

'What? You can't be serious. Do you mean... he groomed

Norah into having an affair? How old is he if he's already in a care home?' Jenna said, her face contorting in disgust.

'He's seventy-five. He told me it was one time only and she encouraged it.'

'Of course he'd say that. Especially as there's no one to back up his story. If it was twenty years ago he was fifty-five and taking advantage of a lonely sixteen-year-old.'

'Was he married at the time?' Clem asked.

'Yes, and he has two children. His wife died last year.'

'Do you think Pike killed the Rundles because Clive discovered what had happened and he didn't want his family to find out, or lose his job?' Billy said, his words hanging in the air.

'Except we haven't found Norah – yet...' Clem said.

'Agreed,' Matt said. 'But that doesn't mean—'

The door from the DI's office opened and she stood in the doorway like a soldier, her face grey and drawn.

Her gaze was focused solely on Matt.

'Sergeant Price, please join me in my office. The rest of you carry on with what you're doing.'

What was so serious that she had to speak to him away from the rest of the team?

He hurried over to where she was standing and followed her into the office. He closed the door behind him.

'What is it, ma'am?'

'Please sit down, Matt,' she said, gesturing to the seat in front of her desk. She sat next to him rather than behind her desk. 'Another child has been taken from a nursery.' Her voice was low.

An icy knot formed in the pit of his stomach.

'Which nursery?' he heard himself ask, dreading what was coming next.

'It's Kid's Stuff nursery, and I'm so sorry, Matt – it's Dani. Dani's gone missing.'

Pengelly's words thundered in Matt's ears. He wanted to scream, but all he could do was stare at her in disbelief, his whole world crumbling.

'But why? She only goes two days a week... Are you sure? There must be a mistake.'

'There isn't. I've just received confirmation. I'm so very sorry. I'm going to the nursery now with some of the team.'

'I'm coming with you. I've got to find her.'

'I don't think that's a good idea. You should go home and be with your parents. They don't know yet.'

A fire burnt inside Matt. He needed to find his daughter, no matter what the cost.

'There's no way I'm staying at home.' He clenched his fists in determination. 'I'm going with you to the nursery. I'm going to be part of the search... we've *got* to find her.'

'Okay. But you must do as I say. No acting without my permission. Understand?'

Matt nodded. His gaze glassy and unwavering.

Pengelly drove them to the nursery. It felt like it took a lifetime. Matt's knuckles were white as he held back the onslaught of emotions.

What had happened to Dani?

His stomach churned as he considered the unthinkable. *I can't lose her as well.*

They arrived at the nursery and Matt ran inside and up to the head, Mrs Lansbury.

'Tell me what happened,' he demanded, his voice harsh and urgent.

'I'm very sorry, Mr Price. We knew about the children being abducted from the other nurseries and took extra precautions. But nothing could have prepared us for this. One minute she was there and the next she was gone… like a ghost. We have no idea how it happened.'

'Show me the CCTV footage,' he demanded. 'Where are the cameras?'

'We have them in various locations outside the building, but none inside. We did address that matter but the parents said no, it was too much of an intrusion to have them in every room.'

What was wrong with these places? None of them had cameras inside. If they had, Dani might still be there. Isla and Violet, too.

'Show me what you have then!' he bellowed. Barely able to contain his anger. 'Take us to the footage.' He turned to the DI. 'Have you arranged for uniform to search the area?'

Pengelly took him to one side. 'Matt, you have to calm down,' she said quietly in his ear. 'We're doing everything we can. Uniform are on their way. If this is getting too much you can leave it to—'

'I know. I know. Please don't make me leave. I'll get it together. I promise.' He sucked in a breath. 'Can you ask uniform to check if anyone living close by has a camera and, if so, to check the footage.'

'I've already done that.'

Matt gave a grateful smile. 'Thank you, ma'am. Also, I know you said that no one had cameras in the vicinities of the missing girls' houses but maybe we could check again just to make doubly sure. I simply can't believe that no one has any. Did uniform ask the entire street or just the neighbours? Because everyone in the wider vicinity should be asked.'

'Leave that with me,' Pengelly said, pulling out her phone.

After she'd made the call, they returned to the head, who took them into the office so they could check the CCTV footage from earlier that day. Once Mrs Lansbury had opened it, she left them to it.

'I'll stay here, ma'am, if you want to speak to the staff.' Matt was convinced he'd discover something from the footage.

'I'll go and have a quick chat with them and then return. We'll watch the footage together.'

'Okay, ma'am.'

Pengelly left and for the first time since it all happened Matt was alone. But he couldn't give in to his emotions. He had to be strong. Strong for Dani and his own parents, even if they hadn't yet been informed.

He pressed play and leant forward until his face was as close to the screen as possible without it going blurry. He slowed the speed to ensure he missed nothing.

He watched parents arriving. Kissing their children goodbye and leaving them with a member of staff.

A surge of anguish washed over him as he remembered earlier in the day when Dani stood on the doorstep with her grandma waving him goodbye and blowing kisses in his direction.

The door to the office opened, bringing his attention back, and he glanced up to see Pengelly heading towards him.

'Anything?' she asked, pulling up a chair and sitting beside him.

He paused the recording. 'Not yet. What did the staff say?'

'Exactly the same as in the two previous cases. One minute Dani was there and the next she wasn't. Continue with the footage.'

He started the recording and they sat together in silence.

His mother arrived, holding Dani's hand.

He gasped.

Pengelly rested her hand on his arm, and he shook it off. Refusing to succumb to his internal torture.

'Hey...' she said softly.

'I'm okay,' he said, knowing he was far from it. 'Let's get on with this.'

His heart ached watching Dani as she took the hand of one of the staff members and turned to wave goodbye to her grandma with her other hand.

A sob escaped his lips and he buried his head in his hands.

'Come on,' Pengelly said. 'Let's go back to the station. We'll ask the head to email us the footage. We'll get the team together and will continue our search back there.'

TWENTY-SEVEN

FRIDAY, 28 OCTOBER

Lauren drove them back to the station. Allowing Matt to remain on the case wasn't a good idea, but when he'd begged her to reconsider she couldn't bring herself to say no. Deep down she knew it could result in even more hurt for him, but it was his decision. She'd support him and be there should he require it.

When they arrived, Matt stopped at the bathroom while Lauren hurried to the office, anxious to speak to the team without him.

'Can I have your attention please?' Her voice commanded the room. 'As you now know, Matt's daughter Dani has been taken from Kid's Stuff nursery. I'm allowing him to remain on the case because he's insisting, but please treat him carefully and make sure he doesn't go overboard. I'm relying on you all. It's a really hard time for him.'

Everyone in the room nodded solemnly and shifted uncomfortably in their chairs.

'Where is he, ma'am?' Tamsin asked.

'He's gone to the bathroom. I don't want him to know we've had this discussion. Have we found any footage from door cams close to where the abducted children live?'

'Yes, ma'am,' Clem said. 'Jenna, Billy and I went out separately, and we each took a uniformed officer with us. We all managed to retrieve some footage from one or two homes in the roads where the children live. Sarge was right to insist we check. We've literally only just got back so we haven't yet had time to go through them. Billy's going to set it up so we can watch together.'

The door opened and Matt walked in, his presence silencing the room.

'We're so sorry, Sarge,' Tamsin said, her voice trembling. 'We won't rest until we find Dani,' she promised.

'Yes, absolutely,' Billy added in agreement.

'Thank you,' Matt said, his voice shaking.

'We've got camera footage from all the areas where the children live, including yours, Matt. We're going to see if there are any cars or people present in all of them. We'll start from the week prior to when Isla Hopkins was taken,' Lauren said.

Lauren stole a glance at her sergeant and her heart went out to him. He stood tall, with his jaw clenched. His face was a mask of stone. She prayed they'd find Dani and this would soon be over.

'I'll shine three screens on the back wall so we can look at the locations together. It will make it easier to spot the same person or car in each of them,' Billy said.

Billy was excellent at IT, which made up for his somewhat erratic behaviour in other areas. Some senior officers might cut him some slack because he was young, but she didn't agree with that. He had to pull his weight or it wouldn't be fair on the rest of the team.

They stood in silence, their collective gaze transfixed on the wall, while Billy played the footage. It seemed an impossible task. There were so many cars and people to check. But they had to keep looking. They needed something. Anything, to help them find Matt's daughter.

'Stop,' Matt called out. He walked over to the screen and pointed at a red Toyota Corolla which had stopped at the lights in the vicinity of Violet Dent's house. 'We've seen that one before.'

'I don't think so, Sarge,' Tamsin said, squinting as she leant forward and inspected the car. 'We'd have noticed.'

Matt nodded slowly, his eyes still focused on the screen in front of him. 'It definitely looks familiar.' He went silent, and then suddenly exclaimed, 'I've just realised I think I've seen it parked along the street where we live.'

'How do you know it's the same one?' Tamsin asked. 'Did you take a note of the registration number?'

'No. I remember noticing the bumper sticker with three cartoon cats. And also the car has a slight dent along the front wing. Can you see it?' Matt pointed towards the front of the car. 'Trace that registration number.'

'I'm onto it, Sarge,' Tamsin said, hurrying back to her computer, her fingers flying over the keyboard.

Lauren's pulse quickened. After nothing but dead ends, did they have a breakthrough? Thank goodness they were able to make out the number plate. So often with CCTV footage it was obscured and they were left in a helpless situation.

'It's registered to an Eleanor Hillman,' Tamsin called out after a couple of minutes. 'She lives in Croft Road, Penzance.'

Lauren's heart pounded in her chest as she nodded. 'Good. Find out everything you can about her straight away,' She turned to Matt, who appeared deep in thought. 'Do you know this woman?'

'I'm not sure. We haven't lived here long enough to make any friends. But remember, we interviewed an Ellie at Redwood. She was the part-time nursery nurse who arrived after Violet went missing. That could be short for Eleanor, couldn't it? I don't recall her giving her surname, though.' He was silent for a moment. 'But there's something else. I can't put my finger on it.'

He closed his eyes for a few seconds, drawing in several long, deep breaths. Suddenly, they flew open, wide with shock and surprise. 'Dani mentioned the name *Nelly*. Maybe she meant *Ellie*. Said it was her special friend who works at the nursery... It's all making sense. We said it was an inside job. We were right. We have to go to the nursery to find out the truth. Find out where she's taken Dani.'

Lauren grabbed hold of his arm, stopping him from taking off. 'Hang on a minute, Matt. The children were taken from three different locations. Okay, there might be a Nelly or Ellie at Dani's nursery and there's an Ellie at Redwood, but we need to check whether they're the same person. Also, there isn't an Eleanor or Ellie working at Acorn. Billy, you checked the Acorn staff. Am I right about that?' She wanted to double check.

'Yes, ma'am.'

'Thanks. Matt, we must remain calm and work this through logically.'

'Easy for you to say. It's not your daughter who's missing. We have to go now.'

His words were like a punch in the gut. She was as much invested in finding Dani and the other girls as the rest of the team.

'I'm sorry. I can't even begin to imagine what you're going through. But you must trust that we'll investigate every single lead. I'm going back to Dani's nursery now. Why don't you go home now to be with your parents. They need you. I'll personally call you the moment we know anything.'

Matt jerked away from under her grasp. 'We've already gone over this,' he said, his voice hard and resolute. 'I'm going to the nursery. With or without you.'

Lauren remained silent, her foolish words hanging in the

air. Despite being unsure, she accepted that he would be going with them. She couldn't be the cause of any more distress.

'Okay, I'll drive. Tamsin, continue researching Eleanor Hillman. The rest of you can help. Someone needs to keep watching the CCTV in case there's anything that we've missed.

Lauren and Matt hurried from the office to the station car park and with the siren blaring, they raced back to the nursery.

'Mrs Lansbury,' Matt said, standing with his hands on his hips, in front of the head's desk. 'You have someone called Eleanor Hillman working here, don't you? She's known as Ellie, although Dani referred to her as Nelly.'

She nodded. 'Yes. Some of the children called her Nelly and it seems to have stuck. She's not on duty today, though.'

'What are her hours? Has she worked here long?' Matt demanded, moving from foot to foot impatiently.

'She's a supply nursery nurse, which means she only comes in when we need her. Well... providing we can get her. She's very much in demand.'

Exhilaration swept over Lauren. Did they have their link? She had to clarify, first, before she got too excited. 'You mean she works at other nurseries in the area?'

'Yes, she does. She's excellent. One of the best nursery nurses we've ever had. The children all love her. And so do the other members of staff. If we had the finances we'd take her on full-time. But we don't. Why are you asking about her?' She tapped her chin with her index finger.

Lauren and Matt exchanged a glance. They had to get out of there quick.

'We think she might have some useful information. It's nothing to worry about.'

'I hope she can help. I've been out of mind with worry about

Dani. How are you coping, Mr Price? If there's anything we can do to help then—'

'You've done enough—'

'Okay, thank you very much, Mrs Lansbury,' Lauren butted in. Not wanting Matt to get side-tracked and start apportioning blame. There was plenty of time for that after they'd found Dani and the other two children. 'We'll keep in touch.'

They left the nursery and ran to the car.

'We have to find her,' Matt said, before opening the car door and sliding inside.

'We will. Leave it with me.' She started the car, turned on the siren and headed towards the station. While driving she called the office.

'CID,' Jenna answered.

'Check with Acorn nursery if an Eleanor, Nelly or Ellie Hillman works there as a supply nursery nurse and if she does, when she last worked. We already know she was working at Redwood during the afternoon on the day Violet was taken because we spoke to her. Matt and I are on our way back; we won't be long.'

'Yes, ma'am.'

Lauren ended the call and turned to look at Matt, trying to comprehend the emotions he was experiencing.

'This is a massive break in helping us to find Dani, Matt. Massive.'

Matt's stomach churned as he hurried behind his boss through the doorway into the main office.

'Right, what else do we know about Eleanor Hillman?' Pengelly asked.

'She's employed by an agency in St Ives that supplies staff to nurseries in the Devon and Cornwall areas. She often works at the Acorn nursery, but wasn't there the day Isla was abducted. Her car wasn't in the car park either,' Jenna said.

'That doesn't mean she didn't take Isla. She might have used a different car, or had help from someone. Have you checked CCTV footage from Acorn to see if she was there in person?' Matt asked.

'We don't have the footage. You checked it when you were at the nursery, Sarge, and said no one entered the premises who shouldn't have done.'

'Well, we need to check again. Tell them to send it to us *now*,' he demanded.

'Matt. Calm down,' Pengelly said quietly.

He drew in a breath and stared at Pengelly. She was using

his first name instead of Sergeant. Had she done so before? He couldn't remember.

'Sorry, Jenna. I didn't mean to shout.'

'No worries, Sarge. I'll get the footage from Acorn and look to see if Hillman entered the building at all,' Jenna said. 'In the meantime, we do have plenty on her. We know that in 2004 she attended a further education college in Bristol where she completed five GCSEs. She then went on to take a two-year course in childcare at the same institution. From there she attended a college of higher education where she took a one-year more advanced course in childcare. She's very well qualified.'

'Then what did she do?' Matt asked.

'She's had various jobs in the sector. All of them in the Bristol area. We've checked her police record and she's clean. Just before you arrived back Clem and I had started contacting the places she'd worked in the past to see if we could turn up anything.'

'What about her family and friends?'

'Tamsin and Billy are onto that.'

Matt turned his attention to Billy, who was sitting close to Jenna and had been looking in his direction.

'We can't trace any family, Sarge, nor any social media pages. Which is weird. Most people have something. We've still got a couple more sites to check.'

'Do we know how long she's been in the area?' Matt asked, turning back to Jenna.

'She moved to Penzance nine months ago and is renting a house in Croft Road.'

'Any partner?'

'We haven't found one yet.'

'I've got something here, ma'am,' Clem called out.

'What is it?' Pengelly asked, her eyes trained on the officer.

Matt held his breath, a mix of dread and curiosity coursing through him.

'I've just spoken to the head of the last nursery where Hillman worked before moving down to Cornwall and she said Hillman left under a cloud after an issue with one of the children.'

Matt inhaled sharply, his chest expanding as he gulped in a deep breath.

'Issue? What issue? And how come this is the first we've heard about it? Wouldn't these things have been reported to future employers?' Matt's disbelief filled the air as the other team members stared in shock at Clem.

'That's exactly what I said, Sarge. From what I can gather, Hillman was accused of being overly friendly with some of the children – nothing illegal, just a bit too emotionally involved, you know? She also accused some parents of neglect.'

'Did Hillman contact the police? Is there a record of her complaint?'

'No, Sarge. She approached the parents directly and it got a little tricky. The head of the nursery had to intervene. Supposedly there was no evidence to substantiate Hillman's claims. It was nothing that had to be reported to the police, or social services. Hillman wasn't doing anything against the rules, but they did suggest that she leave their employment.'

'No doubt with a good reference, so she could get a job somewhere else,' Matt muttered.

'So, how does this relate to our missing children? And why did she end up here in Cornwall? That's what we need to find out,' Pengelly said.

'No. We need to find out where she's taken the children. Dani's been through enough in her short life without this adding to it. She's...' Matt's words fell away.

They all stared at him, concern etched on their faces.

'What happened, Sarge?' Billy asked.

'Billy, it's nothing to do with us,' Jenna said.

'It's okay,' Matt said, the memory of Leigh's tragic death washing over him. A wave of pain surged through his body and he fought back the tears threatening to escape from his eyes as he prepared to tell them. 'Leigh... Dani's mother... my wife... died in a car crash a few months ago. We moved down here to be with my parents so they could help look after Dani while I work.' His voice cracked, and Pengelly reached out and grabbed his hand, giving it a squeeze.

'I'm so sorry,' she said.

'Yeah, me, too,' Billy added, closely followed by Jenna and Clem.

'Thank you. I appreciate your kind words, but now's not the time to talk about my past. We've got to find the children. Find Dani.'

He glanced at his boss, shifting uncomfortably under her scrutinising stare. He could almost hear her inner thoughts: that she should have known about his background. But it had been his decision to keep it quiet. It hadn't affected how he'd done his job.

'Okay, let's move on,' Pengelly said, waving her hand. 'We don't know Hillman's motive, but what we do know is that she's well-liked by her colleagues and she cares about the children she looks after.'

'Which surely must mean that the missing girls are still alive,' Billy said, his words echoing around the room.

All eyes turned to Matt. He wanted to believe the officer was right, but a sinking feeling in his stomach warned him it could be otherwise.

'I hope so, Billy,' Pengelly said. 'It also helps to know that all three girls were regularly in Hillman's care, so if she is planning further abductions we can narrow down the locations to nurseries where she works.'

'Except no way will she get the chance to abduct another child. Because we'll have her locked up,' Billy said.

'Ideally, yes. But our priority is to find the children. Contact the agency to see if she's working today and if so send uniform to bring her in for questioning. If she isn't, then tell them to go to her house. If she can't be found make sure all officers know to be on the lookout for her. I'll put in a request for a search warrant. One way or another, Eleanor Hillman is going to be here to answer our questions.'

TWENTY-NINE
FRIDAY, 28 OCTOBER

Lauren clenched the steering wheel as she sped towards Croft Road, and the house Hillman was renting, with a search warrant. Adrenaline coursed through her veins, knowing that they were one step closer to finding the kidnapped children. Before leaving the station, uniform had informed her that they'd located Hillman at her house and she was being brought in for questioning.

Lauren had left Tamsin on the phone, frantically trying to contact all of the nurseries the agency had told them Hillman had worked, to uncover anything that might assist. Lauren also wanted to search the woman's house before interviewing her in case there was any evidence that could be used.

Matt sat next to her in silence, his whole body rigid. The tension emanating from him was palpable. He was holding up well considering the unimaginable stress he was under.

Why hadn't she known about his wife dying in a car crash? Had he told the interview panel? And if he had, why hadn't they told her? But if he hadn't informed them, should he have done? Her mind raced with unanswered questions as she tried to process the tragic situation he'd been through.

But whatever the answer to those questions, they couldn't discuss it now. After the case was over, and Dani was back with him, it had to be addressed. It couldn't be left unresolved.

Hillman's semi-detached white cottage stood proud, and the red Toyota Matt had spotted in the CCTV footage was parked in the driveway in front of the integral garage. They'd been in touch with the local agency responsible for renting the property and they'd provided a key, which had saved them from having to break in if it had been locked.

Lauren stopped the car in the road, behind the vehicles belonging to the other team members. Before she opened the car door she turned to Matt. 'Are you sure you can handle this? There might be something belonging to Dani inside. You don't have to come with us if you don't want to.' Her voice was low and firm.

Matt's face was pale, his eyes haunted. 'Dani might be in there,' he said in a strained voice. 'And if she is, I want to be the one to find her and make sure she's safe. I won't let you down... I promise.' He clutched at the door handle, fear written in every tense muscle.

They got out of the car, met up with the rest of the team and headed to the front door. Matt kept in step with Lauren and he strode with a gait that was surprisingly upright despite his limp.

Lauren inserted the key into the lock and twisted, pushing open the door. She stepped inside, Matt just behind her, and the smell of citrus air-freshener filled the air. She gestured towards the lounge and kitchen. 'Matt and I will take the downstairs. Billy and Clem, you go upstairs and check out every nook and cranny. Jenna, you head on outside and see what's out there. In particular, look for a shed where children could be hidden.'

'Is there a cellar?' Billy asked.

'Not that I'm aware of, but make sure to check.'

Lauren and Matt pulled on their disposable gloves and

stopped in the entrance of the lounge to scan the area. It was unnervingly tidy, with nothing out of place. It was sparsely furnished with a green leather two-seater sofa, a matching easy chair and a low chrome and glass table in the centre. Along the far wall stood an oak sideboard. Lauren headed over to it, leaving Matt to search the remainder of the room.

She opened the left-hand cupboard and found two large photo albums which she pulled out and rested on top of the sideboard. She carefully opened each one. They both featured groups of children in what looked like nursery settings. Was that normal for nursery nurses?

She studied every photo very carefully but found no clues. None of them featured the kidnapped girls. She then pulled open the middle drawer which contained several manila folders. Inside of these were invoices, a birth certificate, a passport, academic certificates and other personal documentation relating to Hillman. Finally, she opened the right-hand cupboard. Inside was a half-drunk bottle of malt whisky and an unopened bottle of gin. Nothing else.

Lauren pulled out several evidence bags from her bag and inside each one placed the albums and manila folders.

'What have you got, ma'am?' Matt called out from where he stood, flicking through a magazine.

'Personal records. Hundreds of photos of children. But none of our three girls. What do you have?'

'Nothing of any use. In the magazine rack there are several current childcare publications from this year and one classic car magazine that's a few months old. Have we confirmed that she lives alone? I wondered whether the car magazine wasn't hers.'

'Women do like cars, you know,' she snapped, immediately regretting it. He clearly wasn't thinking straight, so she shouldn't get on to him. She could be such a bitch when she was stressed.

'I know, ma'am. I wanted to make sure to cover all the bases.'

'Yeah, sorry. There's nothing in the sideboard which belongs to anyone else, so it appears not. We'll see if the others can confirm. Have you finished searching?'

'Yes, ma'am.'

'So have I. Let's go to the kitchen.'

Clem and Billy were coming down the stairs as they prepared to leave the lounge.

'There's definitely a man living here, ma'am,' Clem said. 'We found men's toiletries and clothes.'

'What about personal items like letters, or other documents?'

'No, none of those.'

'Hmm. I think maybe she has a part-time visitor because there's only her stuff in the lounge. If this man lived here all the time we'd expect some personal possessions. Did you uncover any evidence relating to the missing girls?' She spoke cautiously, mindful not to mention them all by name and risk Matt's despair becoming even deeper.

'Not a trace, ma'am.'

'Did you check under the mattresses?'

'Yes, ma'am. We've searched everywhere and couldn't find a single clue connecting Hillman to the kids. It's like the house is hardly lived in. Everything's in its rightful place. Even the bathroom's impeccable. It's not natural,' Clem said.

'It's the same here.'

'Ma'am,' Jenna said, coming from the kitchen and into the hall where they were standing. 'There's a garden shed, but it's very tidy and nothing in there of any use. The garden's immaculate. Not a weed in sight and the grass cut to within an inch of its life.'

'Typical of the rest of the place,' Lauren said, changing her mind about where she'd next go with Matt. 'Billy, go and check the kitchen. I want to know if it's been recently cleaned. If she's had the girls here, there might be some prints. Also check for anything personal relating to her or this mysterious man. Matt and I will search the car. Jenna, you and Clem take the garage. If it's anything like the rest of the property, it won't take you long.'

'Yes, ma'am,' the team said in unison.

Lauren and Matt strode out to the car, the harsh sunlight reflecting off its glossy paint. Matt tugged on the handle, rattling it in frustration.

'It's locked, ma'am.'

'Damn. Bloody typical. Okay, let's go inside and see if we can find a key. There definitely weren't any hanging up in the hall, nor in the lounge. So, it's unlikely we'll find one.'

They hurried back into the house and straight to the kitchen where Billy was methodically going through the drawers.

'We're looking for her car keys,' Matt said. 'Have you found any?'

'Not yet, Sarge, but I haven't finished searching,' Billy replied, continuing to look through the open drawer.

'Okay, thanks. You carry on.' Matt turned to Lauren. 'They might be in the garage.'

'That's an odd place to keep them, especially if she hadn't actually put the car in there. But we'll check.'

They pushed through the interconnecting door from the kitchen to the garage. As predicted, it was pristine. Jenna and Clem were peering at something on the workbench.

Matt stiffened beside her.

'What is it? What have you found?' he barked, urgency lacing his voice as he rushed over to them.

Jenna and Clem exchanged a glance before turning to face him. 'Sorry, Sarge. Nothing to do with the case. We saw a mouse and were trying to work out which way it had gone and whether there were more,' Jenna muttered.

Seriously? Why would they be focusing on a mouse at a time like this?

'Oh,' Matt said, his voice heavy.

'We're looking for car keys. We can't get into Hillman's car and thought you might have come across them?' Lauren asked.

'No, sorry, ma'am. There are no keys in here. Maybe Hillman has them with her, in her bag. I always carry mine,' Jenna said.

'In that case, call the station and get the car impounded. We want someone out here immediately to collect it. There might be some DNA evidence that will connect her to the children.'

THIRTY

FRIDAY, 28 OCTOBER

Lauren stopped outside the interview room and turned to face Matt. 'Before we go inside to question Hillman, I'm warning you now. You're to remain calm and professional at all times. You may ask questions, but if I think for one second that you're about to lose it then you'll be sent out quicker than you can say your own name. Do you understand?'

Lauren knew that her tone was sharp and unyielding, but she had no other choice. She'd decided to let him interview with her so she could keep an eye on him. She'd considered the alternative of him watching from the observation area but what was to stop him from barging in at any moment? At least this way he was beside her and she had more control over the situation.

'I understand, ma'am. All I care about is finding Dani and the other girls. I've dealt with enough people like this to know that you need to tread carefully. If we put Hillman on her guard then she'll either clam up or start demanding a solicitor. We need to keep her on side.'

He spoke in a non-threatening tone, but his shoulders were hunched and his fists clenched. Had she made a mistake?

Lauren pushed open the door, revealing Eleanor Hillman

seated at the table. She stared directly at them while playing with her fringe.

'Why am I here?' Hillman asked, her eyes darting from Lauren to Matt. 'I already spoke to you at Redwood when Violet went missing and told you everything I know and—'

Lauren held up her hand to silence the woman. 'Before we continue, we're going to record this interview.' She nodded towards Matt, who started the recording equipment.

'Interview on Friday, twenty-eighth October. Those present, DI Pengelly, DS Price, and... please state your name,' Matt said to Hillman.

'Ellie... er, Eleanor Hillman. Am I under arrest? Do I need a solicitor?'

'Miss Hillman, we've brought you in because we think you might be able to help. You're not under arrest. It's up to you whether you would like a solicitor, but remember that takes time. Time we don't have if we wish to locate Isla, Violet and Dani. Which I'm sure is what you want.'

'Do you mean Dani from Kid's Stuff nursery?' Her hand flew up to her mouth.

'Yes,' Lauren said.

'I didn't know she was missing. That's awful, she's such a lovely child. I'll help you in any way I can.' Worry flickered in her eyes.

'Thank you. We understand that you've worked at all three nurseries from where the children have disappeared. Acorn, Redwood and Kid's Stuff.'

Hillman nodded. 'Yes. I work as a supply nursery nurse and go where the agency sends me.'

'Why not work in one place, where you can be more settled?'

'I enjoy working in different places because it means I get to look after lots of different children and get to know them and their families.' Eleanor stared directly at Matt and her eyes widened. 'Oh my goodness, you're Dani's father. I've just realised. What are you doing here when she's missing? Shouldn't you be out looking for her?'

Lauren cast a glance in Matt's direction. On the surface he appeared unfazed by the accusation, but the lines were tight around his eyes.

'I'm doing my job. Now perhaps you can tell us why at various times over the last couple of weeks your car, a red Toyota Corolla, was seen in the vicinity of where I live? And don't insult our intelligence by saying it's a coincidence,' Matt said.

His voice had an edge to it and Lauren gave him a gentle prod with her foot in the hope that he would relax a little bit more. Currently the woman was cooperating and that's how she wanted it to stay.

Hillman's brows furrowed deeply. She shook her head. 'I don't know. All I can tell you is that it wasn't me. I hardly ever use my car. I prefer walking.'

'If it wasn't you driving, then who was it? Does anyone else have access to it?' Matt said, his voice calmer.

'Well... um...'

'Eleanor, this is no time to be protecting anyone.' Matt's voice rose with urgency. 'You must tell us what you know so that we can find the missing children. Now.'

'Yes. Sorry. Of course. My partner, Stuart, sometimes uses it. His car broke down and I've been lending him mine.' She bit down on her bottom lip. 'I suppose it could be him near your house... it wasn't me.'

Lauren exchanged a glance with Matt.

'Does Stuart live with you full-time? Because although we found items belonging to a man, like clothing and toiletries, there was nothing personal,' Lauren said.

Eleanor's mouth dropped open and her hands, which had

been resting on the desk, trembled. 'Y-you've been in my house? Are you allowed to do that?'

'We had a search warrant,' Lauren said, locking eyes with the woman.

'Why *my* house? Did you search the homes of everyone who works at the nurseries?'

'We can't disclose any details of the investigation.'

'You didn't find anything, did you? I know that because I didn't do anything.'

'No, we didn't. Back to Stuart. Where does he work and is he currently living with you?'

'He works for an accounting firm in Penzance. He's sort of living with me.'

'Sort of?' Lauren asked.

'Most of his things are still with his wife at home. They're getting a divorce soon.'

'Where is he today?' Lauren asked.

'He said he was going to visit a client.'

'But I thought his car was out of action?' Matt said.

'He must have gone to work and borrowed one of the pool cars.'

'Do you have Stuart's contact number?' Lauren pressed.

'It's on my phone. May I get it out of my bag?'

'Be my guest,' Lauren said, gesturing with her hand to the back of Hillman's chair where the small black handbag was hanging from its metallic gold chain.

Hillman reached inside and pulled out her phone. 'His name's Stuart Baines.' She pushed a few buttons and then slid the device over to Lauren, who wrote down the name and number.

'Thank you. We'll be back soon after talking to him. You're to stay here until we give you permission to leave.'

'But I have to work this afternoon. I'm covering for someone who's sick at Redwood nursery. I can't let them down. I've told you everything I know.'

Like setting foot in the nursery was going to happen. Not that Lauren was going to burst the woman's bubble yet. For now Hillman was cooperating and that was all that mattered.

'We'll be as quick as we can.'

Lauren and Matt left the interview room and headed back to the office. She'd get one of the team to contact Baines. In the meantime, she wanted Hillman to sweat a little.

'Do you think she's telling the truth?' Matt demanded.

'She's hiding something, for sure. The bigger question is whether Stuart Baines is in on it. What do you think?'

'She does have the means and access to kidnap the children,' Matt replied grimly. 'But her partner... it might be that he's pulling the strings and Hillman's a pawn in his game,' Matt answered with a chill in his voice. 'It wouldn't surprise me.'

If that were true, then Lauren feared for the children's safety. Hillman appeared to love all the children in her care. The nurseries had nothing but praise for her, plus there were the photo albums lovingly put together.

Had Matt reached the same conclusion regarding the children's wellbeing if Baines was involved? She hoped not.

'Hillman said she hasn't used her car today. So, if she did take Dani then what car was used? It had to be one that wouldn't cause alarm.' They continued down the corridor and her phone rang. 'Pengelly.'

'Ma'am, it's Clem. Get yourself down to the impound, quick. Forensics have found one of the children in that car. An ambulance is on the way.'

An icy shiver ran down Lauren's spine.

Dead or alive?

She refrained from asking, not wanting Matt to know. Not yet.

'Okay. We'll be right there.'

'What is it?' Matt asked, frowning.

'They've found one of the children in the car; I don't know who it is.'

'Where's the car?'

'In the impound behind the main station building. Let's go.'

Lauren raced ahead, a mix of hope and dread pounding in her veins. Matt followed close behind, each thud of his shoes echoing ominously as they ran to reach the car.

The rear was open, and Lauren peered inside, her breath catching in her throat as her eyes fixed on a small black suitcase. And then she saw it. A child... still and unmoving.

It was Dani.

A low groan escaped Lauren's lips.

Were they too late?

Matt desperately shoved Pengelly aside, fear churning in his gut. As soon as his eyes landed on the child, he knew it was Dani, curled up in a suitcase, unresponsive and still.

Please, God, let her be alive.

Tears cascaded from his eyes as he scooped her up into his arms, cradling her close to his chest. All hope seemed lost until suddenly he felt it – the shallow rise and fall of her chest.

A wave of relief washed over him as he clutched his daughter to him, rocking her back and forth.

'Dani, wake up. Wake up sweetheart,' he begged, giving her a gentle shake. But she didn't stir. 'Why isn't she waking?'

'They think she's been drugged, Matt,' Pengelly said, softly. 'You shouldn't really have picked her up because of disturbing the crime scene.'

'I don't care about the *crime scene*. I want to be with my daughter.' He held her tightly in his arms and stepped away from the car. 'There's enough DNA in there for you to put that bitch away for life.' Tears continued streaming down his face. 'What has that monster given her? I'll kill her. I will...'

'We don't know yet if it was Hillman,' Pengelly said. 'It could have been Baines.'

'She knew what he was doing then! We have to make her confess and tell us where the other girls are or else—'

'Matt,' Pengelly interrupted. 'The ambulance has arrived. You go with Dani to the hospital. We're going to track down Stuart Baines and bring him in for questioning.'

'What about Hillman? Are you going back to her? I want to be there. To find out what she's done to Dani.' The anguish in his voice reverberated in his ears.

'No. There are still two more innocent children missing and they must be our primary focus. Trust me to take care of everything while you go to the hospital with Dani. Is there anything you need me to do? Anything?'

Pengelly's words echoed around his head. Isla and Violet were still out there, unprotected and at risk. They had no clue whether the little girls were alive or not. He stared down at Dani. She was safe.

'Yes, please. Phone my parents and ask them to meet me at the hospital. They don't even know that Dani's missing because I couldn't bring myself to tell them. My phone's in my pocket and their number's saved under Mum and Dad.' He wasn't prepared to release his grip on Dani for even a second to search for his phone himself.

Pengelly took out his phone and made the call. She was calm and reassuring and explained that Matt was with Dani but nothing else. She returned the phone to his pocket.

'We'll stay in touch,' she said.

The paramedic didn't try to take Dani from Matt, and instead gently laid a blanket around them as they walked silently to the ambulance. The entire way to the hospital he held Dani close. She looked surprisingly content in his arms, almost like she knew she was safe and nothing was going to separate them again.

. . .

The journey to St Ives hospital seemed to take forever and when finally the paramedics opened the back of the ambulance there was a nurse waiting with a wheelchair.

'I'm Lizzie,' she said, pushing the wheelchair slightly forward. 'Would you like to sit Dani in here?'

'No. I'm not letting her go.'

'Why don't you sit in the chair while holding her and I'll wheel you both in. It's hospital policy.'

'Okay.' He sat down and they were rushed to a private room where two people were waiting for them.

'Detective Price.' The tall female spoke. 'I'm Sasha Davis, a consultant paediatrician and this is nurse Karl Hobbs. Will you lay Dani down on the bed so we can check her over?'

Matt gently placed his daughter on the mattress and stood as close as he could to her.

The consultant took Dani's temperature and pressed a stethoscope to her chest.

'How is she?' Matt asked.

'Judging by her vitals she appears to have been given a strong sedative,' the consultant replied.

The nurse, who was standing beside the bed, picked up a syringe from the table.

'What are you doing?' Matt asked.

'Taking some of Dani's blood to find out what she's been given. She won't feel anything, I promise.'

Matt winced as the needle pierced Dani's skin, and while he expected his daughter to flinch she didn't move a muscle.

'Now what?'

'We keep an eye on her vitals and wait. I'm hopeful that she'll stir soon,' the consultant said.

That very moment Dani gave a little moan and Matt crouched down until level with her.

Her eyes blinked open and she stared directly at him. 'Hello, Daddy.' Her voice was hoarse. It wrenched at Matt's heart.

Matt pulled her close and gave a gentle hug. 'Hello, sweetheart. Are you okay?'

'I'm tired.' She yawned and put her thumb in her mouth. Her eyes flickered and gently closed. Matt remained staring at her, overwhelmed by his emotions.

'This is an excellent sign,' the consultant said, jolting Matt back to the present. 'She recognised you and was able to speak. We'll keep her here, and do hourly obs. I expect she'll sleep for most of the next twelve hours. Assuming she continues to make good progress, I don't see why she won't be allowed home tomorrow or the next day. Karl will be in and out for the rest of the day and I'll pop back after theatre. I have several operations on my list this afternoon.'

'Thanks, doc,' Matt said.

The consultant and nurse had only been gone for a couple of minutes when the door opened and his parents rushed in. Tears were streaming down his mother's face and his father was clearly trying to hold it together.

'It's okay. She's going to be okay. She woke up a few minutes ago and spoke to me before going back to sleep. She'd been given a sedative by the person who took her.'

'Matthew, why didn't you tell us?' his mum said. 'Why did we have to learn what had happened from your boss? We've been beside ourselves with worry ever since she phoned. We might have been able to help if we'd known.'

That was exactly why he hadn't wanted them to know. There was nothing they could have done, other than worry. And the stress could have caused a heart attack or something.

'I'm sorry, Mum. I didn't want to upset you. The main thing is Dani's alive and going to be okay. I'm going back to work now. I'll have to take your car. We—'

'No, Matthew. How can you think of work at a time like this?' his father said, frowning.

'Dad, we still don't know who did this, or why – though we're close to the truth. I need to be there to find out. Dani won't even realise I'm not here because she'll be asleep. As long as you're around if she wakes up. Remember, there are still two other little girls missing. I owe it to the parents to find their daughters.'

THIRTY-TWO

FRIDAY, 28 OCTOBER

Lauren's phone rang as she hurried back to the interview room where Eleanor Hillman was located. She'd lied to Matt about not questioning the woman again straight away because his place was with Dani. Although, as it had happened, DCI Mistry had seen her arrive back at the station and demanded an update.

This meant the interview had been slightly delayed, which wasn't ideal. With Stuart Baines still out there, and the prospect of finding the other two children alive becoming slimmer by the minute, every second was critical.

'Pengelly.'

'Ma'am, it's Tamsin. Stuart Baines isn't in work today. He's been on annual leave all this week.'

To kidnap the girls.

'Thanks. Arrange for an APB to be put out, and find out everything you can about him.'

'Yes, ma'am.'

One way or another, she'd force Hillman to speak. The memory of Matt's daughter unconscious in the boot of the woman's car would haunt Lauren forever.

She arrived at the interview room and marched in.

'Can I go now?' Hillman asked, a tremor in her voice.

Lauren glared fiercely across the table, taking in Hillman's panicked expression. The faltering composure had cracked, revealing fear and desperation. This was a completely different woman from the one they'd questioned earlier.

She was scared. But what did that mean, exactly?

'I have more questions to ask,' Lauren began icily, pressing the record button before continuing. 'I've just returned from the impound where forensics were analysing your car. Dani Price was found unconscious and drugged in the boot.'

Hillman paled. 'I-is she okay?'

'She's been taken to the hospital and from what I understand she's going to be fine.'

No thanks to you.

'I didn't know he'd left her there. You have to believe me. I thought he'd...' Her words fell away.

'Do you mean Stuart Baines?' Lauren interrupted.

'Yes.'

'You told us he's at work today. Why?'

'Because... I just thought... you don't understand.'

'You're right. I don't. Stuart Baines has taken this week off work. And I think it's so the pair of you could abduct Isla, Violet and Dani.'

'It's not like that.'

'What is it like, then?'

'Stuart made me. I didn't want anything to do with his scheme. All I care about is the children.'

Lauren paused, then looked her straight in the eye. 'I want to know everything. Now.'

Hillman's face twisted in anguish and despair, her lips trembling. 'It was all Stuart's idea. He asked which of my children I liked the best and when I told him about Isla, Violet and Dani, he said they'd have a better life if we took them.'

'And you agreed with that, did you?'

'Yes, sort of... I mean... he was right that they'd have had a better life with me.'

'You think taking the girls from their families would have been for the best?'

'I suppose that deep down I knew it was wrong. But no way would I say anything to Stuart. Not once he'd made up his mind.'

'Why not?'

Hillman wrapped her arms tightly around her body. 'B-because I knew he'd lose his temper. It's like he turns into a monster when he's angry. I had to go along with his plans and tell him where the girls were and how they could be taken.' Tears streamed down her face. 'I regret my decision every second of every day. I'm so sorry for—'

The door flew open and Matt charged in, lunging towards Hillman. His face distorted in anger. He would have made it if Lauren hadn't jumped up in time and grabbed him by the arm. She forcibly dragged him out of the interview room.

'Where are the girls?' he bellowed, as Lauren slammed the door shut behind them.

'What the hell do you think you're doing? How dare you burst in here and try to attack the suspect when I'm in the middle of her interview! You have no right to do this, no matter how guilty you believe her to be.' Lauren spoke through gritted teeth, her hands balled into fists by her side.

The rage drained from Matt's body and he slumped against the wall.

'I'm sorry. So sorry. I had to find out. I shouldn't have done it. It was inexcusable.'

'Look, I get it,' Lauren said, the tension easing from her body. 'I understand that this is tough for you. But you must stay positive and let us do our job.' She'd have probably acted the same in his situation, so she couldn't berate him further. 'How's Dani holding up?'

'She's going to be okay. She opened her eyes, saw me, and then went back to sleep. They want her to stay in hospital for a night or two, depending on how she is. I left my parents there while she's resting. The doctors think she was given a strong sedative, but we won't know for sure until the blood test results come back.'

Lauren gave him an affectionate pat on the arm. Not something she'd usually do, but it felt right. 'It's a huge relief to know that she's doing okay.'

'I can't believe that we found her. Thank God you had the initiative to send the car to forensics.' Matt gave a grateful smile.

'You'd have done the same in my position, I'm sure.'

'Maybe. But I didn't. It was you, and I'll never be able to thank you enough. What has Hillman said?'

'She's blamed the whole thing on Baines, who, by the way, has taken this week off work and is still missing. She was just explaining everything when you barged in.'

Matt flushed. 'I'm sorry. Do you believe her?'

'If she's lying then she's a bloody good actress. She's scared of Baines. He forced her to tell him how to get inside the nurseries. I don't know yet who actually took the children. I'll find out in a minute.'

'May I interview Hillman with you? I promise not to let my emotions get the better of me again.'

She'd been expecting the question. 'Yes. But I'm warning you, I don't give second chances.'

* * *

Matt followed Pengelly into the interview room to speak to Hillman. He was still reeling over how he'd totally lost it. He'd never experienced that sort of anger before. Not at work or at home. It was like someone had taken over his body and he'd been helpless to do anything about it. It had shaken him to the core.

What if he'd managed to get hold of Hillman?

He'd be facing a charge for assault; would have been sacked; and most likely have ended up in prison. Then what would have happened to Dani?

He shuddered at the thought.

In his defence, though, all he'd wanted to know was what Hillman had done with Isla and Violet. Or what *Baines* had done with them, if her assertions were to be believed.

'What's he doing here?' Hillman said, cowering in her chair, when they returned to the interview room.

'DS Price is part of the interview,' Pengelly said.

'What if he attacks me again?'

'I won't,' Matt said, forcing his voice to remain calm, despite every muscle in his body screaming for vengeance against the woman.

'Eleanor, was it you who abducted the children from the nurseries?' Matt asked, the question lingering in the quiet room.

'Yes,' she confirmed, her voice barely above a whisper. 'But it wasn't my choice. Stuart... he made me do it. I swear I didn't harm them.'

There was something terrifyingly distant about the woman, as if she were a mere puppet, with Stuart pulling the strings.

'You drugged them. How can that not be harming them?' Matt snapped.

'Eleanor, where are Isla and Violet?' Pengelly asked.

'I don't know. Stuart didn't—'

There was a knock on the door and Jenna popped her head round.

What was it with interviews at this place? Every single one got interrupted.

'Ma'am, may I have a quick word please?'

Matt grimaced, stopped the recording, and left the room with the DI.

'This had better be good,' Pengelly said, once they were standing in the corridor.

'Tamsin's discovered that Stuart Baines owns a caravan. The girls could be there. I thought you'd want to know straight away.'

Matt's heart pounded in his chest. Had they finally found the lost girls' location?

'Where's it situated?'

'We don't know, but Tamsin's on the case. If anyone can find out, she can.'

'That's excellent work. Thanks.' Pengelly marched back in the interview room with Matt following.

'Stuart has a caravan?' she said before even sitting down.

Hillman's eyes widened, fear shining from them. 'Yes. An old aunt... she left it to him. It's... it's run down. He doesn't go there. He said he was going to sell it.'

'Where is it? We need to search it. Now.'

'Why?' Hillman's reply was almost a whimper, a stark display of her terror.

'Why do you think?' Matt barked. 'For the good of our health. We're looking for the missing children. Connect the dots, for God's sake, Hillman.'

The woman shrank back into her chair. 'I-I don't know, exactly.'

'What *do* you know exactly?' Matt said.

'I could take you in a car, if I'm allowed? I've only been there once, but I might remember the way.'

THIRTY-THREE

FRIDAY, 28 OCTOBER

They drove to the caravan in two vehicles. Matt accompanied Pengelly with Hillman in the back seat, and Jenna and Clem followed in the other.

The cars sped down the winding roads, past stone hedgerows, fields with cows grazing, and stretches of Cornish countryside, with Hillman giving directions until they were close to Land's End.

'Take the right turn coming up,' Hillman said.

They arrived at the remote High Sands Caravan and Campsite, and pulled in outside the office. The air was thick with the scent of smoke from food being cooked on barbeques, and the grounds were bustling with people.

'Do you know where the caravan is?' Matt asked, turning to Hillman, who was staring out of the window.

'When I came that time, it was dark,' Hillman said.

'I'll ask,' Pengelly said, jumping out of the car and heading to the office. After a minute she returned. 'It's on a permanent site. Baines pays a monthly rent. They've given me the spare key that they keep for emergencies.'

Pengelly started the engine and drove towards the rear of

the campsite, past the tents, towed caravans, and several campervans. People quickly moved out of the way, staring at them open-mouthed, watching as they drew up to a small white caravan in area that was flanked with trees and hedges.

'You stay here,' Matt said to Hillman, clambering out of the car before Pengelly had even turned off the engine.

He raced to the door and tugged on the metal handle but it was locked. He tried peering through the adjacent dirty window but the curtain was shut. He tapped his foot impatiently on the ground while waiting for Pengelly to reach him.

'Mind out of the way,' Pengelly said when she got there, holding out the key and trying to slide it into the lock.

'Hurry up,' Matt said after a few seconds of no apparent success.

'It's rusty, okay?' Pengelly said, turning and scowling at him. After more twisting and turning the key finally slid into the lock. But it wouldn't turn. 'Damn,' she muttered. 'We'll have to break the door down at this rate and I don't want to scare the children if they're in there.'

'Try pulling the door towards you until it's tight against the door frame and then turn the key,' Matt suggested, moving from foot to foot in frustration and resisting the urge to push Pengelly out of the way and try the door himself.

'Okay.' Pengelly did as Matt had suggested and after twisting the key from side to side several times the door finally opened.

Pengelly rushed inside, with Matt close on her heels. A musty smell hung in the air. He scanned the main area but it was empty.

Where were the girls?

He noticed a door to the right. Could it be the bedroom? His pulse drummed in his ears. With trembling hands he pushed open the door and his stomach dropped as he took in the scene in front of him. Isla and Violet were lying on the bed, covered with a duvet, their faces pale and still. He inched forward to their side and held his breath until noticing their chests rise and fall. They were alive. They must have been drugged like Dani. He sank onto the bed beside them, all his energy and determination draining away.

He closed his eyes for a second.

'Matt?' He jumped at the sound of his name, his heart thumping in his chest. His boss was standing over him, her expression tense with worry.

'Yes, ma'am,' he said, his voice trembling. 'They're alive. Thank God. They're alive.'

A look of relief washed over her face. 'We've found them.' She rushed out of the bedroom shouting orders. 'Jenna, call an ambulance and Tamsin, call their parents and tell them to head to St Ives hospital to meet us there. The girls are alive.'

Pengelly returned to the bedroom and sat down next to Matt. 'We've done it, Matt. We have the girls. Go back to the hospital and be with Dani – we can handle this from here.'

'No way. I'm not leaving until we've interviewed Baines and found out what happened. Dani will be asleep for most of the day. This is more important. We need to make sure we have enough evidence to make certain neither of them can get off on a technicality.'

'Okay. I'm assuming that if you're allowed to interview with me you're not going to do anything rash.' She eyed him with a hint of mischief.

He shifted uncomfortably and gave a sheepish smile. 'I've never acted so impulsively before.'

'I might have known you for less than a week, but I believe you. While we're waiting, why don't you tell me about Dani.'

'She's like a mini version of her mum. I know we all think our kids are geniuses, but with Dani she astounded us from day one. She spoke her first word way before most other children do and could hold proper conversations with us by the time she was eighteen months. And now she's two she'll chat to anyone.'

'It's amazing how children develop. I'm not a parent so can only imagine how incredible it must be.'

'It is, but there are times when she drives me crazy. She's so determined and there's no convincing her to do something if she doesn't want to. Talk about battle of wills. That's when I miss Leigh the most. She'd know how to handle Dani.' Tears welled in his eyes, and he blinked them away. But not before he noticed Pengelly had seen. 'Sorry.'

'There's nothing to be sorry about. Dani sounds like a wonderful little girl. Does she have a favourite animal?'

What a weird question. Then again, if Pengelly didn't have children perhaps it was her way of making conversation?

'Umm... yes, she does. She's had a stuffed elephant since she was only a few months old and she always tells us that elephants are her favourite animal. She's already got quite a collection. Whenever we visit anywhere we go to the gift shop and if there's an elephant there she wants it. The way she's heading by the time she's ten they'll need their own room.'

'She might change her mind and like something else by then.'

'Possibly. Or knowing Dani, she'll want a real one for the back garden.' He laughed and it took him by surprise. He didn't laugh much these days. 'Ma'am, I'm sorry not to have mentioned about Leigh to you. I didn't discuss it at the interview, either. With hindsight I should have... but... I didn't want to be treated with kid gloves by everyone.'

'I understand why you didn't tell us, but really—'

'Ma'am,' Jenna shouted through the door. 'Hillman's not in the back of the car. She's escaped!'

'What? Didn't you lock it?' Matt stared open-mouthed at his boss.

'Yes... No... I don't know. Damnit!'

'I'll go; you stay here with the children,' Matt yelled, sprinting out of the caravan before Pengelly had time to answer.

Hillman's figure bounced in and out of view, hidden by the trees, as she scurried away like an animal in search of shelter towards the entrance of the campsite. Matt's chest heaved with determination as he raced after her, his feet pounding against the uneven ground.

With each stride, the distance between him and Hillman grew shorter and shorter until he was within arm's reach.

'Hillman, stop!' His voice ripped through the silence.

He lunged for her arm but she twisted away, leaving him grasping at nothing but air.

'Get away from me – I won't go to prison for something that wasn't my fault!' she yelled, shoving him aside and fleeing once again.

Stumbling momentarily, Matt gained his footing and surged forward in pursuit of her, powering on despite the pain shooting through his bad leg.

'Sarge,' Jenna's voice rang out from behind. 'We'll cut her off at the entrance. You take the left and I'll cover the right.'

Matt followed Jenna's instructions, veering sharply to the left while she made a dash to the right. He tried to track Hillman's movements with his eyes but soon she was out of sight.

As he arrived at the entrance, he realised with a sinking feeling that Hillman was nowhere to be seen.

Had she slipped past them? Was she going to disappear and never be caught? A cold dread trickled through him.

Suddenly, a scream rang out and he turned to see Jenna's silhouette as she tackled Hillman. The two women collided with the ground, a tangle of desperation and determination. Hillman's struggle was fierce but Jenna's grip remained firm.

Matt ran over, and the cold hard click of the handcuffs filled the air as Hillman was restrained.

'What the hell did you do that for?' he yelled, pulling Hillman to her feet, as fury raged through him.

'I was scared of what would happen to me,' Hillman said, her voice choked with fear. 'If I get sent to prison for helping Stuart... you read all the time what happens in prisons to people who commit a crime against children... I'm sorry.'

'Call uniform and get them to take her back to the station,' Matt said to Jenna, ignoring Hillman's comments. 'We'll lock her in your car until they arrive.'

Jenna pulled Hillman to her feet and they marched back to the caravan where Clem was waiting.

'Good catch,' the officer said.

'Can you phone the station and get officers out here to take her back?' Jenna said, opening the car door and sliding Hillman into the back seat.

Matt left them to it and went back into the caravan. Pengelly was still in the bedroom sitting with Isla and Violet.

'We've got her,' he said, smiling.

'I can't believe I left the car unlocked,' Pengelly said, shaking her head.

'I probably would have done the same. We were so anxious to find the girls. Don't beat yourself up over it. No harm was done.'

He wasn't just saying that. It could very easily have been him.

'I disagree. I demand exacting standards from everyone around me, which means I must adhere to them myself. Don't worry, I'll report what happened to the DCI and he can take whatever action he deems appropriate.'

Matt couldn't help smiling at her serious expression. 'Look, everyone makes mistakes. We're not robots. I know for a fact that you'll never do it again. What is it they say about learning from our mistakes? And, anyway, we're stuck out in the middle of nowhere; how far do you think she'd have got?'

'That's beside the point.'

'Ma'am, the ambulance is here,' Clem called out, bringing their conversation to a close.

Matt and Pengelly exited the bedroom, making their way to the kitchen area, watching through the door while the two paramedics took the blood pressures and pulses of the sleeping girls, whose delicate features were at odds with the terror they'd been through. One of them groaned before drifting off back to sleep.

'Are they okay?' Pengelly asked, moving closer to the doorway.

'From what we've seen so far, yes. They're both slightly cool, but not cold enough to suffer from hypothermia thanks to the duvet. We'll take them out to the ambulance now.'

Once the ambulance had driven off, Pengelly locked the caravan. 'Jenna, after Hillman's been collected by uniform, I want you and Clem to go to the hospital to meet the parents and make sure the girls are okay. On the way, call forensics and ask them to come out to the caravan.'

'Yes, ma'am.'

'Matt and I are going back to the station. We must locate Stuart Baines and discover the facts – whatever they turn out to be. One thing's for certain, we'll be making at least one arrest today.'

THIRTY-FOUR

FRIDAY, 28 OCTOBER

'Ma'am, Baines has been picked up and he's on his way in,' Tamsin said, after knocking on Lauren's door.

She'd been with Matt in her office waiting to be informed of Hillman's arrival.

'Brilliant,' she said. 'Now we'll get the truth. Where was he found?'

'At a café in Newquay with his wife and kids.'

Her mouth opened in surprise. 'I didn't expect that. What was he doing with them?'

'I've no idea, ma'am.'

'Matt, we'll interview him first, and then question Hillman. Thanks, Tamsin.' She waited until the officer had left the room, before continuing. 'Well, there's a turn-up for the books. What do you make of that?'

'He's using them as an alibi, maybe? Especially if he discovered that we had Hillman in custody. But... I don't know... Hillman said Baines and his wife were getting divorced. It's certainly odd, for sure.'

'We'll find out soon enough.' The phone on her desk rang. 'Pengelly.'

'Baines is in interview room two, ma'am, and I've just been informed that Hillman's requested a solicitor.'

'Thanks, Sergeant.' She replaced the handset. 'Baines is here, and Hillman has demanded legal representation. Let's go.'

Lauren and Matt entered the interview room. Facing them was a man in his forties, wearing a sweatshirt and jeans. His mouth was set in a firm line.

'Why am I here?'

'I'll explain once the recording is set up.' She nodded to Matt, who pressed the button. 'Interview on Friday twenty-eighth October. Those present: Detective Inspector Pengelly, Detective Sergeant Price, and... please state your name for the recording,' she said, gesturing to the suspect.

'Stuart Baines.'

Lauren scrutinised the man as he shifted uneasily in his seat. 'Mr Baines, I understand that you live with Eleanor Hillman, is that correct?'

He ran his fingers through his hair and cleared his throat. 'It's complicated.'

'Define complicated.'

'Well, I was staying at Eleanor's place, but I'm planning to go back home to be with my wife and kids.' He spoke quietly, almost as if he was ashamed of what he'd done.

'Does Eleanor know you're leaving her?' Matt asked.

Baines hung his head and sighed before answering. 'Sort of. I said I had a work conference to attend but really I went on holiday with my family to Newquay. Somehow she found out and wasn't happy about it.'

What did he expect? Her blessing?

'What did she do?' Matt asked.

'She sent me a few angry texts, which isn't like her – she was upset, that's all. Look, is she okay? Has something happened?'

'We're investigating the disappearance of three children taken from nurseries where Eleanor works.'

'I didn't realise they were *all* from her workplaces. She told me a little girl called Violet had gone missing and I read about the others online. Surely you don't believe that Eleanor has anything to do with it? She loves all the children she works with. She'd never want to harm them.'

'We found one of the missing children in the boot of Eleanor's car parked in the driveway of the house at Croft Road. Eleanor said you coerced her into taking the children and that she was so scared of you she had to do what you asked,' Lauren said.

'What?' Baines spluttered, fear flickering in his eyes. 'It's not true. Why would she say that?'

The body language was congruent with someone telling the truth. No excessive blinking. No touching his nose. No sweating. Nothing.

'We found the other two children locked in your caravan at High Sands.'

The colour drained from Baines' face, leaving him pale and trembling. 'I swear I'm innocent,' he croaked, desperation dripping from his voice. 'You can check with my wife. We've been in Newquay since Monday.'

'You could have planned it all and made sure you had an alibi,' Lauren goaded.

'But why would I do that? It makes no sense.'

'So, why would Eleanor do it?'

Baines slumped in the chair. 'I honestly don't know. She loves children... She always wanted kids of her own, but she can't— Oh... Do you think it's...?' His voice trailed off, as if he was too scared to finish the sentence.

Was that the motive? So she could have the girls for herself?

Lauren glanced at Matt, whose fists were clenched so tight in his lap that his knuckles had turned white. Had the enormity of what had happened finally hit? That he could have lost his daughter forever?

She hoped he could hold it together, because if he didn't then she'd take someone else in with her to interview Hillman.

'Does Eleanor have a key for your caravan?' she asked, focusing her attention away from Matt and back to Baines.

'Yes. I had one cut for her when she said she wanted to help me get it ready to sell. She was going to make some new curtains and give it a good clean. She was most insistent... I guess now I know why.'

'How long have you known Eleanor?' Matt asked.

'We met in the local pub just over a year ago and started up a friendship. Nothing more. When my wife kicked me out and I had nowhere to go, Eleanor offered me a room in the house that she rents. After a few weeks of living together we started a relationship.'

'And would you say it was a good relationship?' Matt asked.

'Yes. She's very easy to live with. We didn't fight and argue like I did with my wife. But it's over and I'm going back home.'

Lauren stared at him. What sort of man was he, to drop his girlfriend like that?

'What do you know about Eleanor's background?' Matt asked.

'Not much, because she seldom mentions it. All I know is she had a difficult and painful upbringing. If I ever asked about her family she'd change the subject.'

That was already more than they'd discovered from her.

'She trained as a nursery nurse and worked in Bristol before moving to Cornwall,' Lauren said, watching him carefully for any signs of lying. 'Did she talk about that time in her life?'

'She said she'd been living in Bristol, but didn't tell me for how long or what she'd been doing.'

'And you know nothing prior to that?'

'No. Look, we focused on the present, not our pasts. Are

you absolutely certain she's done this? It doesn't seem like the Eleanor I know.'

'Maybe you don't know the real Eleanor. The angry texts she sent you could be her true colours. Do you still have them on your phone?' Lauren asked.

He shook his head. 'No. I deleted them. I was worried my wife would see them.'

'Do you remember what they said?'

He closed his eyes for a second. 'That I'd regret it if I crossed her...'

Lauren placed the folder she was holding on the desk in front of her and sat opposite Eleanor Hillman. Matt faced Dawn Groom, Hillman's solicitor, a woman who Lauren had met several times in the past when representing legal aid suspects.

'Eleanor, we've just come from interviewing Stuart Baines and not only does he have an alibi for the time when the girls were kidnapped, but he claims not to have been a part of it. What do you have to say to that?' Lauren said.

Hillman glanced at her solicitor, who nodded. 'No comment.'

'You must be relieved to know that the children haven't sustained any physical harm. That they can go home to their families, where they'll be safe.'

'That's what you think,' Eleanor muttered.

'Of course that's what we think. Keeping them sedated and in a damp caravan isn't healthy for them, especially as Violet has asthma. Did you know that?'

'No, but I didn't mean *that*.'

'What do you mean, then?' Lauren pushed. 'Do you think

the children were in danger at home? Is that why you took them, believing it was for the best?'

'No comment,' Eleanor said, keeping her head bowed.

'For goodness' sake,' Matt fumed. 'Do you know the pain you caused their families? What you put me through when you abducted Dani? And now you're claiming that being drugged and left in an unclean, musty caravan is better than staying with their families who love and care for them?'

Eleanor's head shot up and she stared directly at him, her eyes blazing. 'Home wasn't a good place for any of those girls. And I should know.'

'So you're admitting that you orchestrated and executed the plans to take Isla, Violet and Dani,' Lauren said, glancing at Hillman's solicitor, who was staring, wide-eyed, at her client.

'Eleanor—' Dawn said, in an insistent tone.

Hillman waved a dismissive hand in her solicitor's direction 'These children were failed by their parents. They should have been given love and support, not forced to endure fights over custody or non-stop arguments. And as for you –' she hissed, searing Matt with a look of intense hatred – 'you abandoned Dani at the worst possible time... just after her mother was taken from her.'

Matt countered her words with a hard glare. 'You thought you could give them a better life, did you?' Matt said, scathingly. 'Leaving them alone in a caravan where anyone could've broken in? What if Violet had suffered an asthma attack without anyone to help her? Or Dani – if we hadn't found her locked in your car boot then she could've suffocated.' His voice was thick with accusation.

Hillman slumped forward, resting her head in her hand. 'You don't understand,' she whispered softly.

'Oh yes, we do,' Matt said angrily. 'You thought that because you couldn't have your own children, you'd take away someone else's. That's insane.'

'I was doing what was right,' Hillman said, her voice less certain than before.

'No. It. Was. Not. Right.' Matt accentuated every word.

The tension from Matt's body was intense and Lauren rested her hand on his arm. He had to calm down or the interview would collapse.

'Eleanor, tell me the truth.' Lauren's voice rose as she spoke. 'Was Stuart involved?'

Hillman's chin trembled as she shook her head. 'We were meant to be a family. Me, Stuart and our three girls. I had our future all mapped out. We were going to move away and start fresh in Spain.'

'Did you ever talk to Stuart about this plan?'

'No. I wanted it to be a surprise. But then... He chose her over me.' As tears coursed down Hillman's cheeks, a heavy silence filled the room.

Lauren chanced a look at Matt; his face was expressionless, unreadable. How must it feel to be branded an incompetent parent – even if it had come from Eleanor Hillman?

The woman had been so methodical in her planning, but they hadn't yet asked how she'd pulled it off.

'Eleanor,' Lauren asked sternly. 'Please explain how you did it.'

'Oh... it was easy because I'm so familiar with all the processes. With Isla, I walked from the staff car park along the rear of the building keeping close to the wall. I went inside and hid in one of the spacious equipment cupboards where I could see the door of the room. When Sean and Tina were occupied I crept in, darted around the screen and grabbed Isla. She was very sleepy and didn't protest. We returned to the cupboard where I gave her a drink containing ketamine. I put her in my suitcase, wheeled it out and followed the same path back, avoiding the camera.'

'But someone could have seen you,' Lauren said.

'No, because the staff stick rigidly to their routines, especially when some of the children are napping. The odds of me being noticed were minimal.'

'And Violet?'

'I made sure to be seen upstairs having an early lunch. Then I sneaked downstairs, watched Zoe and Maddie until their backs were turned and then nipped in and grabbed Violet. I took her to an empty room and gave her the drugged drink. After that, I went outside to my car – there isn't a camera by the back door – and placed the suitcase in my boot until I left.'

'But how did you know that Zoe or Maddie wouldn't have turned around and spotted you?'

'I didn't really know, but they weren't likely to suspect anything untoward because my shift was about to start.'

'And Dani?' Matt said, his body tense. 'How did you take her? When did you drug her?'

'I planned it the same as the others,' Hillman said, running her hand through her hair. 'I—'

'Do that again,' Matt suddenly interrupted, pointing at the woman.

Lauren frowned in confusion. 'What are you talking about?'

'Run your fingers through your hair again,' Matt repeated through gritted teeth.

The woman turned to her solicitor, but she gave an uncertain shrug. 'Why?' Hillman asked.

'Just do it,' Matt commanded, his voice cold and stern.

Hillman complied, her movement slow and hesitant.

'Sergeant, what's going on?' Lauren asked.

'Look,' Matt exclaimed, pointing an accusing finger at Hillman's forehead. 'The birthmark shaped like a heart. It's the same one. You're Norah Rundle.'

A chill ran down Lauren's spine. Were they about to solve the murder case too?

'Well?' Lauren said, leaning forward in her chair and staring directly into Hillman's wide eyes, demanding an answer.

Hillman gazed back, expressionless.

'I'd like some time alone with my client,' Dawn Groom said, finally making a contribution to the proceedings.

'Do you want that, Eleanor?' Lauren asked, lowering the tone of her voice.

Hillman gave a resigned shrug. 'No. I'll tell you what you want to know.'

'We uncovered the bodies of your parents. They were murdered. What can you tell us about that?'

Hillman shuddered. 'My parents were monsters. They tormented me from the day I was born, making me sleep in the dark, freezing cupboard under the stairs. Going days without food or making me eat off the filthy floor. Depending on their moods, they would ignore me for days on end. The only place I felt some sense of safety was at school, but even then they wouldn't always let me go.'

'Why didn't you tell anyone? If you'd told someone at school, they could have helped,' Lauren said, her tone more gentle than before.

'Don't be naive, of course I couldn't. We lived in a small community and who was going to believe the *weird kid*?'

Lauren glanced at Matt, who was staring at Hillman, his mouth open. Gone was the anger blazing in his eyes and instead there was compassion.

'Did you kill them, Eleanor?' Lauren said, softly.

Hillman nodded, her body slumped in the chair. 'Yes.'

'Will you tell me what happened?'

Hillman's eyes became distant, and her face contorted, as if she were revisiting those painful experiences from long ago.

'My dad found out that I'd slept with Neville, the man from next door. I don't know how he knew. He said that if I got pregnant he'd kill me, but to make sure he kicked me really hard in my stomach. He damaged me inside. I think that's why I can't have children. I tried with Stuart, but it didn't happen. It's like my dad is looking down on me, laughing...' Hillman's voice faded away and she stared off into space.

'Keep going, Eleanor,' Lauren said.

'I decided to wait until firework night because I knew there'd be plenty of noise to mask the gunshots. We'd had thunderstorms all week, but that night it was clear. I took my dad's gun, the one he used on the farm, and shot them both before burying them in the garden. I packed what few clothes we had to make it look like we'd simply left and grabbed the large sum of money they kept in a secret place. Then I made my way to Bristol where I changed my name to one of a baby who had died the same day I was born – I found her name at the graveyard. It felt like fate because Norah is a nickname for Eleanor. I requested a new birth certificate and became her. It was easy. No one ever questioned it.'

'What did you do next?' Lauren asked.

'I retook my GCSEs and then trained as a nursery nurse. I wanted to make sure children didn't suffer the same thing I did. Keeping watch, I could tell which kids weren't getting enough attention from their parents.'

'And what would you do?'

'Nothing. Just gave those kids more love and care. Well, once I did speak up but it backfired on me and I lost my job.'

'Is that why you moved back to Cornwall?'

'I didn't want to stay in Bristol, not after what happened and Penzance was the only other place I knew. No one recognised me. I look totally different from twenty years ago.'

'Why suddenly did you decide to take these children?' Lauren asked.

'It was after you found my parents. The flood of terror returned, stronger than ever before. My father had taken so much from me... he destroyed my chance of ever having a family. And then when Stuart decided to leave me... What else could I do?'

'What about us? The parents. Didn't you once stop to consider how we would feel?' Matt asked, through gritted teeth.

'You were all too busy thinking about yourselves.'

'You don't know what you're talking about,' Matt snapped. 'You think you've done some good but all you've done is ruined the lives of three families because it'll never be the same again. No one should ever go through what we've gone through and—'

'Eleanor Hillman, I'm arresting you on suspicion of kidnapping Isla Hopkins, Violet Dent and Dani Price. And also for the murders of Clive and Olive Rundle,' Lauren said, interrupting Matt before he went too far. 'You do not have to say anything but it may harm your defence if you do not mention something which you later rely on in court. Anything you do say may be given in evidence. Do you understand?'

'Yes.'

'You will wait here until we arrange for someone to take you to the custody suite where you'll be officially charged.'

Lauren stared at the prisoner, her gaze unwavering.

The case might be over, but the echoes of Hillman's crimes, whatever her motive, would reverberate long after her conviction.

THIRTY-SIX

FRIDAY, 28 OCTOBER

'Hello, Mum, how's Dani?' Matt asked as he got through to his mum on her mobile phone. He was lucky to get a hold of her because she was a great one for sticking it in her pocket or handbag and not checking if it was either charged or turned on.

'She's asleep, love. She woke up once, smiled at your dad, who's been sitting next to her the whole time, and then nodded off again. The doctors have been in several times and they're happy with how she's doing.'

'That's a relief. Thanks so much for staying with her because I'm needed here. What about the blood tests?'

'The results came back and she'd been sedated with ketamine, but there's nothing else in her system. She's just got to sleep it off. They said they'll see how she is tomorrow but she'll definitely be home on Sunday. What about the other girls? Any news?'

He'd totally forgotten to mention what had happened, he'd been so concerned about Dani.

'It's over. We found the other two girls in an old caravan and have arrested someone. I can't tell you who, but... well, let's say it all makes sense now.'

'Thank goodness for that. And are the children okay?'

'Yes, as far as I know. They'd been sedated and were unconscious like Dani. Knowing the person who took them, who had a distorted view about wanting to give them a safer place to live, I'm sure they weren't harmed. Her plan had been to raise the girls herself.'

'Her?'

'You didn't hear that from me, Mum.'

'But why did she take Dani? She doesn't need a better place to live; she couldn't have a more loving home. You know we love the child more than life itself.'

No one could have done more than his parents. He'd never be able to thank them enough for dropping all their plans to travel so they could support him bringing up Dani. To think someone could believe Dani wasn't loved and well cared for... well, it was inconceivable.

'Of course I do, Mum. And Dani loves you and Dad, too. It's complicated and obviously there are psychological factors at play. It was nothing against you and Dad, but more me. She thought I shouldn't be working and instead should have stayed at home all the time with Dani. Look, we don't need to talk about that now. The main thing is that it's over. For everyone. I'm going to finish up here; there's some paperwork that needs doing, and—' He paused at the sound of his name being called and he glanced over to Clem, who was signalling that they were going for a drink and for him to join them.

'Is everything okay?' his mum asked.

'Yes, sorry. The team are heading out for a drink to celebrate solving the case. Actually, both cases. But I'll tell you about that later, too. They want me to go with them, but I won't. I'd rather go straight to the hospital to be with you all.'

'You go with them, love. You deserve it after what you've been through. Dani's asleep and we're here. It's only your first week in the job and it's been extremely traumatic. You could do with relaxing and having a drink.' She paused for a second. 'But obviously don't drink too much. Not with you having to drive.'

'No, Mum.' He bit back a laugh. When had he ever driven after drinking over the limit? But she felt it her duty to say something.

'Are you going to go, then?'

Should he? It would be nice to have some time with the new team in more pleasant surroundings.

'Okay. I'll stay for one. Then I'll come to the hospital and you and Dad can go home. You'll want something to eat and will need to rest. You both must be exhausted. I'll stay overnight with Dani. I'll see you soon.'

He ended the call and went over to where the team, minus the DI, were standing. It looked like the paperwork would have to wait for another day.

'Well?' Clem asked.

'I'll come to the pub for one. Then I'm going to the hospital to relieve my parents.'

'How's Dani?' Jenna asked, as they left the office and headed down the corridor together.

'She's fine now, thanks. Just sleeping it off.'

'That's such a relief.'

'You can say that again. But she's a strong girl, just like her mum, and we'll get through this.'

The Whale Inn was tucked away from the main street. Matt had to duck his head to fit through the doorway – and he wasn't very tall. Once inside, they all ordered drinks and congregated at the far side of the bar. He watched as the team chatted animatedly and it brought back to him his days of working with Whitney. After any successful case they'd go out for a drink together to celebrate. She always insisted on buying a round. Pengelly wasn't there, making him the highest-ranking officer in the group. Should he offer to buy the drinks? He wasn't sure of the protocol here.

'Here comes the Ice Queen. The life and soul of the party,' Billy said, smirking.

Matt glanced over his shoulder and saw Pengelly heading in their direction.

'Stop it, Billy,' Jenna reprimanded. 'Not in front of Sarge.'

'Why? You know what she's like, don't you?' Billy said, looking at Matt.

'Maybe you should give her more of a chance,' Matt said, knowing that already he'd seen a side of their boss the others hadn't.

Before anyone had a chance to answer, Pengelly was in earshot. 'What's everyone drinking?' she asked. 'My shout.'

They all gave their orders and Matt followed her to the bar to lend a hand.

'We'll take the drinks over to the team and then you and I can sit down and have a chat over there,' she said, nodding to an empty table.

'Don't you want to join the rest of the team, ma'am? Celebrate with them.'

'They'd rather be on their own.'

She was right, but it was like a self-fulfilling prophecy. They didn't want her, because she didn't make an effort to join in. But that wasn't something he could sort out just yet.

'Okay. That's fine. I'm only staying for one, anyway. I want to get to the hospital.'

After delivering the drinks, Matt followed Pengelly to a table well away from the others, so that they couldn't be heard. He glanced over his shoulder and saw Billy pulling faces in their direction. He'd let it ride for now. But he resolved to be the person to unify the team. They'd worked so well together when necessity demanded, it would be a shame for them not to solidify it. Of course, it depended on Pengelly playing her part.

Was that likely to happen?

'What do you think of working here, so far?' Pengelly asked after they'd been sitting there in silence for a few minutes, both deep in thought.

'It's been one hell of a week, on so many levels, and not one I wish to repeat. But I think you've got a good team. And I'm sure Penzance will grow on me, once I get to know my way around. By the way, what did the DCI say about Hillman escaping from the unlocked car when you told him, if you don't mind me asking?'

'The same as you. That it was a mistake, we all make them, and that he was sure I'd learn from it. It surprised me. I might not have been so lenient.'

'Tolerance and understanding can often be the best approach.'

'Yes, but you've heard the saying *give an inch and they'll take a mile*. I don't want that to happen in my team.'

'It won't. They're a good bunch. Yeah, some of them – mentioning no names – need more reining in than others, but that's the nature of the beast. Are you happy with my performance so far?'

'I'll be honest. It annoyed me that you were taken on without there being any input from me, but after this week I can see why you had such good references. I'm glad you're here.'

'Thank you, ma'am. I didn't know you weren't consulted about my appointment.'

'No matter. Although your aversion to dead bodies and bones didn't fill me with confidence, initially. Not to mention the fact that you might not be able to chase anyone because of your limp. Although, come to think of it, you did chase after Hillman when she got away.' She paused for a moment. 'I'm sorry, it was inappropriate for me to pass comment.'

'It's fine. I haven't always walked like this. A few years ago I was undercover and got shot in the leg. But I can still run, even if it does look ungainly and it hurts a bit.'

Pengelly laughed. It softened her features and made her green eyes twinkle. She looked entirely different and even attractive.

Guilt washed over him. He shouldn't be thinking like that about another woman. He'd only just lost Leigh.

'I've got to go to the hospital now. Thanks for the drink,' he said, picking up his glass and finishing the remains of his beer.

'Oh... Okay. I'll see you next week,' Pengelly said, appearing surprised at him wanting to leave so soon, even though he'd already mentioned he was only staying for one.

'Will do. Thanks, ma'am.'

He picked up his jacket and after saying goodbye to the rest of the team made a hasty exit, putting all thoughts about how attractive the DI was well and truly behind him.

THIRTY-SEVEN

SUNDAY, 30 OCTOBER

Lauren stood at the top of the short path leading to the front door of the terraced house where Matt lived. Had she made a mistake coming there? It wasn't like they were great friends or anything. But he was on her team and what he'd been through had been so devastating that she'd wanted to do something.

He'd seemed okay when they'd spoken in the pub but she suspected that he'd been operating on adrenaline. By now he'd probably come down to earth and might be feeling different.

She hopped from foot to foot not knowing what to do.

This was ridiculous. Grown women, with responsible jobs, didn't behave like this.

Taking a deep breath, she marched down the path. If Matt didn't want to see her he would say. She had called the hospital to check on the three girls and the nurse had told her that Dani had been sent home. Fortunately, they were all okay and Violet and Isla were expected to go home soon with no lasting effects.

She dreaded to think what would have happened if Hillman had been able to take them overseas. They'd never have located them.

She rang the bell and after a short while Matt opened the door, a bewildered expression on his face.

'Ma'am? Is there something wrong?'

'No. I thought I'd call round to see how Dani is. I've brought her a little gift if that's okay with you?' She could kick herself for sounding so pathetic.

'That's very kind of you; I'm sure she'll love it. Come on in. We'll go into the sitting room. My parents are out shopping for some special ice cream. They're spoiling Dani rotten.'

'Special ice cream?'

'Yes. Strawberry with hundreds and thousands on it.'

'I like the sound of that.'

'I think it's an acquired taste.' Matt laughed, putting Lauren at ease.

She followed him into the warm and inviting sitting room with an open fireplace. Her eyes were immediately drawn to the mantelpiece, on which stood many photos, most of them of Dani. There was one of Matt with a small attractive woman with dark hair, who had an enormous grin plastered across her face. Leigh?

'This room is so cosy,' she said, enjoying the homely atmosphere. 'The whole house is.'

'I love it. My parents bought it for themselves, so it might get a bit cramped as Dani gets older. But for now it's fine. And Dani loves it here, too. I think she's in the dining room playing with her toys. Hang on and I'll get her.' He walked to the door. 'Dani, someone's here to see you.' He looked back towards Lauren, smiling. 'Please sit down.'

Lauren perched on the edge of one of the floral easy chairs, and rested her bag on her lap.

She heard the patter of footsteps on the wooden floor and a little girl with dark curls ran past Matt, who was still at the door, and stopped when she saw Lauren.

'Hello, who are you?' the child asked, staring directly at Lauren.

'Dani, that's not the way we speak to people,' Matt said, looking as if he was trying to hide his grin, but failing.

'It's fine. I like the direct approach. My name's Lauren and I work with your daddy.'

Dani stepped closer to her, her tiny hands on her hips. 'Is he in charge of you?'

'No, Detective Inspector Pengelly is *my* boss,' Matt said.

'Ohhhh,' Dani said, her eyes wide. 'Do you tell him what to do?'

Lauren laughed. 'Only sometimes.'

'Is that because he's very good and behaves himself?'

'Yes, that's right. He's very good... most of the time.' Lauren winked. She looked at Matt, who was shaking his head and rolling his eyes. 'And please call me Lauren when we're out of work.'

'Does he get stars for being good like I do?'

A chuckle escaped Lauren's lips. 'Not yet, but I might start giving them out if you think it will help.'

'Do you know that Daddy saved me from a naughty lady who took me and two girls because she wanted her own children.'

'Yes, I do know about that.'

Lauren was surprised that Dani was able to talk about it so easily. Then again, at her age she wouldn't have known the implications, so it was probably a good thing.

'Did you help him?' Dani asked.

'We all did it together,' Matt said. 'Me, Lauren, Jenny, Clem, Tamsin and Billy.'

'When can I meet them to say thank you?' Dani asked.

Lauren stared open-mouthed at the child. She was barely two and she was asking that. Matt wasn't wrong in his assessment of her.

'I'll arrange a time for you to come to the station, if that's okay with your daddy.' Lauren looked at Matt, who gave a shrug.

'Yes. That's fine with me.'

'Good. I know that everyone would like to meet you. You've been such a brave girl. I've brought you a present; would you like it?'

Dani's eyes lit up. 'Yes, please. What is it?'

'Why don't you come over and take a look? It's in my bag.'

Dani ran over and stood beside Lauren. 'Is it in that bag?' She pointed to Lauren's lap.

'It is. Why don't you open it and see.' Lauren gave her the bag and Dani reached inside and pulled out the elephant that Lauren had knitted.

'Daddy. Daddy. Look. A pink elephant. Lauren's given me a pink elephant. That's my best colour.'

'What do you say?' Matt nudged.

'Thank you, Lauren.' Dani clutched the elephant to her chest and ran over to Matt to show him. 'Look, Daddy.'

'It's lovely. Your favourite animal, in your favourite colour.' He glanced across at Lauren. 'How did you manage to find such a perfect gift at such short notice?'

'I knitted it myself. All I needed was the pattern, which I found online.'

Matt's eyes widened. 'But you only knew two days ago that elephants were Dani's favourite animal. How did you manage to knit it so quickly?'

'Knitting's my hobby. Well, that, cycling and my dogs.'

'What sort of dogs?' Dani asked.

'I have two border collies called Tia and Ben.'

'I want a dog but Daddy said we don't have room. Will you bring them here so I can meet them?'

'Yes, I'm sure we can sort something out.'

'Dani, don't hassle Lauren. She's very busy.'

'It's no trouble. You don't mind, do you?' she asked, not sure whether she had overstepped the mark.

'Of course I don't. I just didn't want to impose.'

'You're not.' She glanced at her watch. 'I'd better go now because the dogs need walking. It was lovely to meet you, Dani.' She stood up to leave.

'I'll see you out,' Matt said. 'Thanks again for the lovely present for Dani. It's perfect, but you shouldn't have gone to so much trouble.'

'It was fun and I enjoyed it. But for goodness' sake don't let on about my hobby to the rest of the team or I'll be forever called the *Woolly* Ice Queen.

A LETTER FROM THE AUTHOR

Dear reader,

Huge thanks for reading *The Lost Girls of Penzance* – I hope you were hooked on Lauren and Matt's first case together. If you want to join other readers in hearing all about my new releases and bonus content, you can sign up for my newsletter.

www.stormpublishing.co/sally-rigby

If you enjoyed this book and could spare a few moments to leave a review that would be hugely appreciated. Even a short review can make all the difference in encouraging a reader to discover my books for the first time. Thank you so much!

I was drawn to writing the book for a few reasons. I have many happy memories from holidaying in the southwest corner of Cornwall, and I wanted to revisit the area through my writing. Then Matt entered my mind. He'd been such a vital part of the Cavendish & Walker series even though he left mid-way through. I thought it would be great to team him up with Lauren Pengelly because they complement one another perfectly to make an outstanding pair of detectives.

Thanks again for being part of this amazing journey with me and I hope you'll stay in touch – I have so many more stories and ideas to entertain you with!

Sally Rigby

www.sallyrigby.com

facebook.com/Sally-Rigby-131414630527848

ACKNOWLEDGMENTS

First, I'd like to thank Storm Publishing for the opportunity to collaborate on this new series. As one of the first authors to have signed with them, I am thrilled to be a part of their exciting development in the publishing world.

I am incredibly lucky to have worked with Kathryn Taussig, one of the most talented and insightful editors I've ever had the pleasure of collaborating with. She's helped me from the inception to completion of this book and we've had some brilliant brainstorming sessions.

Thanks, also, to everyone who works at Storm, from editing and production, through to sales and marketing. This really is a huge team effort.

To my sister-in-law Jacqui and my brother-in-law Peter, a heartfelt thank you for your invaluable help in providing insights into the area, and for spending time with me checking out all the local places of interest.

Last, but not least, thanks to my family for their unwavering support. It's much appreciated.

Made in the USA
Middletown, DE
31 August 2024